LEFT HAND OF THE MOON

Alexis Brooks de Vita

LEFT HAND OF THE MOON

DOUBLE DRAGON

DEDICATION

For my children and my readers, with great love and appreciation.

*

In New Orleans' French Quarter, there is a tale about the ghost of an enslaved mistress who can sometimes be seen walking the rooftop of her former owner's home in the winter sleet, where she froze to death two centuries ago.

Table of Contents

CHAPTER ONE
HEAVEN'S DYING TIME

This was the story that would never be known, never be told. That's what I couldn't stand. That the real story, the story that told who I'd been all my life and what I'd lived through, would be known only to me.

Dirty little secrets, whispers and lies. Jules's mother had won. Our love and our hope to be together were finished.

Jules and I broke up under the left hand of the moon, when all things can't help dying. But I didn't know the moon was waning when I let Jules catch my hand on the stairway.

He whispered, "When the clock chimes ten, Aurelie. I'll be at the servants' side of the fountain," which meant the dark side facing the servants' quarters, where no torches burned.

I tossed my head and climbed the stairs with the freshly washed chamber pot for his grandmother's room in the attic, where she lay like an uncovered corpse and had lain all our lives. *Let Jules wonder*.

He had not spoken to me for days. I hoped my cold jasmine water splashes had kept the swelling out of my eyes, long and slanted. "Enchanting," one of the family's dinner guests had called them. I couldn't afford not to be beautiful and sweetly scented, now that Jules's only remaining promise to me was abandonment.

But I would always love him. So I did trail slowly across the courtyard well after the chime's beats lay silent under the patter of droplets in the fountain's bowl.

I unwound the sweat-heavy turban from my hair and dabbed the fountain's water across my forehead. Being there was all the mercy I meant to show Jules.

He paced, a dark shape that shifted the darkness ahead of me. I swished my fingers through the fountain's pool to make him turn.

He jumped, startled out of his distraction, and strode to me. "Aurelie. You have to understand."

I smoothed the black wings of my eyebrows and coaxed tendrils of water into the fine hairs along my hairline. I lifted my face, eyes closed, to the cooling night.

I didn't have to see Jules to know that he had crossed his arms and spread his legs. He began to drone in that tone he had learned from his father.

I crossed my arms, dangling the turban, and turned my back on him.

He stumbled in his speech but rallied and plowed on about the importance of his engagement to marry this other girl his mother had chosen for him. I wanted to whirl and snap at him, *Not for you! For your brother, you fool!* But this was not last year, or even a few months ago, when I could have gotten away with saying-or doing-anything I could think of to Jules.

This was different. We both faltered, unsure how to proceed with both of us hostile and refusing to apologize.

Jules had always loved me. He had held me and cried into my neck, hot tears that madethe fine hairs at my nape slip from my smooth chignon, when he first heard of this same engagement. *Why should I even listen to this sudden change of his fickle heart?*

It didn't matter what Jules had made up his mind to say to me. It didn't even matter that he betrayed our sweetest memories by saying all this on the dark side of the fountain. *Where we first admitted, nearly three years ago, that what was humiliating us and driving us from each other was love. Has he forgotten what standing in this place means to us? Commitment, not betrayal!*

Jules couldn't want to marry that other girl. *He'd cried and dug into the space between my arms and my breasts like the baby he's always been with me.*

And European men, even exiled Frenchmen, didn't have to do anything they didn't want to do. We'd had a lifetime under the shifting rule of transient governments in Louisiana to learn that. *So there isn't even a reason for me to be here, listening to him.*

Except for my patience. My loyalty in the face of his efforts to prove himself. I was just standing in front of one more rehearsed speech, like the one he made last summer at his cousin's wedding with-thanks to my listening and clapping-hands dry and still enough to lift the champagne glass without spilling it or dropping it.

That was the wedding where his mother met the girl she had just engaged Jules to marry, wearing the ruined finery of her fallen titled family.

I, too, could tell them a few things about being fallen. I had no pity for Jules's fiancee and no sympathy for his mother's social climbing. *And when he never marries this other girl, we'll both see that I suffered, poor fool listening to Jules play the man with his chest stuck out, for nothing.*

The fountain gushed a song behind his thoughtless words. I swayed to the rhythm of the water as it carried me into that safe place that drifted through my mind. *How can he enjoy being so cruel? Jules always had his family's selfish streak.*

Despising him, denying that he was there saying these hateful things to me, I opened my eyes and looked up into the night sky.

I meant only to divert myself, to force the time to pass until even Jules couldn't take the sound of his own voice anymore.

But what I saw stunned the breath out of me.

For there we stood under the slender left hand of the moon. *The waning moon. The dying moon. The power of death is spreading over us.*

This was no game.

So this is why Jules isn't reaching out to me, taking my hands to beg to be forgiven! This is why he is pushing himself to say such hurtful things. He is driven by the power of heaven's dying time.

This is the end.

I unlocked my arms and spun around, flung my turban to the cobblestones, and threw myself at Jules to still his lips with my fingers. "Don't speak, *mon cher ami.* No more. Not tonight." Only two more nights would see us into a safer time to play this tiresome charade.

Am I too late? Even in this faint light, I could see that Jules's face was closed against me. A stranger rose up in him. My fingers touched a tight, dry line.

He pulled my hands from his mouth. "You will never again address me without saying *'maitre,'* Aurelie. I won't have my wife-my whole family-humiliated by you. Is that understood?"

And then, mercifully, he was gone. He didn't wait for an answer he must have known I couldn't give. *Master? Jules?*

I'd cleaned Jules's scraped knees of gravel and blood when we were children and he couldn't beat me at footraces around the courtyard. I'd teased him out of being a sissy who ran with tears, blood, and snot on his face to his mother every time his older brother battered him. And I'd sewn his ripped breeches back together when he finally learned to climb the wrought iron gate and sneak out to play and steal with the street children, saving him many a whipping from that same mother who only thought to use him now for her own social climbing. *In fact, I've been more of a mother to Jules than she has ever been. I've been his sister and his best friend, too. And I will always be his first love. No matter to whom she marries him.*

We had hidden for hours at a time, days in a row, in the servants' quarters, while Jules taught me to read so I could enjoy the beauty of the poems and love notes he wrote me. We had known for nearly three years now that someday we would have a small home of our own, away from his family, where we would make love for the very first time, raise our children to be freemen, and live quietly.

For that, we could make sacrifices. *I've sacrificed.*

I'd bitten my cheek and called Jules "*Maitre*" enough times, in front of his parents and friends and waited table, serving the wards, nieces, and plain, penniless younger daughters that important families paraded in front of Jules's mother.

But Jules was never my master. It was just a game, like all the others.

I stared across the courtyard to the tall glass doors Jules had just gone through, back to his parents' quiet evening in the library. *He is my admirer and my slave. His poems say so. He never wanted to be anything else.*

I fell to my knees, meaning to pick up my dirtied turban. But now I felt oddly weak and maybe a little nauseated.

I'm shaking. I never shook. Fear was for Jules, facing the world of a free and wealthy Frenchman and frightened, reaching back for my hand and my faith in him. I was supposed to be the brave one.

I was still on my knees in the blackest shadows behind the fountain, bent double with my face in the soft ball of my turban cloth, hacking up tears, when *Tante* Clothilde came to me. "Hush, *minou*. All this noise. Do you want *Monsieur* Jules to look down on you? One more sobbing female at his feet!" She slid her arms around me.

I raised my scrubbed face. Fresh tears washed it as I spoke. "He doesn't want me, *Tante* Clothilde.

He's changed, and the moon-" I pointed-"Oh, just look what we've done."

Tante Clothilde looked and sighed. Then she smiled, as if making up her mind, and shrugged. "So what? So much the better-"

I pulled away. Would even *Tante* Clothilde turn against me, now?

Now it will begin. The three African women who lived in the servants' quarters, and their lovers who stole in with little gifts of ribbons and chocolates for them, and a piece of ripe fruit or sugar cane for me in exchange for promises to be silent and keep secrets, they would all turn against me, now that Jules had abandoned me. They'd say I'd thought too highly of my position, my influence over Jules, the power of the secret that made Jules's father keep me here despite his wife's screams and hatred.

Tante Clothilde grabbed at my hands and frowned into my face. "*Petite.*" These were almost her names for me, she used them so often. *Little one. Kitten.* "Aurelie, yes, I see the dying moon. And what does it signify, *minou*? That now is the time to kill, and the time to cleanse." I stopped fighting.

Tante Clothilde pulled me closer. "This is the time to purge, to purify. It all depends on what is before you. You're not too young to understand that this is the end of nothing but hiding and waiting and daydreaming about Jules taking you away from here. Death tonight is a good death that brings life." She kissed my hair. "The love of a girl and a boy

15

dies to make room for the love of a woman and a man."

Dare I believe? "Really, *Tante* Clothilde?"

She laughed, and the world turned and was again as it always had been. "Have I ever told you wrong, *ma petite*?" She shook her head as if such a thing were impossible.

And, indeed, it was. *Tante* Clothilde never told me anything that did not come true or prove to have been true all along, when only she could see it. Her vision of the world walked me through a lifetime of being needed by Jules when I envied him, and of being hated by his mother, whom I resented in return. *Tante* Clothilde always knew. She could not be wrong.

She was, again that night, not wrong. But I was unprepared for how suddenly Jules would prove *Tante* Clothilde right.

Jules appeared in my room in three nights' time, under the silver sliver of the growing moon. He waited for me just inside my opened door.

His hand shot out of the damp darkness and put out the lamp I carried. Then he gripped my wrist and pulled me into the room that smelled of sweaty skin and the breath of tired sleepers.

I was ashamed of this room, though *Tante* Clothilde had cared for me in here ever since I could remember. Most nights, I looked forward to the woody darkness and my familiar cot above the mildewed and softly splintered floor, ruined by summer floods. But a year ago, as I read Jules's awkward, yearning poems, I also began to feel ashamed that Jules might see me in here, someday.

I did not want him to follow me in here, as I heard from *Tante* Clothilde that most owners did with the women they liked. A year ago, I refused to allow him in here any longer.

Mistaking my shyness, *Tante* Clothilde had offered to sleep in the kitchen, creeping with her visiting husband through the courtyard shadows. This was sensitive of her. For she had only asked that I turn my back, eating the little gifts her husband brought me as I fell asleep listening to the sweet thoughts in my mind rather than the sounds that followed her husband's soft scrabbling at our alley window.

"The *Madame* will never allow Jules's father to buy or rent him a *garconniere* of his own, some nice little apartment where you two can set up housekeeping," *Tante* Clothilde reasoned. "You must learn to strike while the iron is hot. Let him come to you in our room. The kitchen floor can be quite comfortable for me, for one or two nights. Don't let your concern for me keep you from snatching with both hands at a chance for happiness." She snatched at the air to show how it must be done.

Tante Clothilde meant well. But I had always thought that Jules's and my love would never need a *garconniere*. Jules and I would never share our love in sneaky stolen moments spent clutching and crying out.

I would be bedded like a bride. Our love would have a home of its own. We would wake together over coffee and sleep again after brandy, for the rest of our lives.

I was sure Jules felt as I did. I'd memorized his wistful poems.

Stars in the fountain.
Study the brittle
nature of illusion:
Illusion that you and I
Could part,
Your soul separate from mine,
And I remain whole.
My wholeness
Is in you ...

Until he pulled me into my own room's darkness and put a hand over my mouth. Suddenly, I was unsure that Jules was not really the stranger at the fountain saying I must learn to call him master. How far was he willing to take this game?

I held the darkened lamp and wondered if I dared hit Jules with it. *Or should I just break away and run?*

Jules released me with one hand and shoved a bundle into the crook of my arm. "Aurelie, you must forgive me for everything I've said to you. I'm mad with regret. I've been thinking about what you said that night. We will escape together. No, don't argue with me. And don't waste time making me beg. My mother is watching. She'll have my father empty my account, if she suspects, and we will need that money. Now, I must go." He pressed his lips to my forehead. "My good girl," he whispered. "I owe you my sanity."

I watched him slip out through the heavy wooden door and into the fragrant night.

Suddenly, I could smell again the potted flowers that adorned the courtyard. All white, for pure love: jasmine, honeysuckle and magnolia. I could hear again the musical notes of the fountain, like a harp played after dinner. And were those nightingales singing?

I had not been about to argue with him. I only wanted to ask him what I said at the fountain that had suddenly changed his mind.

But as he disappeared into the singing night, I let the question go and took the bundle with me to my cot. *She is always right.*

I slept with the bundle pressed to my stomach, just where I'd held in the pain of Jules's rejection only three nights before, doubled over. *What is in the bundle?* I hoped and fell asleep dreaming that it was a bridal gown and veil, more light and fine than the one I had unpacked and aired for the *Madame* to entice Jules's fiancee.

My bridal gown would be draped with tatted lace and float free of stays, as my figure was trim and perfect, and I would drift down a church aisle trailing silk and dreams like an angel.

In the morning, *Tante* Clothilde ignored me feigning sleep in my cot and hurried across the courtyard to the kitchen, having washed herself quickly with splashes of jasmine water that steeped in a clay jar in the corner. Only when she was gone did I crawl from my cot to shake out Jules's bundle.

It was not a bridal gown. I should not have been so disappointed. *But what the bundle is not isn't nearly so surprising,* I argued with myself, *as what the bundle is.*

19

It was a masquerade costume.

I held up the cascading pieces. They were meant to disguise a Frenchwoman as an enslaved woman. But few enslaved women dressed in such fine fabrics. Bright satin flowers shimmered in the rippling skirt, and fine lace edged the lavender apron. The bleached cotton blouse would fall below a woman's shoulders, to be caught up and held by a bow tied between her breasts. A scarf of blood-red silk curled in a pool at my feet. In my hands were a silver-spangled satin shawl and gilded mask to cover the wearer from face to feet and convince others that she couldn't possibly be the penniless captive woman she pretended to be.

I tied the costume back in on itself and sat on my cot. I had to work up the courage to go into the house and ask Jules what this meant.

I didn't find him. Instead, Jules found me dusting the chess set after setting out the brandy decanter and snifters in his father's library, that night. His family had dined unusually late.

He pulled the curtained glass doors shut and came to me. "I pretended an upset stomach. My mother will follow me to my rooms soon, bringing some vile concoction or other." He smiled and shrugged a little. "To be truthful, I can use it. I've been sick with worry. Have you put the costume in a safe place, where you can get to it easily?"

I said nothing. I never did, when he apologized badly, no matter the questions I was desperate to ask.

Jules grabbed at my hands so that the dust of the rag puffed into our faces. "This is no time to punish me, *mon coeur*-my heart," he insisted. "Remember. On All Saints' Eve, put on the costume and wait in your room until you hear the cathedral bells sound midnight. You can hear them in your room, can't you? There is a window to the alley. At midnight, if you hear no one outside that window, leave your room and go to the street gate. You know how my mother has all the fires and lanterns put out on All Saints' Eve. She's very Old World, that way. Don't be afraid. Even if you cannot see me, I will be there. I will protect you. You must not fail me."

"As you planned to fail me, *Maitre*?"

Jules winced. "I deserved that."

The rap of his mother's fashionably heeled shoes sounded on the marble of the foyer. "Jules? Is that you in the library, *chou-chou*?"

"Damn. Still a cabbage, at twenty years old." Jules pulled the rag from my fingers. Then he lifted and kissed both my hands. First the backs. Then the palms, closing my fingers against the stubble-prickly, baby-smooth curves of his cheeks and chin.

His lips hovered over the dry palms of my hands and whispered something into them until I yanked them away, as his mother passed right outside the curtained library doors. Then Jules turned and slipped through a doorway that would wind up the servants' stairs, to avoid his mother as she doubled back to the grand staircase.

She opened the doors this second time. "Have you seen my son, Aurelie? I fear he is unwell."

I had retrieved the rag from the floor. "No, *Madame*." I looked, as always, through her eyes to the world beyond her head.

Don't fail me, Jules had said. But I never failed him. I could not.

Tante Clothilde kissed my forehead with a murmured, "Good luck, Aurelie," and watched for me as I ran across the unlit courtyard on All Saints' Eve. The cathedral's chimes drowned the jingle of my shawl's spangles and the brush of my feet on the courtyard's cobblestones.

I turned toward the unlit gate. There, he waited with his pallid, handsome face turned to watch for me. Jules in the darkness was even more shadowed by a top hat and long cape. But I could see when he held out his hand.

The movement flipped back his cape, and I thought I saw the glint of his fencing sword strapped below his slender waist. What costume was this?

"Come," he said and shoved open the gate as the last notes of midnight carried above the creak of its hinges. It clanged shut in the sudden silence, and Jules cursed the noise as he reached through the bars to jam the padlock closed.

"Come!" And he seized my hand and pulled me down the damp night street.

He strode, but I ran, taking light steps as I dodged trash and piles of rotting waste to keep up with him. The lovely skirt and costly shawl, which I hadn't spared a thought to enjoy when I was dressing, were soon spattered with something wet and weighty that made them cling about my ankles.

People sat along the streets, some drunk, some drowsing, and turned to watch us leap over and around them. Some lifted their goblets of what should have been pale wine but smelled like urine, their stink all around us. They called out and laughed as I turned my masked face away.

We ran through the press of elegant and grotesque bodies and grinning, grimacing masks, clustered around small bonfires to draw the wandering spirits. Spirits in scowling red demon masks and gilded courtier masks, their pearl droplets quivering, and warm human bodies in purple robes and blue togas as in Jules's history books, walked into me and through me or burst into comment on contact with me, as though startled to find that I was solid. Dancing women, their pale or bronzed curving torsos bared between islands of gossamer fabric, silk flowers, or dyed feathers, and men flaunting huge grotesque body parts, spilled from wide-open doorways and surged up from the ground all around my flying feet. Blocked from Jules's view by his cape as he passed, they looked at me, rose toward me and flowed around me, before they laughed and fell back, pointing, in our wake.

As tired as I was, unused to being on my feet at midnight, to say nothing of on the public streets, I began to wonder if I was in fact asleep and running through a nightmare or awake in a back alley of Hell. *Is Jules that stranger at the fountain again, pulling me away from the safety of the only home I have ever known?*

Toward what? Into what?

Our fingers slipped. Jules clutched backward at my hand without looking and jerked me forward.

I called out, "Where are we going?" But I was careful not to shout out his name. For he now used

23

his free hand to tug down the brim of his top hat and shield his face from stares when he wasn't using it to brace his sword and keep it from striking his thighs and breaking his stride.

Jules ducked his head under the tilt of the hat and behind the screen of his fingers and turned back toward me, his jaw and lips golden from the flames of the dimming bonfires lit to cleanse the city of its sins. His cape lifted and flowed, black and liquid, between us.

His voice was harsh in the thick air. "Can't you keep up?" *Did I hear contempt?*

I was pulled between two thick twisting bodies in black and red, painted with flames or really on fire-I couldn't tell-and suddenly we were out of the lamplight.

Jules now led me down a darker street, its *banquettes* stacked with soggy piles of garbage crowned with feebly licking flames. These were the fires of the night set by people too poor to gather enough wood for bonfires. Dogs snuffled hopefully at the smoking piles or at my scraped, muddy feet as we flew more smoothly, now that there were no crowds, or they tucked their tails and scuttled, hunkered down, away from Jules's feet, as he pounded on.

I was suddenly terribly afraid in these unlit streets. I wanted to call out to Jules to stop, to turn and go back to the main streets, despite the masqueraders and the demons. But what could I call him, if I mustn't call out his name?

He had never *said* I couldn't call out his name. "Jules?" I whimpered.

He turned, still holding the brim of the top hat down over his eyes. He stopped and frowned, studying my face.

I woke from the feeling of nightmare. Here was Jules, concerned as he'd always been, worried either for me or about what we were doing. *What are we doing?* I would share his worry. "Where are we going?"

His face relaxed. "To get away from my parents. Do you want me to be recognized? Stop pulling back. Stop calling me."

"It's just-" I started, but there was no chance to finish before we were on the run again.

Now tiny chunks of broken glass sliced into my bare feet. *Why couldn't I have a costume with shoes?*

The broken glass must have been left from bottles of wine and rum and imported delicacies, for the slouching wild dogs pressed their soft black noses to the shards all around us on the cobblestones and licked at them, dribbling blood that ran into the urine and murky water that trickled at the edges of the street.

"The dogs will kill themselves," I called out to Jules, "eating the glass." And when he said nothing, I insisted, "Jules, chase the dogs away from here."

Jules dropped his gaze from some point up ahead in his mind to the dogs scattering before him. "They'll pass it," he lied to me. "It will go right through them."

It would not. But the slivers and chunks were going right through the tender skin of my feet. I had always gone barefoot, but on the clean, smooth cobbles of the courtyard and the marble and wooden floors of the townhouse. Never like this, stumbling over broken, discarded and filthy things. When was the last time I'd been on a public street?

Not since Jules had overcome his fear of escaping his mother's house.

How I wished-suddenly-that I could return to my hostile, safe home.

As if he'd heard my thought, Jules's hat and cape turned and lifted toward me in the darkness once more, and his voice floated to me through the night and the regret. "We are almost there." He watched me, slowing almost to a stop as I danced around the last of the glittering bits. *He could have carried me. No one would have known what kind of girl he was carrying, with the mask and the costume.*

And why should he have to hide his care for me? Hadn't we gone to all this trouble to flee the only people who wouldn't allow him to love me?

Out here in a small dark street, he watched as I cut my feet. It is enough to make me wonder...

We had doubled back through these alleys toward the bright main street along the river that we'd left. Its light now spilled forward, pulling us to the corner and back to the bedraggled people who leaned on each other, their arms around necks and waists, limply lifting toasts to lips that mumbled things to make them throw back their heads for a last laugh. "Only the demons are still out here, and the damned Americans," a woman murmured in my ear as Jules pulled me down the last stretch of *banquette* along the black river. Then she shouted after me, "Get inside, *cherie!*"

And all at once we were inside a quiet foyer under the flickering candlelight of a crystal chandelier.

A man lifted his head from a wide desk where he sat writing notes. He inquired politely of Jules, "May I help you, *Monsieur*?"

Jules lifted a heavy key from a hidden pocket. The man waved us on.

"You have a room here?" My fear quickened yet again as we started down the hallway behind the foyer.

The hallway spilled us into a maze of courtyards. Jules finally stopped his headlong dash, lifted off his top hat, and took a deep breath. "Good God." He sighed. "We did it, *mon amour*. My love, welcome home."

He ran a hand through his hair by way of combing it and turned a serious face to me. "We are on our own now, Aurelie. Can you believe it?" He reached for my hand but, instead of pulling me on, he pulled me into his arms.

I went willingly, lowering the mask, and let go of the edges of the shawl at last so I could press my cheek to his shirt front.

I sagged against him. *So tired. So frightened, a new feeling for me. Cut and bleeding, also new.* I needed to wash the glass from my feet, to wash the offal from this skirt and from my ankles. I thought with a start of *Tante* Clothilde going to sleep alone in our room in the servants' quarters, her clay jars of jasmine-scented water sitting full in the corners. She

27

would have gladly washed the blood from my feet, clicking her tongue in dismay.

She has always taken care of me.

"What is it, Aurelie?" Jules asked tenderly. "Come. Let us get out of this night air."

This time his pull on my hand was so gentle I barely felt it. He kept looking back to make sure I followed him willingly across the courtyard and up the thin wooden stairs, and then down a narrow gallery that brought us to a slender door. "Our room," he called it as he again pulled out the massive key.

Our room?

The tall thin door swung open on the new life Jules offered me with a toss of his cape and a wave of his hand. "After you, *cherie.*"

I hesitated. "Our room, Jules?" If this was what he intended, then I was going back to his hateful parents.

His arm lowered. "What's troubling you?"

"This is an inn. I've heard of such places."

"Yes?" Expecting more.

Must I explain what should be plain? "I cannot do this. I never meant to be this to you."

His face, as well as I could see it in the night, covered by shadows thrown as the lanterns in the gallery were blocked by courtyard trees and vines, was still. Surely Jules was becoming this sober stranger who kept emerging.

I had come here with a stranger. I began to back away.

Jules caught at my hand. I made a small sound that meant, "No, don't."

He coaxed, "Only to talk. Come in and talk with me, Aurelie. I don't understand." He bent and lifted me and carried me, not over the glass, as I'd wanted him to, but over the threshold. Then he kicked the door shut and made his way to the bed in the center of one wall.

It was a plain but prettily covered bed, mosquito netting tucked around it. I lifted a little of the netting away, so as not to tear it with my weight as Jules set me down on an edge of the feather-stuffed mattress.

A lamp sat on a table near the room's only window, open over the gallery and courtyard we had crossed. "I didn't bring a light from the bonfires outside. You don't mind if I don't wait for a priest to bless the fire before we light up our new home, do you, Aurelie?" Jules asked.

He didn't wait for an answer. He was already striking a flint he'd pulled from a pocket as he chatted. "You don't believe in my mother's superstitions. You're nothing like my mother." He lit the lamp's wick and replaced the glass. Then, by the lantern's light, Jules knelt and lifted one of my feet.

I said, "I don't want to be here," just as he said, "Hush. Hush."

Then he pressed his lips to the dirt, to the mud, to the breaks in skin and flecks of clinging glass. "Of course you want to be here." He wiped his lips and ran his hand just above the cuts. "I am here. Where else would you want to be, Aurelie?" He squeezed the foot, and I cried out as he clutched it toward him. "Don't ever do this to me again."

I snatched my foot away. "Do *to* you? Is this what I should have expected *from* you? An inn? Men take girls to an inn-"

"For reasons that have nothing to do with you and me, Aurelie." Jules looked down now at the floor, as if confused, his voice low. "What is this all about?" He shook his head and turned away from me and to me again, as though he'd lost something and needed my help to find it.

Then his voice rose. "Do you have any idea-no, of course you don't; you couldn't-what trouble I've had doing what you said you wanted-"

I jumped to my feet to scream at him, "What *I* wanted, Jules?" and fell back from the sharp pain, still screaming, "When did I say I wanted to throw our love away on an *inn*?"

Jules stood. I thought he would turn away, but there was nowhere to go in the small room, and so he stayed there, fists on his hips at my eye level. His rising and his posture swept his cape back behind his shoulders. "Throw our love *away*?" he shouted back at me, but I wasn't listening.

I stared at the sword.

That was his brother's sword he was wearing. Not a fencing sword. A deadly weapon. What had possessed him?

Worse, what had possessed me to come away with him?

"Oh, my God," I said and leapt onto the splinters of glass still in my feet to run to the door.

It was shut, not locked. I could get out, if I was quick. I could always outrun Jules. I would outrun him this last time, all the way back to the townhouse, if he chased me.

The door wouldn't open. Jules caught me against it, pulled my hands from the knob, and dragged me to the table by the window.

He pulled me down into one seat and knelt again in front of me, still gripping my wrists. "Yes, what you said! Have you lost your mind, Aurelie? Why did you say the things you said if-"

I snatched my wrists free and shrieked at him, "What did I say, Jules? You're making no sense, and you're frightening me!"

Silence fell between us like a steel blade. He continued to kneel there with his mouth open.

Finally, "Frighten you?" Jules repeated. "I have never. I *could* never. Aurelie, this is Jules you're talking to! *Your* Jules."

"Well, now you can frighten me, and you are frightening me. Explain this, or have the goodness to take me back to *Tante* Clothilde, and I swear I'll say nothing about this"-what was it? This escape? This running away?-"to anyone."

"Stop." Again, he shook his head. Only now, as his gaze swept the floor and my feet, he started to look as desperate as I felt.

Then Jules raised his face and held out his hands to me as if he held the truth just there, where I could see it for myself. "At the fountain," he pleaded. "When I explained to you the financial arrangements my parents made that bound me into that damned marriage, and you finally listened to the bind your own demands had always placed me in-"

31

"*My* demands? Liar!"

"No. I'm not lying. I'm finally telling you the whole truth, Aurelie. I couldn't do what you wanted. We could never have been together if you'd kept fantasizing that I would afford a house, or even the down payment on a house. I'm not my father-"

"What does *he* have to do with this?"

Jules now searched the walls, still with that shake of his head. "What does my father have to do with my love for you? Only that everything you want would need my father's approval, signature, blessing, and financial backing! Houses, Aurelie?"

"One house. The smallest, simplest house! Not your father's mansion."

"And promises of emancipation and education and small business shops for all our children? Aurelie, be realistic!"

Now he was shaming me. Ridiculing my hopes. Destroying the beautiful promises he'd made since our love was new, when we were children. If he couldn't do these things, why had he promised to?

For this. To bring me willingly to an inn.

I am betrayed. Doubly betrayed. Not just to be abandoned. First to be used and only then to be abandoned.

Anger is stronger than fear. I stood and didn't run. "Get away from me. I am going home, Jules."

He stood, too, and moved to block my way. "No. You will not do this to me. I have seen this through, and you will see it through. Just as you said that night."

I said patiently, as though to his grandmother, wrapped in white cloths in her attic, "You keep

32

saying I said something. What did I say?" I only remembered trying to stop his mouth with my fingers at the sight of the waning moon. *Had I said anything?*

"You said not to go on telling you ... You know, Aurelie. Why are you forcing me to repeat this?"

"Repeat it or peacefully let me go."

Jules put his hands on my mouth, as I had tried to put mine on his that long ago, strange and distant night. "I told you that if you would not accept what I could offer, you left me no choice but to obey my parents and give up-" He grabbed at me again as I sank to the chair.

He went on. "You wouldn't let me finish, and when I thought about it later, I thought you were asking me not to give up, that you were finally willing-"

"It wasn't that. I wasn't even listening to you. It was only the moon. Our love was dying."

"Not our love, Aurelie," Jules beseeched me at last. "Never our love. Our love cannot die. Only our chance to be together, as we've always wanted. Won't you take this one last chance with me?"

How could the cuts in my feet suddenly be so much more painful than when I had been walking? I tucked them away from where Jules knelt again, so he wouldn't bump them. They felt swollen to bursting.

Tears shot from my eyes.

Jules swarmed forward, engulfed me in his cape, and rocked me in his arms as *Tante* Clothilde used to do.

33

Used to do. I had left my old life. By morning, I could no longer return. Not without punishments. Whippings would probably be the least of it.

Jules murmured, "Oh, *mon ame,* my soul, no, no. Don't cry. There is no reason to cry. Look around you. This is ours. It will last. I will make it last. I've wracked my brain and planned everything, Aurelie. You will see. You shall kill me, if you turn away now. Don't go."

CHAPTER TWO
BECAUSE I HAVE YOU

We fell asleep as we were. The last thing I knew was that Jules's head rested on my knee, and his hand loosely clutched my ankle because I wouldn't let him have my foot again.

The cape spilled around him in a black swirl on the floor and carpet. The black curls that grew from his head cushioned my fingers as I stroked him, trying to comfort his frustration.

It was an old habit. I remembered another time we had been in this same pose, I seated, shocked, hurt, trying to comfort Jules, who was overcome. His brother lay dead.

I closed my eyes to shut out the unwelcome memory and the unfamiliar room. Hopelessness welled up in me. *What have we done? Can we fix this?*

When I opened my eyes again, it was to find Jules trying to ease my foot into a porcelain basin of water.

I pulled it back.

He looked up at me as he took the foot in his hand again. "You have to, before the cuts get infected. We don't have your witch, Clothilde, to treat you, if the foot swells."

I let him take the foot. He held the ankle, so small, curving, and coppery, caught in the ghostly circle of the long fingers of his right hand, as the fingers of his left hand ran lightly over the sole,

35

brushing glass and pebbles into the water's muddying pool.

Dawn lightened the lamp-reddened blackness that had made the room so eerie in the night, gilding it pink and gold with early sunlight. I could see in a far corner a screened-off dressing area where Jules must have found this basin and a pitcher of wash water.

Sounds from the courtyard below had probably wakened him. Noise carried up to us through the slightly opened window of calling, laughing women, setting out breakfast on the woven willow tables. The scent of strong coffee and fresh croissants drifted through our window and mingled with the staler smell of last night's streets that still clung to our clothes and hair.

Jules, as if reading my thoughts, said shyly, "Let's wash and dress to go down to breakfast. I have a surprise that should please you."

He worked his way up stiffly from the floor and went to a large dark wardrobe against the wall opposite the unused bed. I dunked my other foot into the filthy basin of water and gingerly picked at the things embedded in the skin while I watched him.

The wardrobe swung open on a small collection of a gentleman's and lady's clothes.

The cape and sword slid from Jules to the floor as he turned to me, smiling and spreading a hand that invited me to enjoy the sight. I said a little stupidly, "Does the inn provide clothing, too?"

Jules laughed. "No." He worked open the buttons of his shirt and pulled it off. It joined the cape and sword on the floor, and Jules went behind the dressing screen.

I heard him wring out a towel in the pitcher to scrub his face and teeth. While he washed, I tiptoed-why, I couldn't say-to the wardrobe that opened onto a new life for me.

Jules's clothes were the soberly colored, tasteful trousers and blouses becoming fashionable for young gentlemen that year. Following the Revolutions in France, young gentlemen discarded the foppish fashions of their grandfathers and had tailors make them the sober new clothing of the changing age of machines and sciences.

The clothes awaiting me, however, were only simple in color. Peach, cream, and apricot shades poured over a base of ruddy chocolate.

But the fabrics were far from simple. Intricate layers of fine Belgian lace adorned the bodices and hems of a day gown, an evening gown, a dressing gown, and a modest selection of silky underthings. It occurred to me that I might be expected to sleep in these fragile undergarments, finer than the stained satiny bloomers I picked up from *Madame*'s floor on the mornings that followed her husband's rare visits to her room.

I was still hot with blushing when Jules came around from behind the dressing screen.

"How do you like them?" he asked softly. "I didn't have time to order them. I had to buy them ready made. But they seemed made for you."

Suddenly, the extravagant costume that had seemed so sadly neglected in its brief beauty, arriving mud-spattered at the inn last night, seemed tasteless. I picked at the bow tied between my breasts, to loosen the blouse and pull it over my head.

While my hands were still above my head, I could already feel Jules's palms and fingers cup my back to pull me toward him. The warm wetness of his mouth pressed to the outer edge of my left breast, just where it swelled above the ribs.

This was not what I had planned ... what we had promised each other. This was ... not!

I lowered my arms, still trapped in the blouse turned inside out, and gently pushed Jules away with the flat of my palms. He held on but straightened to listen to me say, "We still might go back, Jules. They might not know yet that you are gone."

"I didn't do all this so we could go back, Aurelie. You've known for years that I could not give you up. Would you really have stood by, refusing what little I could give you, to see me go into a marriage that would drive me mad with loneliness? This is the last time I'll ask you, *mon amour*. Will you go back? I will not. I'll stay until I have no more money to pay for the inn. If you stay with me, it will strengthen our case when we finally return to my parents." But he could not keep up his stern tone.

He nuzzled my nose with his own and tried to get me to imitate his smile. "My fiancee's family will be irreparably offended by my running off with you, *cherie*. My parents will be forced to admit that they can make me over in my brother's image in every way except in the choice of what woman I shall love. I owe them everything but that."

This argument was dangerous territory between us. I could not win it. Whenever, after his brother's death, I questioned Jules's sense of what he owed his parents as their sole surviving son, he told me I had no understanding of a French gentleman's sense of honor.

I have no sense of it, perhaps, because I have seen so little of it practiced by those same French gentlemen.

But taking up such an argument, this lost and searching morning, seemed little more sensible than slicing my own throat with the fallen sword. I let his words fall away from between us.

"May I wash now?" I tugged the blouse off my arms and slipped behind the dressing screen.

There was another towel to dip, wring, and pat across my face and neck. I unpinned the thick bundle of my chignon and let the hair spring free, light and bushy, all down my shoulders and bare back. I scrubbed it between the ends of the damp towel. Then I unfastened and dropped my skirt and apron and sighed as I sponged off the rest of my stale, dirt-crusted body.

My towel came away so filthy that I had to search for a clean corner of Jules's to wash my teeth.

Neither of them was clean enough, when I was through washing, to wrap around my body, so that I could rejoin Jules on the other side of the screen. I remembered the dressing gown. Peach silk, flowing from its hanger, running with beige lace trim.

If I put any of these clothes on, would I be committed to stay? Surely not. Hadn't *Madame* returned clothes that had been cut and sewn especially for her, after more than one wearing?

I asked Jules to hand the dressing gown over the screen. He waited on the other side to see me come through, wearing it. And when I did, he smiled the smile of our childhood, the breathless tender smile of the first time I read one of his poems all by myself.

Tenderness
Is the breast that hides
Your heart from me.
Come close,
And let me touch the love
That waits.

"You're beautiful," Jules said and held out his hands to me.

This time, it took forever to walk into his embrace. All along the way, I wondered if I should turn back, for both our sakes, and leave us room to return to the safety of parents and owners who didn't know us, didn't know who we were and what we had lived, who would order our lives without reflection and doubt and regret.

Order, instead of this mad escape to build our lives around a murderous, secretive turning toward each other that was beyond our control or understanding.

In his arms, alone together in the passing morning, this last hope to be redeemed in slavery and obedience fell away, never to be picked up in

40

my mind or heart again. We had waited, hoped, and given up. There would be no more giving up.

His lips bathed my throat and breasts with dry, hot kisses. His breath warmed my heart, sent it racing under his whispered words of love, pet names and endearments that tried but couldn't reach the hope and loneliness that had pulled us together and kept us separate, groping toward each other's deepest feelings, for as long as I could remember.

I could remember nothing of my good intentions, my firm resolutions to taste, to share, to entice, but never to give in. Somewhere, there was a house of my own he could have bought me.

His lips traced a burning line down the vein inside my thigh.

A house with shutters against the summer's scorching sun and steamy heat.

His lips found a searing point of feeling just as his fingertips freed the last tiny alabaster buttons of the dressing gown, sliding them, unresisting, between the holes.

A house where my children would run through the flower garden on flagstones Jules laid with his own hands in the early days of our living together, when there was no extra money for hiring workmen.

The silk ran from me like the resolutions and the house and the children on the flagstones.

And then there was nothing but burning, and tight muscles straining toward the tenderness he offered, and lifting and joining lips, hands, and hearts through crushed breasts as he surged up onto me, into me.

We could not get close enough.

41

And after we had brought down the mosquito netting, tangled between our bellies and legs, and had to rip at it, tearing it away, it was only a breath, not even a thought, not even a moment, to rush together again, against not netting but years and insults and hurt and his brother's death ... *No, no. Not that. Don't think of that.*

The pain that I had always heard of was a rush of agony that found my deepest secrets, and it was those, the lumps of hopelessness and loneliness crumbling inside me, that made me cry out and cling, shuddering, to Jules, as he held me and said ... He said ... But I could not understand a word of whatever he said.

For the promises fell away in the incoming flood of his closeness. He was here at last, mine at last, and we were not two but one. We had always been meant for this moment, our forever.

This was who we were, and who we had fought against. In the end, the only one we had not killed, had not betrayed, was this one that was all that was left of the two who had so foolishly resisted.

But there would be no more resistance.

Everything that I used to be escaped me in the bloody flow that soaked the mattress beneath us as we slept and woke, heart to heart beating more slowly now, bathed in cooling sweat sweeter than water to lazy searching lips, wetting dried lips in drowsy kisses.

We loved each other. We could only love each other. No one else.

And as the morning passed, we moved again in that closeness that was at last familiar, for we had become ourselves, that one being we had always known ourselves to be. One in each other, more each other than ourselves, and more each other's than our own.

Jules's heartbeat on mine was mine. When he rose to search for the pot under the bed, I felt bereft. I sat up in the tangle of torn netting and bloodied, sticky bedclothes to watch him kneel and urinate into the flowered porcelain chamber pot.

He replaced the cover and slid the pot back under the bed.

I asked, "Did I hurt you?" and nodded toward the pale blood, diluted, matted and drying in the dark curls of his pubic hair. I remembered the clench of my muscles, that spasm like dying.

He shook his head. "Did I hurt *you*?" he said softly. "It's your blood, *ma chere*."

"You didn't hurt me." *Not until you got up and left me lying alone.* That movement had ripped the heart, beating, right out of my chest. "You were gentle. Weren't you?" I couldn't be sure. My feelings had raged with more desperation than I had ever borne in the courtyard, in the quarters, in the townhouse when ...

"Should I go find us something to eat, *cherie*?" Barely whispering. He didn't want to go. I didn't want him to go.

"Can't I go with you, Jules?"

He looked away. "It might be best if you stay here, so that no one may think-"

"I understand."

He looked up at me quickly, to see if I really did understand.

43

I tried not to be hurt hearing that, already, there would be people who would say that I was just this, the girl who was taken to the inn.

"I love you," Jules said and crawled back onto the mattress, onto the netting and the drying stains, to hold me.

And we kissed and rested, wakened and tried to find again the peace that waited for each of us at the passionate center of the other's body and being, as the sun arced, blazed, and fell from the sky outside.

In the rosy darkening, Jules insisted, "*Mon amour,* my love, I should go find us food. We will starve."

"No." Thoughtfully, "We would die of thirst first."

He chuckled in the spreading darkness, beyond my sight. It startled me. I had not been joking.

He slid an arm around me and pulled me to him. "We cannot die now. We must live, now that we have each other." He kissed me.

In the end, in the burgundy lamplit night, we had to wash in the rank used water and dress in the fragile, lovely new clothes, meaning to go out together and find what we needed.

We decided that we would need food that we could bring back to our room at the inn. As perfect as our escape would have been if we could have made it a honeymoon and dined in a restaurant with pressed linen and fine silverware, every minute spent in public together endangered the security of our hiding place.

Jules had bought me a light wool chocolate cloak to cover my head, face, and the day gown.

Unfortunately, he had neglected to buy a quietly colored scarf for my hair, as the law required of women of any African descent at all. So once we'd rinsed the last shreds of glass from the soles of my feet and soothed the burning skin with ointment, we dressed and stood before the full-length mirror, considering what to do about my abundant hair.

Rolled and repinned, it still pushed indignantly at the cloak's hood, threatening to leave me bareheaded in the slightest breeze.

There was no question that I could ever get away with going bareheaded. I was golden-skinned, obviously not of purely French, Spanish, or English descent. For all I knew, though *Tante* Clothilde teased me as a "little quadroon putting on airs," I might be a mulatta, descended from a pure African woman and a European man. It was my beauty and my love for him, not a pale skin, that had won me Jules.

And the law was notoriously hostile to beauty as dark as mine.

Jules lifted the raging scarlet turban of the costume he had bought me from the floor. He couldn't bring himself to suggest that I ruin the pastel dress by wearing this turban.

There was no hope for it. "I'll stay," I said. "I might be able to clean up our room, if only I had something to wear to the well, to get fresh water."

Jules said sternly, "You are not to go to the well. The inn has women who clean the rooms. We must not have heard their knock. I didn't buy you the kind of clothes you would need for servants' work."

He had not, it seemed, bought me the clothes I would have needed for a freewoman's way of life, either. But I couldn't say so.

"Maybe you will see a suitable scarf while you are shopping for our dinner," I suggested. "I can go with you next time, *mon amour.*"

Jules dropped the scarf and hugged me. "Do you know," he said into my ear, "that is the first time you ever called me your love instead of your dear friend."

"No!" I didn't believe him.

"Yes. You've gotten so used to the sweet names I call you that you've taken credit for saying them in return. But you don't. That is, you haven't until now." He smiled.

I returned the smile.

And stood in the doorway, still smiling as he went down the gallery and down the stairs, to return to my view as he crossed the courtyard below our room.

He looked up to where I watched and waved me back into the room. I went reluctantly and closed the door.

Alone with whomever-whatever-I had become. Jules's lover.

I didn't clean the room. I sat by the open window, my hands restless on the unlit lamp, and watched the people who came from and went into all the rooms that faced our courtyard.

Who were they? Why were they here?

I had heard that gentlemen took young women to inns to use them without embarrassing their mothers and wives. Some freewomen and

Frenchwomen made a living by going to inns with gentlemen.

That was not what I had done, I insisted to myself as I watched and waited. Jules and I were not strangers. We had grown up together, playmates and fast friends.

A woman knocked at the door. "The innkeeper sent me, *Madame*, to clean your room and fetch you fresh water. It has been all day, and we saw the gentleman step out, so we thought, perhaps now ... "

I let her in. She surveyed the scene of my and Jules's coming together and said she could not replace the mosquito netting tonight. She doubted we would suffer, as the weather was cooling and there were so few mosquitoes.

I returned her smile and sat out of her way as she worked. I felt rude, watching her clean without offering her my help. But in my new dress, so fine and delicate ...

She asked me to put down the dirty clothes I had picked up from the floor. When I stared, unsure what to do, she took the bits of my filthy costume and Jules's abandoned clothes and shoved them into a sack dragging at her side. "They'll be cleaned and returned, *Madame*," she assured me. At hearing that title applied to me without benefit of any wedding ceremony or home of my own, sitting awkwardly in *deshabille* in an inn ... I thanked her with a wave of my hand.

Yesterday, I had still been a hopeful, resentful girl. Today I was *Madame*.

I was still seated at the table by the window when Jules returned. My heart leaped and beat more

47

fiercely when I saw his dark curls glide below our window, crossing the courtyard. My hands trembled by the time I watched him approach our room through the window onto the gallery.

He smiled through the glass at me. He looked as relieved to see me, still here, as I felt to see him, returning.

He came through the opened door into my arms.

His bundles pressed against our ribs, between us. Curious strangers might have been watching us from other inn windows. But we stood, close and unwilling to move, until one of his bottles of water slipped.

He clutched at it and upset a pink-wrapped paper bundle that had rested on his bent arm. I juggled it, grasping with first one hand and then the other, and caught it before it fell.

"It's yours." Jules nudged the door shut behind him with his foot. "Did the maid come to clean? She did a nice job, don't you think?"

This was so clearly a hint that I said without thinking, "It's a lovely room, Jules."

He went to put his other purchases on the table and said without turning toward me, "I'm sorry it's only a room. But it's not where we have gone that counts, *mon amour*. It's the statement our leaving together makes to my parents."

Not now. "Yes, yes, *cher*. I understand. I only meant that this is a lovely room." I considered telling pretty lies about making our bedroom just like it in the house we would have someday, but I couldn't. Instead, I unwrapped the pink package.

It was a shimmering silken cloth, the bronze threads shot through with scattered strands of gold that outlined flourishing blossoms and birds with trailing plumes. "It's very fine." I could watch my fingers play on the other side of it.

Dismissing the scarf and his hurt at my disappointment, Jules said, "I've lit the lamp. Come eat with me."

We sat in the glowing circle of light that shut out our world of new feelings, too intense to describe to each other, and touched hands as we ate.

The paper that had wrapped the spicy sausage, protecting Jules's cape, was our platter, spread to hold a small round of cheese, a loaf of that morning's bread, and a cluster of grapes. We drank the water and wine from their bottles.

We kissed the drops of wine from each other's lips. What did it matter if we couldn't tell each other all we felt? We could show it.

We saw it in each other's eyes. We felt it and knew that it could not be spoken without putting the speaker through unbearable pain and fear.

Love was not enough of a word. Existence was what we had found in each other. As we ate, we watched each other's eyes and understood.

"Don't speak," we said to each other sometimes, and "Don't try," at others. "I understand."

"I feel what you feel."

"You are my heart," Jules said at last and closed the paper on the picked-over food. "I feel because I have you inside me."

"I live-" I began, and he finished for me, "because I have you inside me."

"Where there used to be-"

"Nothing. Not even emptiness."

"Can we survive this?" I stopped his hand as he reached to trim down the lamp's wick. Another change. I was never the one who asked. I was always the confident one who knew.

Jules said, "I am going to survive because I have this. *This* cannot be taken from me. Even if I die. Even if you die. You will always be in me, making me who I needed to be, even before I knew who that was."

"Will we survive together?"

"We can only survive together. Even if-"

"Even if I die. Even if you die."

Jules said, "I have died in you. There is no more me that is separate from you."

I said, "Even before we came here."

"Even before we came here. We came here and came back to life. We found life again because-"

"Because we found it in each other."

"Yes," Jules said. "We have found life in each other."

This time, we undressed slowly. We watched each other's faintly glowing shapes in the flickering light of the courtyard's torches as it warmed the slowly revealed curves of our bodies, finding pinpoints in our eyes.

"I love you."

"I love you."

"I only want to love you."

"I want nothing else. There is nothing more than this moment, here with you."

Our fingers traced the lines reddened by distant firelight. Touch told too much now. Every pore of our skin felt jolts like electricity. We threw ourselves together, resisting the shock, and tore at each other in our desire to be close. But there was too much pain between us now. This time, our lovemaking was frantic, and we fell away from each other at the end, spent and stunned. Do starving beasts take pleasure as they feed their hunger?

We lay, exhausted and confused in the dark, and reached for each other's hands. We looked away from each other, frightened and panting, as we fell asleep.

We woke covered in the morning's sunshine and wondered at how timid and breakable we were the night before.

Everything would be fine. It must be fine, for we had each other. We flowed together, tasting, touching, and soothing each other's pleasure points.

This feeling of pleasure and joy lasted for months.

But it was mine only when Jules was with me. It left me whenever Jules left the inn without me.

I never learned if he had that feeling that everything would be all right when he was without me. I assumed he did.

For he was eventually emboldened to go out with a few friends he made at the inn. Some of these young men were friends he or his older brother made at school. Even these did not perturb Jules, as he was sure they would never betray us to his parents.

For they, like he, had come with lovers. Their lovers should have been female companions for me.

But their lovers, women who sat luxuriously dressed at the height of French fashion in the courtyard and even came to call on me in our room, women whose lovers rode them, held them, displayed them naked in the inn's windows to impress passersby with their manhood, all passed from our lives within days.

When Jules realized the impermanence of these relationships, he apologized for having ever introduced me to any of these women. "I thought at least some of them would be like us," he explained. "Lovers trying to get away from his parents' expectations and start a life together."

I could have told him this would not be so. The first of these young women proved to me that serious relationships had permanent homes. They did not come to an inn.

She asked, pouring me tea at breakfast one morning in the courtyard as the men smoked over by the wall fountain, "So, is the *Monsieur* your steady, or are you fishing, like the rest of us?"

"Fishing?"

"You know, *ma chere.* Throwing out a line to see what you get."

I was winded. I stared at my hands, resting in my lap, until I could breathe again. *Fishing?*

Soon Jules was at my side. "*Mon amour, qu'est-ce que c'est?*"

I said, "It's nothing, I think."

He didn't like this and took my arm to help me to our room. As we started up the stairs, I heard the young woman tell her escort, "I had no idea. But could she be-?"

Once in the room, Jules watched helplessly while I cried.

When I could stand the lie, I assured him that I preferred to meet his friends' lovers, passing faces though they might be. For one thing, they were my only company when Jules was gone and the fear of what we were doing descended upon me.

Secondly, the scarf had not done all for us that we had hoped. It did not give us courage to go out together, even at night, and risk being recognized in public.

I hated the lovely thing and didn't wish to go any further than the courtyard, where I didn't have to wear it. The management was not so strict in the case of women who clearly were descended from the African race.

The owner explained his policy to Jules one morning when we came down to breakfast too late for me to work with the hated scarf, so that it trailed from my shoulders. Jules had whispered to the innkeeper, "Is it all right?" And he had answered with a courteous nod and a chivalrous comment to Jules about what a shame it would be to cover such lovely hair as mine.

Jules turned and watched me, wishing, I suspect, as I raised my coffee to my lips with a trembling hand, that I had not heard.

What was it to be a woman of African descent in New Orleans as English America took over Louisiana? It was to be encased in a beautiful body and cling to a lover like the moat that surrounds a besieged castle.

I learned to steer the women's conversations toward subjects I needed to discuss with *Tante* Clothilde but couldn't. *This pain that is starting deep inside ... This desire to have him suck my nipples ... Why do men cry? If they must cry, why not forgive us for having seen it?*

The women were of all races and every mixture I could imagine. They faded away with the passing of the warm weather.

By Christmas's cold, a new wave of visiting young men with their lovers came to the inn. I refused Jules's invitations to drink with them or dine with them in the courtyard or in their rooms.

"I'm not up to it, *cher*. You go ahead. I've gotten used to going down to the courtyard alone when I want some fresh air. No one bothers me."

This was not quite true. I should have said, "No one bothers me any longer."

For there had been a woman. A pale, angry woman, who came to the inn with a bent and aged man, evidently her husband, and followed me about the courtyard whenever he left her alone, until I fled to my room.

She had followed me one morning, looking more venomous than usual. I was stubborn and stayed in the courtyard despite her sitting within mere feet of me, glaring at the side of my head.

But I grew anxious. Was she a friend of Jules's mother? Was I unwise to sit as if I didn't see her there and read the newspaper Jules had left me, baring my head to the sun?

She finally broke through her few last reserves and shuffled across the bit of courtyard left between us, after me.

"Harlot!" she shrieked in a dry English voice like tossed straw. I looked up at her, astonished. She advanced on me, balling her vein-threaded hands into fists.

This could not be happening.

But it was. The elder woman, all dignity shed, stood before me, quivering and reddening and spitting with rage.

The flecks of her spittle struck me along with the viciousness of her words, which I could not understand, other than the one she had troubled herself to translate: "Harlot!"

I rose and backed away from her.

The maid who had cleaned our room the first day and, by now, become my only friend, Else, a large woman who regularly escorted visitors who had drunk too much or dressed themselves in too little to their rooms or to the street, came from the direction of the front desk, down its far hall. I ran toward her.

Else saw the anguish in my face and the fragile fury bearing down on me. She went straight past me to the woman and used the force of the other's movement to turn her without fighting her. They left the courtyard to find the woman's room, Else's voice soothing away the anger of the elderly, shaking woman.

The innkeeper came to the doorway where I cowered. "Americans," he said, smiling but afraid to offer me his arm for fear of appearing to be too familiar. I waited until Else returned and asked her if she would help me to my room, as well. She slid an arm around my waist.

Else helped me into my bed, opening and spreading the new mosquito netting so that I might lie down. "Perhaps, *Madame*, you will forgive me when I say it is time to tell the *Monsieur*."

"Perhaps, as you say, Else, it's time to tell him." But I did not tell him. Not about the incident, and not about the other matter.

But the innkeeper told Jules about the incident and suggested that I not come downstairs unaccompanied anymore. Jules stormed into our room that night and demanded, enraged, "Who is this man who let his wife insult you? What do they look like? Where do I find them?"

"Who told you-"

"That cowardly innkeeper. He would not identify them, so I can have no satisfaction until you do."

"He cannot identify them because they have gone. They are no longer here."

Jules hesitated, uncertain what to believe.

I pushed my advantage. "He made them go. He has taken a loss, as they did not pay. He did not want to tell you, I imagine, for fear that you would try to pay up their account, for them. For him. To reward him for protecting me." I had never before lied to Jules in all my life.

Silenced with shame that he could not perform such a gallantly contemptuous act as paying off the debts of his enemies to protect the honor of his enslaved lover, Jules turned away.

I stayed in our room for days afterward, to ensure that the couple might end their stay at the inn before I ventured out to the courtyard and was spotted by the wife again.

Jules stayed with me for those days. They were heavenly. Only when I found him pacing the room, biting his fingernails one morning when I woke, did I suggest it wasn't good for him to miss his friends and his outings. "I am fine. As long as you are discreet and stay away from the places frequented by your parents and their friends, I prefer that you get out now and then."

Christmas morning, he woke me with our first crackling fire and gave me a volume of new poetry that he had written, evenings and early mornings while I slept. He had had it bound by a bookmaker in the city, so that I might have a real book to read while he was out, like a fine lady.

My gift to him was the news that our first child would be born that summer, secure in our love.

Summer, the season of death in this city by the sea.

I drowned my dread in Jules's joy.

CHAPTER THREE
THE DEATH SUMMERS

The fireplace was tucked into a corner of the wall furthest from the door, hidden behind the white wrought iron of the bed's headboard. It seemed uncertain, cowering from the room as it did, that the fireplace was to be used. Could it heat anything from there?

But when, Christmas morning, Jules called a maid from the gallery to ask if a bundle of wood and kindling could be delivered, she answered so cheerily and delivered it so swiftly that I could see Jules wondered why he hadn't thought of lighting a fire before.

He hadn't thought of it because I had dissuaded him.

Else had become my confidante and explained to me that pregnancy could make a woman burn. I had made Else something like what *Tante* Clothilde had been to me. But instead of being the wet nurse who called me "kitten," Else was my friend who told me of her pain when her babies were born dead. "Crushed," she said, by the strength of her muscles shoving them from floating warmth to the steamy city's heat.

Else's owner, the innkeeper, told her that she was too large and strong for childbearing. Too much like a man. He meant to comfort her and accustom her to her work restraining women guests.

Else said she was accustomed and thought perhaps barrenness was best for an enslaved woman. But she had a very tender spot for my pregnancy and seemed to wish to share it with me. "What will it benefit me to envy you?" she asked with a shrug much like Jules's. "If I can help you, I can be near you and your child." She did not say that Jules was a fool to keep himself apart from me and the child I was so obviously, to Else, anyway, already carrying.

We generally didn't discuss Jules. He did not exist between us. When I hurried to the public latrine in my dressing gown, preferring that humiliation to the greater one of carrying out a full chamber pot in the sunlight of broad day, or quickly sipped down hot tea in the courtyard in the morning, my hair wildly thick about me with the trailing scarf only a suggestion of my recognition of the hair-covering law, Else always appeared and offered me her arm, her smile, her unmoving gaze that held me up for a moment, above my feeling of being lost in a place where I could not stay.

Any time I approached telling Jules of anything Else had told me or done for me, a twinge of something like guilt overcame me. The pregnancy and what it did to my body and my feelings were secrets I shared only with Else. So I had not yet told him that the heat of a fire would make me burn, by the time a small fire blazed in the fireplace, late that Christmas morning.

I had no chance to tell him.

He threw himself at my knees where I sat at our table by the window. I stared and breathed shallowly, not only from alarm at his impetuous gesture but also because of the binding of my evening gown just beneath my ribs.

I had risen earlier than usual, but still much later than Jules, and washed and dressed in my loveliest gown, a small token of the festivity that Jules would miss from his home.

The pregnancy had brought me to a point where I wanted nothing more than to sit in one of the silky chemises Jules had lined the wardrobe shelves with, gazing lazily out of our window and sifting my memories for those most acceptable to the future I wished to build.

And as soon as I had Jules's book of poetry unwrapped on the table before me, its velvet ribbon tied around my hair to lift the bulk of it off my sweating nape, and the silhouette of our baby drifted in the prickly firelit heat between us, Jules threw himself at my feet.

I managed faltering smiles. "I could not have planned a better coup!" Jules assured me. He seized my hands and dampened them with kisses while he urged me to see the beauty of our predicament. "I was becoming desperate," he confided. "The money, oh, you would never understand such things, but what to pay, and whether or not to go into debt, waiting out my parents, all has been answered, *mon ange*-my angel! With the money that remains, I will continue to buy us food, and no matter that none of the gentlemen of my acquaintance at the inn has produced an offer of temporary employment-"

"Employment?"

Jules shook his head abruptly. "Too risky, too risky by far. Had I trapped myself in some small office, had even one of my parents' friends espied me, can you imagine the superiority of my parents' position when they finally approached me? Ha! I would have sunk inestimably below all that they had offered, becoming dependent upon the dictates and whims of an employer, having to display my scholarly skills not for intellectual showmanship but for the gaining of subsistence-"

"Jules, please." I shifted away from the chair's arm that dug into a seam under my breast. "I cannot follow your argument."

Jules pulled himself to his feet, loomed forward over me and kissed away the sheen of sweat across my forehead. Bracing his arms by holding the armrests of my chair, he gazed into my eyes. "All will be well, now, *cherie*. You have given me the greatest of gifts: new life and a new hope for our just cause." His face crumpled with concern. "Are you in pain? What can I do to help you through this?"

At last. "*Cher,* please leave me and go out to find us a nice Yule dinner that we may share later this evening. I need to rest." I squirmed away from Jules's closeness, his eyes fixed deep into mine. *Oh, please just go.*

As soon as he had been persuaded to leave and let me sleep, not to return until the sun had set and the holiday had fled, I worked myself out of the dress. Relieved at last of its confines, I swore to myself that I would not don either the day or evening gowns again until after the baby was born.

I slouched in my chair, one leg lifted to an arm rest, its foot held in the softness of the bed's mattress, panting from the work of undressing and the heat of the clinging chemise. When I could rouse myself, I stripped off the chemise, as well. Then I continued to sit before the window, its glass opened for cooling air, its curtains parted to my face's width, so I might gaze outside.

I would have thought that relieving myself of the discomfort of my clothes should have ended my misery, but it did not. Once I was bare, turned to the steadying draft of the open and uncovered window, tears came in a rush.

I placed my head in my arms on the table and sobbed until my shoulders shook.

When the worst of the sadness passed, I raised my face to see if anyone outside the window might have been watching me. I felt watched. But no one was there.

I extinguished my lamp and opened the drapes and curtains wider. *If only I could be out there in the courtyard below, or even in the tree limbs across from me, naked as I am in my chair, free, a bird, to lift my arms and fly.*

This must be pregnancy insanity. Else had told me of such a thing.

I turned my chair slightly so that no one outside the window could see more of my body than my bare shoulders. I poured myself a goblet of watered sherry from the decanter Jules had left on the table to refresh me. I would have preferred water, but he wished to sacrifice, and so I must accept the gift of sherry.

I raised the goblet to my lips. My fingers would not hold steady. The drops like watered blood, like running body fluids, sprinkled my opened lips.

I spit it back into the goblet and pushed the prickling heat and the color and smell of the watery liquid aside. *Watery blood. Heat. The death summers.*

Three death summers haunted Jules and me, so far. *And what next?*

Could I keep fighting off the memories of the summers? I had fought them for Jules's sake for so long. But why did it fall to me to fight them off?

Perhaps if I let them overtake me at last, weakened and grounded by my body's work to grow the baby, lost in this strange place, I would find that the death summers carried some sense of home and hope. I drifted into reverie.

The first was three years ago, the first summer Jules and I knew that we loved each other and searched only for an opportunity to experience our love as fully as we dared.

But I had been given the care of Jules's endlessly dying grandmother. Hers was the death of that long-ago summer.

So I sat in the heavy wet heat of her third-story room, unrolled the rush mats at her windows to shut out the dragging thick air of midday, and rolled them up again to let in the evening breeze and the storms' cooling rage. All day, I sponged his *grandmere's* hard, thin forehead with damp cloths and sprinkled her sore-covered body with *Tante* Clothilde's scented waters.

63

And, endlessly, I collected the sour-smelling trickles of fluid that flowed from every puckered hole in her body, sluiced into a white porcelain container as though the gummy mass of it were an offering of suffering to be poured back into the brown earth from which we all had come.

I had heard from *Tante* Clothilde so many stories of who I might be, how I might be related to this family through this woman's son, my owner. I used sometimes to kneel by *la grandmere's* side, as she lay and stared open-mouthed at the ceiling that blocked heaven from her view. I would take the fragile chill bones of her hand in my warm, soft one.

"*Grandmere,*" I said, trying out the truth of her relationship to me. I dared only because she was beyond hearing, possibly beyond caring, and we were alone.

"*Chere grandmere, souffres-toi?* Dear Grandmother, are you in pain?" I crooned, so used to babying Jules when he needed comforting. "*Vois-tu ce que votre fils a fait avec la vie que tu l'as donnee*? Do you see what your son has done with the life you gave him?"

"What do you say to her?" Jules asked once, coming suddenly upon us.

I held my finger to my lips. "Shh. I try to ease her thoughts, if she is thinking. I try to make her feel that her thoughts are not her burden, alone."

Jules raised me to my feet and put his arms around me.

That was our first kiss of mouths and desires. When we parted, turning, breathless and sticky with shared sweat, to the grandmother on the bed, we started.

For she no longer stared at the ceiling. She stared directly at us, at where our lips must have met only seconds before.

As we fell apart from each other, stunned and denying, she continued to fix the air between us, the spot where our passions had come together, with her horrified pale stare.

"Jules, how can her eyes be so white?"

"My mother says she has gone blind with age. She cannot see us. She did not see us, Aurelie." Jules reached for my hands and followed me as I backed to the head of the dying woman's bed, to escape her stare. "Aurelie, even if she had seen us, who do you think she could tell? She has not spoken since before I was born."

I pulled the back of one hand to my lips, to still everything that waited there to be said.

What if she told, not what she had seen, but what she had heard from me? Some of it was soothing, like a lullaby, but some of it ... That day, I ceased speaking to her.

As I pressed cooling cloths to the veined pallor of her forehead, as I waved my water-laden fingers in an arc over the jutting bones and sweltering skin and weeping sores that entrapped her, whoever she was, whoever she had been when she truly lived, I stared as silently and sullenly as the other women who were forced, in alternating turns, to tend her.

I had been given her for the summer, that first summer, because I was most expendable. I did nothing that others could not do as well or better throughout the house. I could be shut up with *la grandmere* for all hours of the day and most hours of the night, until exhaustion excused my collapsing onto a pallet on the floor at the foot of her bed. I rose at the first stabs of morning light at my eyelids, with a start, to see if she still breathed. As soon as it was warm enough, I started in again at my endless task of fanning away the flies from her eyes, her sores, her un-sipped foods and her ceramic pot of stored wastes.

No one would miss me who did not love me.

Tante Clothilde brought me cool foods, bread spread with heat-melted cheeses or slices of fresh overripened fruits clustered in rough wooden bowls, fresh water clear of the color of the dying woman's fluids, her amber teas and urines and liquid feces.

Tante Clothilde would set my bowl of food and my bucket of water with a ladle on the floor by my chair. She hugged my head to the tight band of the apron that circled her waist. "*Pauvre minou,* poor little kitten, surely this will end by driving you mad. Run out to the latrine. I will watch her for a few moments."

I ran into the hallway and down to the gallery that ran around the second-floor rooms. I would soar. I was more than alive. I was young and strong and whole. I would live, and my life would open before me like the sky to a soul on its way to heaven. No! Like the sky to a bird.

I could fly.

I pirouetted around the gallery, arms out like wings to embrace the harsh sunlight and the blistering heat because I could bear it. I could catch the smallest breeze and be refreshed.

I began to climb up drainpipes to third-floor balconies and down vines to the courtyard cobblestones. Flying.

Until the day I slid from a mossy vine into the waiting arms of Jules's older brother, Franchot.

He laughed as he caught me. "You are a wild thing, aren't you?" Suddenly, I felt as if I had been violating the place.

I looked up to the grandmother's window where death and *Tante* Clothilde waited. The rush mat, raised to give someone a view of me sliding down the vines, dropped back into place.

Franchot had not released me. As I looked down from death's window to his face, flushed, smiling, and glowing with sweat, he lowered his mouth and kissed mine.

This was weeks after I had waited a lifetime, not knowing what I waited for, to be kissed by Jules. How could I receive this mockery of Jules's kiss within the same lifetime?

Within the same summer.

Now I felt that it was I who was violated.

Franchot said, "Wild little animal. Come with me, and I will show you what do to with all that passion."

He laughed almost indulgently, as if I were a child, released me, pretended to grab at me, and ran lightly into the house through the glass doors that let out onto the courtyard.

I hid in the room I shared with *Tante* Clothilde until she came there herself, scolding me, to get back upstairs to *la grandmere*. She had had to leave one of the other women there in my place, and if the mistress found this out because of a late dinner or dirty stairway or cold bath water, heaven help us all.

"I cannot go back," I insisted, oddly afraid to tell *Tante* Clothilde about Franchot's kiss and teasing, though I told her everything that had ever passed between me and Jules.

Maybe if Franchot never saw me again, the summer would end and he would be back at his hated Spanish military academy without further incident. Disgraceful education for a young Frenchman, his father always said.

Jules now came daily to *la grandmere*'s attic room to relieve my watch with food, poetry, and even kisses. Neither Jules nor *Tante* Clothilde mentioned my incident with Franchot in the courtyard, so I began to tell myself that no hand had dropped the mat back into place before the window. In my anxiety, I must have imagined it.

Nothing watched in that room but the bored angel of death, indolent and irresponsible. So that summer limped by, burdened with the heat and stench of *la grandmere*'s room where death lingered but would not strike.

And I was given a new job. As the youngest and prettiest of our owner's women, I was washed, lightly perfumed, and nicely dressed to serve table when young ladies of fallen titled families were brought to dinner to be paraded before Franchot.

Jules was silent at these dinners. I would have liked to talk with him about one young woman in particular whom I came to think of as The Ward.

The Ward sat delicately straight, her neck framed by dry wisps of hair that refused to be caught up in elaborate curls. She turned her small face to all the men who spoke, in turn, except Franchot.

She was serious, dark-haired, and clearly not happy to be there. So, obviously, it was she whom Franchot announced as his choice in marriage.

She had no choice. She was a Ward, orphaned but left enough status by her titled parents to be shipped to the Americas and found a suitably wealthy husband.

I should have sat in her seat and been served by someone such as she.

For had I not heard all my life, from *Tante* Clothilde, that our owner himself shared blood in common with me, and his parentage was higher than that of his wife, whose parents had secured him in marriage to her only through sacrificial donations of all their wealth?

Tante Clothilde insisted that the dying grandmother had hated the mistress and blistered her pregnancies with accusations of infidelity and contemplated infanticides. This was why the mistress had only carried two of her pregnancies to term. All the others were driven from her body by despair, near starvation and cruel purges, and her mother-in-law's evil wishes.

I wished I had heard those long-ago accusations fly. I wished I had seen the mistress run, weeping, to lock herself in her rooms, screaming insults back at her unborn baby's grandmother, trying to drown

69

out the accusations that flew at her through the barred door.

But I had to content myself with the reality of *la grandmere*'s outstretched body and the women's whispered stories, told to make the tedious hours pass. These things had all happened, and ceased to happen, long before I was born, as orphaned as The Ward but raised by *Tante* Clothilde.

Had *la grandmere*'s curses stripped the mistress's womb of the other children she should have borne, raised, and wed to the titled families of our isolated city? I liked to think so.

Maybe, if she had known of me, she might have thought more curses into the ripe summer air to further bring low my hateful, hate-filled mistress and raise me, descendant of the grandmother, to my rightful place in her son's family.

At least, so I loved to dream.

I had not slid down the vines but walked as sedately as The Ward to an agreed rendezvous with Jules on the dark side of the fountain, released from watching for a few moments by *Tante* Clothilde, the night Franchot caught me again.

Jules came upon us, struggling with each other in the darkness, and fell upon his brother, pounding him with his fists. Franchot surged away from Jules. The thrust of his escape knocked me to the ground.

With me out of the way, Franchot doubled back and came after his brother with his fists flying. I saw Jules stumble, backing away too quickly to secure his footing. Jules crumbled to his back by the fountain, knocking his head against the basin's stone edge as he fell.

He lay, flat and still.

And Franchot bent, drove one knee into his brother's chest, and shot his right fist again and again into his brother's face.

I ran screaming through the kitchen and into the library for help. "Franchot is killing Jules!" My owner threw aside his chess table and cheroot to leave an ugly burn in the carpet as he ran to the fountain to save his youngest son's life.

Tante Clothilde, who knew herbs and the healing of near-dead bodies, was given the tending of Jules while I ended the summer's death watch alone with his grandmother.

Franchot left early to return to his *execrable* Spanish military school, rumored to be the ruin of French gentlemen. ("But what choice is there, stranded in the Americas?" his father demanded of his mother.)

I clutched *la grandmere*'s death near me, each day begging it, *Take her; take her!* so that it would not venture down the stairway and take my darling Jules.

I will burn my books,
Useless words that crowd you
From my mind. What I need
To know, to study,
Is my happiness ...

That was the first of the death summers.

The following summer, I could read on my own, thanks to Jules's escapes from all tutors except his fencing master.

I thought it was odd when a second slip of paper appeared on *la grandmere*'s threshold, after I had already received the book-burning poem. The second slip of paper was a blunt note that said, "You will come to me. Wait in your room when my mother excuses you from your deathwatch at my grandmother's bedside."

I held the note and stared at it, confused. Had I misread it, somehow? Gotten words wrong?

For this note was odd on two accounts. Jules never wrote again before we had had a chance to meet in secret and discuss one of his new poems, just written for me. He didn't like to leave my understanding of his poetry to chance. We met and read over the poem together, so that he could see for himself that I understood not only the words but their sense.

He never let anything distract me, not even a second poem.

And a simple note? Jules never wrote me notes. *Only poems.* Something must surely be amiss.

I couldn't think what.

The second odd thing about this note was its assumption that the mistress would relieve me of watching *la grandmere*. She didn't. No one did but *Tante* Clothilde or another of the maids, for brief bouts with the fresh air, or Jules himself, for our plunges into ecstatic touching and the sharing of hopeful words. He knew this. Why would he write such an odd, mistaken note?

This second point had no convincing answer, in my mind. Maybe something was afoot in the family, and Jules had heard that his mother would be coming up to *la grandmere*'s lonely room on the third floor to sit with her mother-in-law, despite the summer's heat and the resultant stink of slowly dying flesh.

It would be just like Jules to jump at the first chance to discuss his poem with me. *Now, let's see. Have I understood it?* I pulled it out again and went over the spare words. He spoke so much more fully than he wrote.

But something else troubled me, and I could not concentrate.

Still, I didn't know what it was that niggled at the back of my mind until I was in the darkness of my and *Tante* Clothilde's room, and I felt the door close behind me.

Then I thought, startled, *It's the writing. The poem and the note look so different. Why did Jules's smooth, well-trained handwriting change, become so jagged and stark, when he wrote that strange note?*

As the door clicked shut and I heard fingers fumble along the wood for a latch or lock, I decided, *Jules did not write that note.*

But who might have written it, then? *Who else knows that I have been taught to read?* I thought with panic.

And worse, *Who else wants to meet with me out here alone in the dark of my room with my aunt, across the courtyard from everyone in the main house?* The answer flashed through my mind.

I turned and yanked open the door, scratching aside the hands that already fumbled at my apron ties and my dress's buttons. Franchot, sprinting close behind me, swore at the pain of the scratches.

I had never heard of an enslaved girl fighting off her owner or her owner's son. I didn't know if such things ever happened.

I only knew, as I raced out of the servants' quarters and into the courtyard, that Jules would be hurt and our promises to each other would be somehow broken, I didn't know how, but I could feel it, if Franchot had his way with me.

As I streaked past the fountain, the nerve of what I had done suddenly terrified me. What if one of my owners, furious, met me on the other side of the glass doors where I was headed? Stopped me and ordered me to turn around and face Franchot. Gave me to Franchot ...

It would be just like the mistress to hand me over to the son I hated.

I veered to avoid the downstairs rooms, which were haunted by my owners every evening from dinnertime until they retired for bed.

And I turned and leapt, instead, at the heavy vines, tangled with moss and white blooming flowers that climbed up the courtyard trees and hung down the townhouse walls.

I scrambled up the vines to the lower branches of a flowering tree, and from there leaped at another cluster of vines along the second-floor gallery, intending to climb from there to the third floor, hopelessly heading back to five minutes ago, before I'd left the wretched safety of *la grandmere*'s room to answer the note's summons.

But then I realized, *No, the note said the mistress is in there!* And hadn't she, somehow-I didn't know how-made this whole deception possible? That I should give myself to Franchot, instead of to Jules, who loved me? Though why she should want me to be with the one brother more than the other, I could not imagine even as I scrambled like a rat fleeing a kitchen cat.

I had thrown a leg over the gallery railing and called out, probably to *Tante* Clothilde, when Jules appeared.

I didn't know at first it was Jules, coming out, as he did, from his brother's glass door rather than his own.

He walked stiffly, oddly straight. I hesitated, looking between his shape in the gathering gray of late twilight and the open railing.

But then I heard Jules shout, "Aurelie!" and I broke out of my stupor and ran to him, calling, "Jules, I didn't know. I didn't know!"

Jules came toward me on the balcony with that stiff, straight gait, holding something up by the hilt. His fencing sword?

He pulled me away from the gallery rail just as his brother climbed over it, still coming after me.

When he caught sight of Jules, Franchot's eyes, I could see in the new darkness, shifted from his brother to me. Franchot laughed. "Keeping the little piece to yourself, are you, Jules? Well, I'm the firstborn heir, and first pickings should be m-" Franchot was saying as Jules, still dragging me with his free arm, came upon him.

I felt a swift hard swipe of Jules's muscles above me and to the other side, as his arm tightened around my shoulders.

As the swipe reached its highest point, Franchot sank to his knees.

Even through the moist blanket the darkness had become, I could see Franchot's eyes roll upward into his head. And as Jules's arm descended to his side, Franchot fell forward on his face at his brother's feet.

It seemed then that Franchot's shadow crept out from under him and grew beneath him, spreading. When its warmth touched my toes, I pulled from Jules, knelt and bent over Franchot. But he wasn't oozing his shadow.

He was losing all this blood.

Jules dropped his brother's sword and, without a word, bent and hefted the heavy legs and helped me carry Franchot through the glass doors to his own room and bed.

There Franchot lay as I ran to the stairway, calling *Tante* Clothilde and the other women to come help. "Franchot has been hurt! Jules has carried him to bed, but he is bleeding. Oh, come help, everyone!"

Then I ran back to Franchot's room, past Jules, standing stunned and still, to the gallery. I picked up the sword, surprisingly heavy, which tilted and threatened to clatter from my hands. I ran it across my skirt, slicing the fabric a little, on both sides. I dropped it to the ground, where it clanged and made me jump. I knelt and wiped it, turned it, and wiped it again.

Then I went to Franchot's side, to work off his soft leather boots and work open the clinging shirt, only one button sliced from its collar and yet so unbelievably soaked with blood.

How could this happen? *This has not happened. Has it?* I kept turning back to Jules, where he swayed as if he would fall and stared, to tell him so.

By the time the women and our owner and the mistress assembled in Franchot's room, crying out, shouting, shushing and tending, the story that would become the official story for everyone but Jules and me had been chattered into existence.

"I tell you," the master bellowed at the mistress, who sobbed, wrung her hands, and threw herself forward into the seeping blood that pumped more richly from her son's throat each time she fell on him, "I heard it! Franchot must have been in the alleyway, you know how he fights, and Jules came to save him, but he was too late. You cannot blame Jules. Jules carried his brother to his room, and you want to accuse him of fratricide! I heard the negresses screaming as soon as Jules appeared, carrying his wounded brother."

I would have gladly tended Franchot, to ease Jules's pain.

But he had already died.

He was dead while Jules waited alone with him, watching death settle and claim, and while I leaned over the stair rail, calling for help.

La grandmere, the constant offering that death disdained, was forgotten for a full day and night. No one thought of her. No one thought to send me to her, or to go to her without me.

Police were summoned to search for cutthroats in the alleyways. A doctor was summoned to

77

examine the wound and dose the mistress with laudanum to keep her asleep, mumbling through her agonized dreams, until the funeral. A judge came personally to the townhouse to assure Jules's father that this would be ruled a death by misadventure.

When *Tante* Clothilde found me, holding Jules in the dark of his room the next evening, away from the further questions his father and the police might ask, she sent me to check on *la grandmere* and give her water if she still lived.

Tante Clothilde went into the darkness, where I had been, to hold and speak to Jules, who would speak to no one after he was forced to speak to the police. When I went into *la grandmere*'s room, her stench, heavier and hotter than ever, thrust me back.

I leaned on the doorframe and breathed air from the hallway until I was steadied enough to try again. I went into the blackness and fumbled, past the bed, for the rush mat pullstring. I found it, clasped it, and tugged up the mats from the windows.

Night air, scented with jasmine, magnolia, and honeysuckle, rushed in. The stench lifted, dissipated around me. I went to the bed.

The open eyes. The opened lips.

I went to the bucket and ladle, left for me a day, a lifetime ago, and brought a scoop of rank water to *la grandmere*'s lips.

It trickled in. It stayed inside her. She did not choke. Maybe she lived, after her fashion. Seeing her, I asked myself, *What is life? What is death?*

Was Franchot, downstairs, truly dead? Could he, the center of this family, really die?

Much later, I knelt, with Jules, through the smallest night hours of Franchot's wake, the hours when Jules began to speak again.

Jules turned to me in the blackness burned by candle flames and whispered, "I cannot live through this. I will kill myself."

"If you must kill yourself, Jules, have enough mercy to take me with you. Don't condemn me to live without you, unless you hate me. Do you hate me?" *Franchot chasing me across the courtyard.*

Jules turned back to his prayers, head bent.

But he turned to me again as I nodded, exhausted, on my knees. "I cannot bear what I have done, Aurelie. Don't make me bear it for your sake."

"You have no need to bear it. I am bearing it for you." *Franchot's open mouth on mine.*

Jules sand into the silence of his meditations. Then, rousing, "I must kill myself. It is the only honorable thing for me to do."

"Very well." I sighed. *Franchot's hands tugging at my ties and buttons.* "I only ask, Jules, that you kill me first. Then you are free. Maybe you will kill me to avenge your brother, and then choose to live, after all." I shrugged. In that moment, I really did not care. *My fingernails caught and dragging through the skin of Franchot's hands.*

In the morning's darkest hours, Jules got up from his knees and came to me. With his head in my lap where I sat on the floor, my knees swollen and burning with the ache of the vigil, Jules said into my mended skirt, "Aurelie, how can you bear it for me?"

"With my life. With every word I say and every thought I think, I can bear it for you, Jules. I killed your brother. You did not. You cannot take that honor from me."

"I held the sword."

"For me."

"The thought was mine."

"The wish was mine."

"But I killed him."

"But you did not wish your brother dead. I did. Franchot's death is mine. I claim it. I bear it for you, Jules. Now, live. If you choose, kill me and live for me. If you choose, kill me and live for your brother. But you cannot blame yourself for the death that only I wanted."

Jules's arms went around my legs. My skirt grew damp and warm, then damp and cool, as his tears gave up the burden of his brother's death to the disappearing border between us.

Long ago, I had gloried in Jules's need of me. Now, I watched fearfully as the boundary between us melted, dissolving us into each other.

What was Jules and what was me? After the wake, it became difficult to tell. His poems searched.

You are the eye,
The still center of my being.
At the edge of your smile
Lie hell and my destruction,
Leaping as I sleep, warning,
Why wander? Mad traveler,
Go home.
Embrace your savior.

In the fall, Jules went away to Franchot's *execrable* Spanish school. When he came home at Christmas, The Ward was brought to meet him.

Then began the parade of young women. Jules promised his parents he would fulfill his brother's promising future. And yet, Jules also promised me that his life, which I had saved, was mine.

When he promised to marry The Ward if I were given a home of my own and my freedom, his mother first produced The Lie. "Choose some other negress or mulatta, Jules. That one you cannot have. Perhaps some lovely freeborn woman? Shall you attend the Quadroon Ball, this season?"

What she could not bring herself to say-but planted in Jules's mind, all the same-was a lie. Our owner had already told Jules so. Or so Jules said to me.

And, anyway, Jules said it did not matter. Things were different between the races. Blood changed, when Europeans and Africans mixed.

Tante Clothilde was suddenly silent.

And the Ward became engaged to marry yet another man. No matter; I continued to envy her.

For, if blood counted so, I should have had choices such as The Ward's. Somehow, I was descended from my owner's family, whether or not he denied it. I just knew it.

And I should not have to be here, alone and pregnant in an inn, wondering if I carried my brother's child.

81

CHAPTER FOUR
INTO THE DREAD

I raised my head from my arms. What was the use of these exhausting, discouraging thoughts? Here we were, and what would come, must come.

I wished I felt like crossing the room to wash and slip on a silky chemise. I did not. Instead, I dipped my fingers into the goblet of watered sherry and my spit and dabbed the wetness around my face. *Wash away the worry.*

The sun had gone beyond the front of the inn. The day grew late. Cursed holy day. I flipped open the cover of Jules's book of poetry and gently turned the front pages.

Too twilight to read. I reached for the lamp and box of flints and lit the wick. *Won't that oppressive fire in the fireplace ever die down?* I wished the room were not so well tended. *A nice bucket of ashes left by the hearth would solve at least one of my problems right now.*

As the lamp light flared and was lowered, I turned my head to look out of the window.

There stood a man, watching me.

He was dressed like a gentleman. He held a cane but did not lean on it.

Maybe not a gentleman, for, as I watched him, I realized he looked as if he was just about to strike with his cane and shatter the window between us. He glared as if I had lied to him, and he wanted to chastise me.

Who is this man?

We held each other's gaze through the glass, and it came to me. This was the visitor to Jules's parents' home who had told me, long ago, that my eyes were "enchanting."

I had turned away and returned to the kitchen for another tray of sweets. What need had I of a strange gentlemen's pretty words? I would never be the enslaved girl who must hope and fear that an admirer will give her a dress, a scarf, a baby for her owner to sell. Not as long as I had Jules, who wanted to give me a house of my own and freedom of the best kind, with education and small businesses for my future children.

Jules does still want to give me all that, doesn't he? I asked myself now, distracted. I shifted under the man's gaze. *I should get up and close the drapes.* I fidgeted, nude and embarrassed, working up the nerve to rise.

At that long ago dinner, the man had followed me out of the room and caught my arm to say that I must pardon his forwardness, as if I were a gentlewoman: "*Mademoiselle, je vous prie de me pardoner.*" Making fun of my low station, I was sure, at that time.

I had hated him.

And here he was now, intensely hating me. He would not release my eyes.

I rose boldly from the seat as if I were not naked and backed to the side of the window, where finally I could reach forward and drag the inner curtains shut, and then the drapes.

There. Gone.

But I heard the man's heeled shoes march to my window. Stop. Retreat. Stop. Return.

Tread slowly past the window to the door.

I thought of running to hide behind the dressing screen or, better yet, in the wardrobe. But I only stood there by the window, frozen with panic.

Now the steps came quickly back past the window. They clattered down the stairs and across the courtyard.

Truly gone. Why did he not knock, after all?

And now what had I done?

Daydreaming over useless pain, forgotten incidents, I had exposed my and Jules's whereabouts to a family friend. One of their social superiors that Jules's mother courted so earnestly. He would go to them and tell them where to find their son.

And they would come.

Would the baby be enough to keep Jules from going back home to his family? For, if he went back, what would become of me now? *They will sell me as far away from their son as they can get me.* One heard of girls and women worked to death in cane and rice fields, in the swamplands at the edge of the sea.

This did not bear thought. I would not think of it. *I have to warn Jules. Oh, where is he? Where does he go, for all these hours and days? I thought we ran away to be together, not to imprison me in this no-place.*

Soon, I would be sniveling, and Jules would return to a swollen-faced girl with a bulging belly under protruding ribs. I would look disgusting. Better not to cry.

I seized my Christmas gift up from the table and crawled into bed with his book of poetry propped open next to me on Jules's empty pillow. I stared at the pages and watched the firelight play in lights and shadows upon the carefully inked words.

So that when Jules opened the door, heartily juggling warm packages of cooked food and even a real Yule log, I turned to him and smiled.

"*Ma chere*. You are a sight for sore eyes, Aurelie. Come and help me lay the table. You won't believe what happened," he said.

As we spread the table with the wrapping paper, I was careful to exclaim over the delicacies Jules had brought for our Christmas dinner. Duck tenderly roasted with an orange sauce that left its thick skin faintly crackly and sweet. Pungently pickled tender artichoke hearts. Orange, mango, and papaya, and purple-skinned passion fruit hauled off a cargo ship arriving from the southern Americas. Small squares of dark and white chocolates, blanketing little clusters of nuts and scented creams. *Can we eat all this before it spoils?*

Jules was ecstatic. "Aurelie, you must forgive how long it took me to return to you. But it was extraordinary. I came home with the poorest pickings-a scrawny goose cooked so quickly the skin was burnt black and yet the bird was so raw inside as to still be cold through its wrappings!- when I stopped at the front desk to pay for our room. You will pardon a little financial talk, *mon ange*-my angel! But I had not paid our bill in several weeks, trying to decide how best to use the last of our money. No, don't worry. Look at me.

Imagine my pleased surprise when I discovered that, somehow, our bill has been paid! Not only for the past few weeks, but for the next several. How could I have afforded this without even noting it to myself?"

I looked up to see his face radiant above the lamp and the duck. "Jules, clearly you did not afford it. Someone must have paid it for you. A friend you've met at the inn?" I asked hopefully.

Jules frowned, still smiling. "No, I can't imagine. Who would have such goodwill?" His face lit. "Might it be my parents? Do you suppose they could have found out our whereabouts and be trying already to reconcile, Aurelie?"

I sank into the chair where the gentleman had discovered me earlier that day.

Jules threw off his cape and came to kneel at my feet and hold me. "No more worries today, *cherie*," he crooned. "We will feast and be joyful. You see, I've given the goose to the maids-I looked for that friend of yours but couldn't find her and don't know her name, so I left the goose at the desk for all the negresses to share-and I went back out and bought a spread fit for royalty. We will celebrate our baby." He kissed my belly, uncomfortably bloated from sitting around the room every day for all these weeks. He whispered into my skin, "Our future is bright. We will be happy."

He smiled back up at me. I had no choice. I didn't have it in me to warn him about the man at the window or share my misgivings about the paid bill.

He brought me a chemise so that I might dress enough to have the curtains and window opened on the cool winter air. We ate, dimming the lamp and reading Jules's poems to each other.

The poems were collections of promises and fears we had shared in the fleeting hours of night, alone in the inn like lost children. Why had he written them down? They were secrets better left to the darkness. To hear them again, to see them written on paper, saddened me.

Jules said that these were poems we had written together, finding words for our need to be close. The bookbinder had begged Jules's pardon for having read some of them, but he wanted Jules to know that they were truly extraordinary in their sensitivity and vulnerability, and did Jules know that this was becoming a rage among French poets?

Away with rigid form and formula. Into the dread and addiction to the unknown.

Not even the masters of paint and pen, back on the continent, had Jules's daring, the bookbinder claimed. How he cast aside propriety and ripped open his heart with his hands!

Jules touched my hand on the book. "You have taught me honesty and every good thing I know." *What is he trying to tell me?*

Annoyed, I took my hand away. "Jules, I was sitting in the window today."

His eyebrow lifted. His mouth opened but he said nothing, in his obvious effort to control his irritation. "As you were when I returned, *ma chere*? Naked?"

I turned my head away and slid my fingers from his book and back to my lap. I wrapped my fingers together so that he couldn't pull one of the hands into his grasp.

If he disapproved already, how could I ever finish what I had to tell him? The man at the window had probably paid for our room, and what would this mean to our hiding here? *We have to talk!*

Jules worked my fingers apart until I gave in and surrendered to him one still hand. He said, "Aurelie, why won't you understand? Until we have the money for a house of our own, I don't want visitors to the inn to misunderstand what you mean to me. You are not here for me to display my manhood in a window, as you have seen men do with those other unfortunate women."

"Those women don't seem to mind."

"Aurelie! I did not bring you here to teach you to condone such attitudes."

"No, Jules. It's just that-"

"Just that the danger is too real that the outside world, my parents' world, might come to define our love through our actions, even to define it to us, and we could be fatally misunderstood. There is too much that they cannot know, cannot take into account. There is too much that is only known to us-"

"Jules, this is not what I wanted to discuss with you." I rose from the table, hesitated, unable to remember whether or not I was dressed. I looked down and saw the creamy spills of silk and lace about my thighs.

Jules said, "Don't talk. Listen. Aurelie, there is hope, and more than hope. Our honor is defended and will soon be the talk of the city. Don't you wonder why I had money to go pay for our room?"

"You said-" I lifted my fingers to my forehead. I felt dizzy. The secret of the man at the window was beginning to oppress me. This was not a secret I wished to keep. Why wouldn't Jules listen?

Jules caught me as I sank and eased me over to the bed. He lifted my legs and helped me lie down with my head on the feather-stuffed pillows. I must have been faint, as it took me a moment to recall what it was I needed to tell Jules.

But he was already telling me, "Aurelie, do not be distressed. This is for our good, financially and honorably. We will be vindicated. I have given permission to the bookbinder to show my work to a publisher, and that publisher will sell copies of my book here in the colony as well as in France. If I translate the poems into Spanish, he will market them also in Spain! Of course," hand clutching a cluster of black curls, "my Spanish was never as elegant as my bro-"

Would Jules be foolish enough to mention Franchot here in the inn, dragging his bloody memory into our escape?

Jules stopped himself. "Anyway, *mon coeur*-my heart!-here is my news. The publisher has paid me-rather handsomely-for my poems. We have money to continue living on our own. And we have the satisfaction of knowing that soon all of the French-speaking world will be shedding tears over our plight and praying for our deliverance from my parents' tyranny!"

Now I was listening. "How is that, Jules?"

He knelt beside me and took my hands. "The poems tell the world who you are and how much I love you, and how right it is for us to be together. The whole French-speaking world is rising against oppression. The French love beauty of feeling and expression."

"Your verses are rather bare. You have told me so."

"But daring. Weren't you listening? Never mind. Soon, Aurelie, we will have friends and champions. Let that be enough to help us through these lean times."

Friends and champions? I should say something.

I did say, "Jules, perhaps I was seen today through the window by a friend of your parents ... "

But Jules was already bending to touch my lips with his. I felt the pillow warmth move against my mouth and breathe into it as he said, "You will drive me mad. I will not share you. I will not have other men thinking of you, of how you look, of how it feels to ... "

His mouth, his lips, his tongue came into mine, pulling at my feelings.

We left the food where it lay on the table with the open book and flowed into the discovery of what had become of our love in these past weeks.

Time ceased to mean anything.

When we were hungry and thirsty, we ate and drank whatever lay upon the table until it rotted or was finished, the bones and peelings drawing vermin in the night. Sometimes, one of us opened the door to the knock of a maid, bringing fresh water and towels, asking for our bedclothes, our laundry, our chamber pot. Didn't our room need cleaning?

So, once in a while, we dressed, Jules in his trousers and open shirt, I in my dressing gown over a rumpled chemise, and went down into the courtyard while the room was cleaned.

Most days, we did not.

There was too much of touching, of listening to whispered words, of feeling with our fingers how we had grown, how Jules's muscles had thickened and hardened, away from the sadness that clung to his parents' home, how my body had softened and filled out, rounding at breasts, hips, thighs, the skin moistening. "Am I fat?" I asked with concern.

Jules smiled. "So soft, so much of you." He smiled and returned to kissing my belly. "No. I am lost in you. As small as you are, you are my world and there is nothing beyond you that I want." My body became measured in spaces the size of Jules's kisses.

His lips found and touched every piece of me. I had not known that the soles of my feet could tingle, that a kiss brushed lightly up my knee could make my stomach flutter, that lips trailed along my hip to the curve of my waist could make me cry out.

"Here are the peaks and valleys of my earth," Jules whispered along my thighs, "the rivers where I drink, and the oceans where I drown," into the rushing, running, pooling place between my thighs, my mind, and my soul.

Sometimes I lay and felt and wondered at the feel of Jules along my heavy, hot body. Or I cried out and snatched him to me, to kiss his mouth and feel the length of him all along the passions he had raised in me, spreading with the beat of my heart.

There was no pain, as Else had described. Sickness fell away. I lay and dreamed in the world made by Jules's kisses, by the lazy stroke of his warm tongue, by the trickle of feeling following his fingertips. Warmth ran in me and through me as the winter wept its sleet and misty rain outside our room.

I stayed away from the window.

The crowd of visitors at the inn dwindled after the Yuletide. The mornings we went down-breakfasting with Jules, I regained my taste for coffee-we had the spread almost to ourselves. Else, lurking in the doorway to the foyer and front desk, watched but did not come near. She did not respond to my gestures of welcome.

Maybe she, too, did not like to share our closeness with Jules. It was a pity, but when I saw her, I remembered to miss her.

I missed no one and nothing else. Only Jules, when he left, more and more rarely, to buy us food.

He had found a woman willing to be paid a little on the side to slip from the inn and buy us what food she could.

"It is a shame," Jules discovered, "that a good negress on a reasonable errand with coin of the realm in her hand can't buy whatever she has been sent to buy." This was said as Jules counted his change and glared at the simple spread of day-old bread and molded cheeses that had been sold to the woman who ran our errands. Clearly, someone had mistaken her for a freewoman and felt it safe to cheat her terribly. "This is robbery," Jules decided. He dared not complain, of course, for it was he who had robbed her owner-our innkeeper-of her services by sending her out on our errands.

"I will have to leave you to do the shopping myself," he decided. "We cannot afford to hand out money to greedy merchants this way."

The first time Jules dressed fully to go out again into the city, the day was gray and windy. I went into the courtyard to sit and reread Jules's Christmas book of poems. My dark cloak covered my chemise and dressing gown. The open-heeled slippers warmed only my toes, but I could not be chilled.

I fought against the flipping pages and clutched the whipping ends of my scarf as the words raged past me, gray and undecided as the storm blowing by.

Safety I have left behind
To follow you, I must follow
You to the ends of reason.
What was the reason
You eluded me so long?

Else's hand came down around me and flattened a page.

I looked up and smiled. "It's good to see you again," I assured her.

"Are you happy, *Madame*?"

I shrugged and had to clutch at the hood of my cape and the unwinding scarf again. "He is happy. I am hopeful. That is enough for me."

Else gave her languid shrug, loosing the page from under her hand. I watched the gray swirl around her head and didn't want to hear what she might say about my hopefulness.

So I said like a ray of sunshine, "Was that your husband I saw you with in the doorway the other morning? I've never seen you two together. He held you so affectionately."

She interrupted. "Someone has been paying your bill, *Madame*."

My smile died. I closed the book.

Then I was angry with her. What right did she have to question my few good feelings or force me to question them? Jules would have bought us a house by now, if he could have. He could not, and if we had friends to help us, that was nothing to be ashamed of, was it?

I said as much to her.

Else listened to this as she tied my scarf around my hair and wound it into a turban. I felt her tucking in the ends as she answered, "I only thought you might want to know, *Madame*."

I caught myself about to say something such as "This is men's business and none of my affair," or some such nonsense. *How like the real Madame-Jules's mother- I am becoming*, I thought with shock. I snatched up the book and would have fled to my room.

But Else's arms went around me. "Let me help you with the stairs," she said. "The heels on those slippers." I could feel her shaking her head.

At the door to my and Jules's room, I thanked her. "For helping me up the stairs and for telling me about our bill," I explained. "If the man comes again to pay for our room, do you think I should talk to him? Does he leave a name?"

Else shook her head. "No name, *Madame*. I don't think it would go well, if you spoke with him. I only thought you should know."

I was restless in the room. After hanging my cloak and scarf and kicking off my slippers, I threw the book on the table and paced. Maybe it wasn't *that* gentleman who was paying our bill?

But if it was, what could he want in return? *Jules must have known for weeks now that someone else keeps coming back and paying our bill.*

The next time Jules went out for food, I begged to go with him. "I want to see the city," I pleaded. "I've never seen shops and, oh, the crowds, the windows. I've heard it's beautiful to go out shopping."

"Who told you so?"

"*Tante* Clothilde."

Jules laughed and shook his head. "It's only wonderful to shop when you're spending someone else's money."

"But this is my chance to see the city!"

"Aurelie, no." Jules took my chin in one hand. "This is not your chance. After we have bought a house and are living in no fear of discovery, that will be your chance."

And he was gone.

When he used to be gone with his inn friends, he stayed away a long time. As the winter moved toward Mardi Gras and he was forced from our bed to the streets for our food, alone, he began to stay away too long, again.

Jules would return with food even more meager than the maid had gotten us, his face bleak and gray from cold. Or hunger. Or worry.

He told me nothing.

My eyes and hair shone, my skin was shiny and moist with kisses, sleep, and hope, since Christmas. But now Jules's gray edged over me like a shadow.

I began to creep to the window to watch while he was gone.

As the inn filled again with Mardi Gras revelers, I felt I was losing him. I could not shake the feeling.

Our passion began to scorch us, drive us apart from each other's bodies in bed as though we were heated irons. We reached for each other too hard, tore at each other's mouths and feelings with harsh kisses and devouring words.

"Where were you, Jules? I watched for you."

"I told you to stay away from the window!"

"I asked you to let me come with you!"

Fists in his hair, Jules shouted, "But you don't understand anything, Aurelie! You just have to trust me."

"Trust you? Have I not come away with you to this place?"

"Stop it!"

"Answer me!"

Angry kisses, biting into each other, fierce weeping, and our painful coming together at night, whipped on by our shared lonely fear of losing each other, ended these confrontations.

Sharp pains doubled me over after every battle between Jules's need and my desperation. I began to wonder if I would lose the baby.

Jules woke one night to find me bowing on the bed, my forehead pressed into the mattress, rocking the baby inside me into stillness.

"Have I hurt you?"

"For two weeks now."

"Forgive me."

"Help me."

"How?" He touched me in the dark.

"I don't know." I raised my face to him. My lip was bleeding. In the light through the window, which I never wanted closed any more, he caught sight of my broken, swelling lip and kissed the blood.

"We cannot go on this way," Jules said.

"What happened? You were happy."

"I've been working on translating the poems," Jules explained. "My Spanish is not good, and such close work with the poems takes me back."

"You wrote these poems here in the inn."

"No. We brought with us to the inn everything that had happened before."

"Stop writing them in Spanish, then. It demands too much of you." I kissed Jules's face, and my kisses left smears of blood.

Jules held me but looked away from me, avoiding my eyes. "It's the only way I can get more money. The money goes so quickly. I have ordered you a gown so that you may go out with me on the town. How could I even think of taking you in a dressing gown and cloak? I've seen that you can't wear these others."

"Oh, Jules."

"But, even without the cost of the new gown, the money goes so quickly."

"Jules, I don't need to go out on the town with you. Can't you get back your money for the gown?"

"You don't understand."

"Then make me understand. Explain to me."

Jules pulled at his hair again. I tried to pry his fingers out of the tangles. "It can't last!" he shouted and shook me off. "I just don't see how we can make it last."

"We have the baby coming. Should we go back to your parents, now?"

"Oh, God!" Was he laughing? Jules had thrown back his head and now made sobbing sounds. "Aurelie," he said, sobbing and shaking his head when he could speak again, "you just don't understand anything. This can't work."

"But you said-"

"I *hoped*. I *dared*. I *tried*, for your sake. For my sake. For the sake of our love. Because I need you." He turned to me and crawled into my arms again, his head bowed so that his ear pressed to where the baby grew.

He was crying. I shushed him. I tried to still his shaking shoulders, holding him tightly like a straitjacket. Nothing helped.

He said, "There will be no more money for the poems until the books are published and have sold out. A second printing will get me more money. Or this Spanish volume, if I can complete it. And it is destroying me. It reminds me of Franchot's school-"

"Why? The poems were all written here, Jules."

He raised his head. "The *language*, Aurelie. Franchot was such a hero there. Oh, God, even the people who hated him wanted to *be* him. I'll never be free of him." He shouted, gritting his teeth. Flecks of spit foamed at the corners of his mouth and flew at me with each word. "We'll never be free of him. How I hate him. And look what he's done to my life. Even dead, he has the last laugh!"

"Jules, you're making no sense!" I couldn't keep my grip on his shoulders or arms.

He flung himself into pounding the bed. "It won't work!" he yelled through his teeth. "I can't be him. I can't make it up to them. I don't want to make it up to them!"

I scrambled off the bed and dropped to my knees over by the table, ready to hide under it if he continued to rage. He was scaring me.

Maybe if I lit the lamp, someone outside might see the flailing, come to check, hear the shouts, and rescue me.

I reached up to work at lighting the wick, just in time to see Jules bound off the bed and head for the wardrobe. I stopped working at the flints and the wick to watch.

He snatched open the wardrobe, reached in and opened a panel in the floor. Then he stood and whirled to face me.

His arm was behind his back. But he was naked, and I could see plainly enough in the moonlight through the window what he was holding.

Jules saw that I knew and swung the sword before him. He said, "I saw your panic when you realized I'd brought the sword with us. You always could read my mind and my heart, know my secrets. Why did I bring my brother's sword-yes! I will say it! my *brother*-to the inn? Yes, for protection in the streets. But why were you afraid when you saw it?" He advanced on me slowly on bare feet, easing his weight forward, sword first, as though I were an opponent.

I had seen Jules with his fencing master. I would not be able to escape.

I looked toward the door, so distant. My hands fumbled at the lamp.

Jules went on, "You noticed I've left the sword here more often than not, even when I'm out at night. You're clever. You know so many things. You know me. What is the other reason I brought my brother's sword to the inn?"

Jules stood above me now. I had my mouth open to speak. I wanted to speak.

Jules slowly lifted the sword. "You said you wanted to die at my hand," he said as the sword reached its arc above his head.

I screamed.

I rushed up from the floor to the window and threw myself at it, scrambling to open it-how did it open? I couldn't think-and screamed to get out. I beat the glass with my fists. "Help me! Oh, help me. He's gone mad."

Jules must have flung the sword aside. I felt his hand in my hair, pulling me from the window, and his other arm braced against my stomach, doubling me forward, choking off my air.

I was flung away from the window and landed on the floor near the abandoned sword. I saw it and screamed again, crab-walking backward away from it.

Jules flew to his knees beside me. His hands grabbed at my face, covered my mouth, held the back of my head.

"Shh! Hush," he hissed at me. Then, "Hush!" he bellowed as fists banged at our door.

Jules swung his head around to study the locked door. "Who is there?"

"The innkeeper, *Monsieur*. People are concerned."

"Tell them all is well."

"*Monsieur,* certainly. After I see for myself that all is, indeed, well."

"I am disciplining my mistress. It is no concern of others."

"Discipline is necessary. Death is against the law."

"Death?" Jules rose, released me and flung my dressing gown from the wardrobe backwards at my face as he stomped to the door. He opened it and stood, naked and outraged, in full view of the men and maids who had come to my aid.

Else was one of the women. She peered past Jules to me, where I cowered, dazed, on the floor next to the sword.

I cannot escape it. There is not far to go. The room is so small.

I had draped my dressing gown over me, as there was no time to put it on. Else murmured to Jules, "*Monsieur,* let me go to her and help her. She has not been well," but he was shouting at her owner, "Our room is paid for! You presume out of curiosity and disrespect-"

The men behind the innkeeper jostled and stared, agreeing, "Who has the child or wife or slave who will not cry bloody murder when struck?"

But the innkeeper said, "*Monsieur,* I see you have your sword drawn. May I point out that discipline with a sword might be excessive, particularly when dealing with a woman in a delicate state?"

Someone laughed. The men began to disperse.

Jules was livid. He stared at the innkeeper and said nothing.

The innkeeper looked past him to me. Else slipped past Jules to my side.

As she propped me up and worked the dressing gown onto me without ever completely uncovering me, I stared at her in confusion. She whispered, "Come away to the servants' quarters for tonight. You have friends. The innkeeper will let no harm come to you. He is paid well to look out for you. Besides, he is more afraid of the man who pays your bill than of your lover."

But I no longer listened to her. I was listening to the part of the innkeeper's speech that had gotten Jules's attention. "You know that famous case? Anything that smacks of torture, murder, no, no. This is not the way of the French colonies. The Americans, perhaps. One reads of atrocities in their republic all the time. But we believe that even inferior creatures have rights, and this is why our colonies may be less lucrative, but they allow us to hold up our heads among civilized nations. One must not employ barbarity against the barbarian."

Jules was disdainful. His arms folded against his chest, his head high, he stared at the innkeeper until he turned and said to me, "Well, *ma chere*, you see what your screaming has brought down upon us? I fear you have cost us our good reputation in this place."

The innkeeper laughed and patted Jules's arm like a father to get his attention and reassure him. "No, no," he assured Jules. "Nothing of the kind. These things, among the young, and what is this I have heard? You are a poet? Well! Inspiration, passion! Only, you must remember, *Monsieur*," and here the innkeeper's voice sloughed off his hilarity to become stern again, "murder, even of a negress, is against the law."

Else, watching me watch the men, had stopped talking. Her owner continued persuading Jules. "Might it not be best to send the negress to friends for the remainder of the night? A chance to rest and put problems aside until morning?"

Jules watched me. He looked down from the superior height of being unafraid, not pregnant, not

103

owned by anyone or anything but his desires and his sense of obligation. His folded arms blocked me from welcome in his embrace.

If I left, how would he feel? *Abandoned.* Just as I felt every time he left.

If he felt I had abandoned him, even for this one night of his strange anguish, what would become of our relationship? Of our hiding away in this room?

Worse, where will I go if he does not want me back in the morning?

Jules said, "Of course, I will not put my mistress out into the streets or your servants' quarters. She will stay here, where she belongs. I will go stay with friends for the night."

He closed the door on the innkeeper and the watchers, saying, "Excuse me while I dress."

I sat still while he approached me. Would I ever lose this sudden, icy fear of him? For now it seemed to me as if I had always feared and hated Jules. *But I have not! I have always loved him.*

He threw his clothes from the wardrobe to the floor and sat down beside me to snatch his clothes on. "You said you wanted to die at my hand," he spat through his teeth.

Understanding hit me. "Only if you were going to kill yourself," I whispered back. My voice shook and caught in my throat as though he had choked me.

Jules stood and shoved his feet into his boots. "And if we cannot make it work here? What do you propose? To go limping back to my parents?"

Long after Jules had gone into the night ahead of the innkeeper's men and torches, I sat in the darkness by the sword. I listened for Else, hoping she would return. But she did not. I wished for something to drink besides stale water and watered brandy. Maybe a cup of one of *Tante* Clothilde's soothing teas. But there was no one to ask or send.

"To go limping back."

Our mad dash here had been shattered like the glass in the street on All Hallows' Eve, and I, like those dogs, lapped at it, bleeding and greedily eating my own destruction.

CHAPTER FIVE
SOMEONE IS COMING

At some time in the night, I must have crawled into bed. It was there that I woke at midday to the sound of Jules pounding at the door and asking if I was all right.

When I opened the door, trailing my half-buttoned dressing gown, he dragged me into his arms.

"Oh, God, oh God," he said into my shoulder, into my tangled hair.

Beyond him, the courtyard trees and the city struggled to appear through a clinging mist. "Come in," I said to Jules. "It is chilly here."

He hesitated, looking into my eyes and reaching for my hand as I backed away. "Are you sure I should? I don't wish to frighten you any more."

"I can see that, Jules. Come in."

Jules paced as I washed. "I need something warm to drink," I murmured into my handfuls of water. "I've caught the city's chill. How odd to feel cold at last."

Jules must have heard me, for he said, "When you didn't come down to the courtyard for breakfast, the innkeeper sent for me. He thought maybe I'd hurt you more than I'd admitted to myself. And I thought so, too."

I dried my face and came to stand before Jules. "You want to kill me. Why?"

"Oh." He groaned and turned away from me. "I should have killed us both at my brother's wake. How mad to think we could live with this and make a life for ourselves."

"I'm making life-" I started.

But Jules went on. "The guilt. The hatred." He had his fists at his eyes. At his temples. He shook as he said, "I have nowhere to go with the hatred."

"You hated your brother with good reason," I said so low I was not sure he heard me.

But he had. "My brother is dead. Let him rest, Aurelie."

"It is you who won't let him rest." My fear of Jules's raving crumbled into frustration. "I am going on with life. My life. My baby's life. Your life inside me, if you don't want it for yourself. It's you who want to keep resurrecting your brother. He's gone, Jules, and he is not coming back. Not in you, no matter what you do, and not at all."

Jules hollered. Not at me. Into the air, into the room. "Ah!"

I hollered as loudly. "You cannot live the life he was meant to live! You are not Franchot." I jabbed my heaving chest with a stiff finger. "*I* hate Franchot, dead as he is! *I* hated him when he was alive, and *I* am glad that he is dead!"

"Stop!" Jules raised his hand as if he would strike me. But he did not. He stood there, trembling, staring down at me as I stared back up at him.

I said, "You want to kill me? Are you going to die? Then I will hold your head while you die by your brother's sword, as he always wanted you to. But I will not go with you. I'm staying behind, with my baby. Write some kind of will or such thing that grants us our freedom from your parents."

Jules's hand struck my face so sharply and suddenly that I didn't know why, for a moment, I was on the floor, dizzy.

Jules was at the door, watching me. When my eyes swam up to meet his, he said, "I will send someone to bring you something warm to drink. I will leave them money for your meals. Surely, the maids can share their meals with you."

He shook his head as if to clear it. As if it were he who had been struck. "I must give up the Spanish translations," he resolved. "They are too hard on me. I can't think why. Maybe, once I give them up, I can come back to you." He looked over at me again. "I'm going to come and get the sword now. Don't come near me."

The sword?

The gleaming thing still lay on the floor where it had been dropped the night before. I crept onto the bed and to the far end of it, away from Jules as he came on.

He picked it up and held it to the light. He smiled, studying it. "Such a beautiful, simple, deadly thing," he said. He went to the wardrobe and got the sword's sheath, buckled it on. Sheathed the weapon. Went to the door with a lighter, gladder stride.

His head was high as he watched me, cowering, from the way out. "I don't know what else to do, Aurelie," he said and closed the door.

I didn't know the maid who brought me a tray of coffee and croissants left from that morning. I thought I should eat but could not. I sat at the window, sipping the bitter, creamed coffee and watching the Mardi Gras revelers who came and went.

They were noisy in their mad costumes, and they laughed as if they were shrieking at each other. As the courtyard darkened into night, its lit torches and still fountain pools, silhouetting the misshapen, dancing bodies, put me in a strange state of mind. *I have descended into hell with Jules to retrieve his brother. But I have been abandoned here.*

In the falling twilight, men dragged and carried the women they honored all the other days of the year toward my window and past my window, on their way to other rooms at the inn. The women they normally disdained, tonight, they gave their arms and helped along the gallery.

In the failing light I could see that all these women, most of them as ghostly pale as Jules's dying grandmother, were baring pale parts of their bodies that were normally covered. Inviting, flaunting sex and the power it gave these women over their men.

If Jules had waited one more night to kill me, surely no one would have come to help me. Even with my door and window shut against the noise, I could hear that the inn resounded with screams tonight. They echoed off the waving leaves of the vines and trees, off the still waters of the fountains, off the high walls of the courtyard maze.

A man stood before me on the gallery.

In the darkness, I could only see that he was cloaked. Booted. Watching.

I pulled at the unbuttoned edges of my dressing gown. Surely there were more interesting sights abroad tonight than I, a pregnant girl sitting alone in a dark window. I rose slowly from the seat and backed behind the drape, reaching for its pulley string to close it.

As the drapes rushed forward to shut out the night, I saw, beyond them, that the cloaked man hurried past my window.

Now he banged on my room's door.

"Oh God," I said into my hands. "Oh holy mother," imitating *Tante* Clothilde, wishing for her, wishing I were small again and had never come here, never thought to escape with Jules.

"Aurelie?" a strange voice called at the door. A deep gentleman's voice. "*Mademoiselle* Aurelie?"

I pressed my back against the wall between the window and the bed, staring toward the door that blocked the voice.

A gentleman. A friend of Jules's parents, no doubt, addressing me as Jules's mistress rather than his servant.

They will come here and find me alone, without Jules, and take me back with them, and then what will happen to me and my baby?

"Aurelie, is *Monsieur* Jules with you?"

The pounding and gentle calling went on for some time.

What can I do?

Maybe, as soon as he left, I could go to the front desk and ask to sleep with the maids until Jules returned. Maybe I could ask for a message to be sent to Jules, warning him, begging him not to leave me alone here.

What will happen to me?

I sank to the floor and drew up my knees to shield my baby, staring at the door that jerked with every strike of the gentleman's fist.

"Oh, Jules." I began to cry. I bent my forehead to my knees, folded my arms over my head, and waited to be discovered.

The knocking changed.

Now it was the polite tapping of someone who worked at the inn. "*Madame?*" A new voice called, a man's voice, rich with tone and humor. "*Madame*, I'd like to check on you and see what you need."

I called from across the room, "Are you alone?"

The voice chuckled. The light sound rose over the shrieks that came all around it from the courtyard and the other rooms. "I'm all alone till I get to my quarters with my woman," it said.

If it had been a European, I would have screamed and hid again. But this man sounded like an African. I ran to the door and opened it.

It was Else's husband. I was so glad to see him, it was all I could do to keep my hands to myself.

I wanted him to stay. Protect me. Tell me what was going on. "There was a man here," I rambled, "and he wanted to get in. He knew my name. He kept pounding on the door."

Else's husband was still smiling at me as he shook his head. "Come, now, *Madame* Aurelie," he said. "Else tells me you know a thing or two about your situation here. You don't lack for friends, *Madame*. If there's a gentleman knocking at your

111

door who knows you from past times, maybe you should answer and see what he wants."

"Oh, but *Monsieur* Jules would kill me."

The man raised an eyebrow so high I could see the ripples of his mahogany forehead even in the dark. "From what I hear, he may do that anyway. Begging your pardon, *Madame.*"

Dignity. I was making a fool of myself. I scrabbled at the buttons on the dressing gown that had been open, now, ever since Else tried to dress me. "Don't call me *Madame*, please," I said. "I'm not a freewoman. I'm just like you and Else, and I need friends. I thought Else was my friend."

"She is, *Mademoiselle* Aurelie."

"Then you be my friend, too." This was not working. My voice wavered to a stop.

"I'm trying, *fillette*. Little girl."

"I am afraid, without *Monsieur* Jules here. I don't know what to do. Can you send for him? Tell him about the man at the door, please?"

"I can, *Mademoiselle* Aurelie. But are you sure that's what is best for me to do? Maybe you should wait and talk to the gentleman, if he comes back."

"Oh, no." I leaped backwards and started to shut the door on Else's husband. He blocked it with one hand.

Then he waved me down from my panic. "Now, *Mademoiselle* Aurelie, don't you do that. Don't worry. There's no harm coming to you here. You let me go get Else. She'll know how to talk to you."

I waited with the door locked to let only Else in. She came in with a tray and a crisp, "Good evening, *Madame*. It's crazy out tonight, isn't it?"

"I'm frightened."

"So am I. Why don't we eat a little something together and wait for your *Monsieur* Jules to come home?"

Was this the first time Else had called the inn my home?

She set my tray with the morning's leavings on the floor, thought better of the stale croissants, and plucked them up to arrange them on her fresh tray, surrounding the two bowls of stew she had just brought. "I never get these," she explained. "But I love them." She sat in the chair opposite mine and dipped a croissant into one of the bowls of stew on the table.

She brought it up dripping pungent juices and watched me while she bit into it. "Mm," she murmured. "Give me some good leavings, and I sure can cook."

I locked the door and left it to sit with her. "What if Jules isn't coming back? I don't want to be left here alone, Else."

Else finished one whole croissant and licked her fingers before she answered. "Excusing my forwardness, *Madame*," she said.

"Please don't call me that, Else. I'm not a freewoman. I'm just like you. And I need friends right now."

"So my husband tells me. Excusing my forwardness, but what you need today, you may not appreciate tomorrow. And I love my life the way it is. So I won't presume to advise you."

"Oh, God." I turned back to the window and reached for the pulley string of the draperies. Out there somewhere was Jules, who had brought me here. We were in this together. He should be here to help me figure out what to do.

Else rose and opened both the draperies and lace curtains for me. Then she took her seat again. "As I was saying," picking up the conversation along with another croissant, "I would never advise the mistress of a wealthy Frenchman. Who knows what would happen if he heard of my advice and didn't like it?"

She laughed and dipped this second croissant into her bowl of stew.

I watched it drip brown broth and slices of garlic, slivers of onion, and-what was that?-minced bell pepper and basil? It smelled good and soothed my nervous stomach.

Else bit again and said around the tasty food, behind her hand, limp at the wrist with the delicious weight of the bitten buttered bread, "But if it was anyone *else* alone at an inn with a gentleman acquaintance-not her lover, mind you, I know that-knocking at the door, I would ask her what she thinks she has to lose by answering. She couldn't get more abandoned and sick and hopeless than she is now. But why should I bother *you* with what I would tell *her*?" Else shrugged, smiled, and dipped again. "You know that your *Monsieur* Jules will always come back to you. You're not alone." She extended the rich roll toward me, dripping butter.

"Have a bite? I suspect you haven't eaten in at least a day, *Madame*."

We finished the two bowls of seafood stew and all the croissants, together. I don't know how, but Else had me laughing over the demon shapes outside my window by the time her husband brought us sherry.

I asked who had sent it. Else cut off her husband's reply to say, "The innkeeper. I hope you won't mention it to your *Monsieur* Jules."

I had no taste for wine, but I wanted them to stay. So I invited them to drink it with me.

We shared from the bottle.

As I drank, though I laughed at the hideous shapes outside, bending to leer in through the glass, then straightening with upraised hands in ripping screams of laughter, they began to disturb me more than ever.

I eased myself from the seat, inviting Else's husband to take it. He rose from the floor and eased himself into the chair, smiling at his wife, as I stretched out on the bed.

Jules had loved me there. There were no decisions to make and nothing to do but wait, nothing to think of but poetry and finding more ways to share and say our love.

"She's had a hard time, *Monsieur*," I heard Else say.

"I know. Thank you for watching over her." It was Jules's voice. I tried to waken.

Else's husband said, "Thank you, *Monsieur,* but it was the only right thing to do."

I sat up but couldn't see. Darkness? Dreaming?

Jules insisted to Else's husband, "Take it. I've cleared it with your owner. It's all right."

I must have slept again, for suddenly I felt Jules's arms gather me up in a rush, waking me and shaking me. "Oh God, Aurelie. What have I done?"

I gave in to the fatigue and slept until morning.

When I woke to find Jules in bed beside me, I said, "If it helps you, let's name the baby for your brother, and in honor of everything about him that was best. Franchot if it is a boy. Fanchon if it is a girl."

Jules shook his head. "There is no need. We may name her Fanchon or Fanchette if she is a girl, because I like the names. (Do you? Good.) But whether or not we mean to honor my brother, we will live. I have thrown the sword into the river."

We moved awkwardly into each other's arms.

"Forgive me," Jules murmured into my hair. "I have never had your faith. Have patience with me, and teach me to believe."

I couldn't cry. I couldn't speak. I stared past his shoulder, at the cold fireplace, the dressing screen, the closed wardrobe, and wondered what it would be like to leave this place-and all the hopes we'd brought here-behind us forever.

Jules wanted to go to Mass and mourn on Ash Wednesday.

I sat at the window in a blushing chemise, my feet poised in the open-heeled slippers, idly flipping the leaves of Jules's poetry book as the cathedral's chimes called to the repentant. I felt beautiful, desired, and devastated.

116

I had rinsed and wrung out the fading dressing gown and draped it over the dressing screen, which was getting warped from such treatment. I reached for the silver-handled hairbrush and a jar of scented hair creme Jules had bought at some point during our stay at the inn, and I began to dress my tangled, drying hair as the last notes of the cathedral bells faded. *How much did such luxuries cost Jules before he began to worry about his money?*

The sound of the chimes, lingering in the courtyard and in my memory, recalled to me that strange, long-ago escape from innocence and murder that had brought Jules and me across the courtyard of our childhood home as the chimes sounded the end of All Hallows' Eve, when evil abounded, and the coming of hope with the Feast of All Saints.

"And here we are, All Sinners," I said and laughed, oddly, alone in the silence.

There was a knock at the door.

I had seen no one coming to our door along the gallery. Where had my mind been?

On the escape. The chimes. All Saints, All Souls, and Ash Wednesday.

The knock sounded again, more insistently.

I went to the door and opened it without asking who was there. I must have assumed it would be Jules, having changed his mind and turned back from repentance.

But it was Else's husband. He smiled at me, a broad curve that invited confidence.

I said, "I don't even know your name. I'm glad you're here. I need to thank you for all you've done for me."

Else's husband said, "Archaimbaud. A tough, old-fashioned name. You can call me Arc. But use it to call on me for whatever you need, not to thank me. Else's gratitude is thanks enough. She worries about you."

I smiled. "I'm fortunate that way. I was so alone, when I first came here." And then I closed my mouth, confused that I could so betray the happiest days that Jules and I had ever shared.

Arc said, "I know. It's all right. You aren't alone any more. As a matter of fact, that's why I'm here this morning. Your friends have saved you some breakfast"-I finally noticed the tray he must have been holding balanced in one hand when he knocked-"and sent you a message. The message is"-he spoke slowly now, as though I might be stupid-"you do have friends." He waited.

Not knowing what else to do, I reached for the tray. I could make nothing of his message.

"May I come in and put it down for you?" Arc asked with great patience.

I stepped back out of the way and followed him to the cluttered table, leaving the door open, in case Jules returned. It wouldn't do for him to think ...

Arc settled the tray and turned back to his task with me. He was trying to make me understand something. I could see that. He said, "*Mademoiselle,* you do know, don't you, that you needn't stay here, frightened and half starved?"

"Half starved?"

118

He grinned. "Well, by the standards of a woman as big and healthy as Else, anyway. But she could never speak for a dainty lady like you, could she?"

"What are you saying? I understand nothing of this." I shook my head. Where was my mind? Why did he seem so sure of a certain meaning, when I could grasp nothing?

Arc sighed, folded his sinewy arms, and threw back his head to think. I watched him and thought, *Why not? Why did my aunt raise me with thoughts of Jules and a house and freedom, instead of thoughts of a man such as hers and Else's? Someone gentle, giving, loving, who understands what it is to be trapped and secretive.*

The thought made hot blood rush to my cheeks. I looked away and began to mumble thanks to Arc for the breakfast. "Please thank Else for saving some breakfast aside for me."

"*Madame* Aurelie, it's like this. You need to know that there are people who want you to come away from *Monsieur* Jules while he figures out what he needs. Maybe even to stay away, after he's figured it out. Maybe some of these people are the very gentlemen you thought *Monsieur* Jules could be for you, someone to protect you-"

"*Monsieur* Jules can no longer protect me." *Am I mad? This kind of talk will surely get one of us-or both of us-in trouble.*

Arc must have thought the same. He flinched, as if I'd struck him, and began to back toward the door. "It's not my place to say if that's true, *Mademoiselle*. But if you feel that way, all the more

119

reason to go to your friends until *Monsieur* Jules's affairs are settled. And if you never want to return to him, well, there are friends who can help you with that, too. But keep this to yourself, for all our sakes." He looked me in the eye.

"Does Else know these friends?" For I would go to anyone she trusted or recommended.

Arc flared with something like real anger. "Else knows nothing. Nothing." He pointed at me from the doorway. "She cares for you, and I've delivered messages that would set her mind at ease, if she knew of them. But she knows nothing. And she can't have anything more to do with you ... " Arc faltered into silence.

He was protecting Else from me. From contact with me and whatever trouble I was in, too blind to see it for myself.

"*Monsieur* Arc-" I began but didn't know what, of everything in my heart pounding to get out, it might be safe to say.

He reached to shut the door to my room but paused to say, "If you decide, *Mademoiselle*, that you want to go away for a while and stay with those friends I mentioned, the gentlemen who can protect you, where no one can find you until you're ready to be found, you just let me know. A freewoman like you has choices, *Mademoiselle*."

"Arc, I'm not a freewoman!" *Else knows I'm not free. Doesn't Arc know this?*

If he didn't, then his advice and information were useless to me. I didn't have the choices of a freewoman.

A cup of chocolate, still warm, and little chocolate-covered cakes had been sent up to me on the tray. Surely, these were not the remnants of the inn's breakfast. They must have come from some expensive shop, the kind I had thought I might visit someday on Jules's arm.

I sat to sip the chocolate and nibble the cakes, still brushing and dressing my hair, glancing now and then at the offensive poems with their rages about love and torment.

When Jules returned, he wore a cross of ashes on his forehead.

I started when he bent into the lamplight and the ashes gleamed. *How like a sword the cross of ashes looks!*

He didn't ask about the chocolate dregs in the cup or the little flakes and crumbs on the tray. "Aurelie, we must repent." He pressed his forehead into mine until the skin burned, squeezed between our skulls. "This Lent will be a season of restraint and contemplation for us. We will come to understand our destiny and shape our souls to deserve the blessing of love we've tried to wrest from God's hands."

This tangle of talk went on until he tore himself from me and, throwing off his cloak, burrowed his long body into our rumpled bed.

We began to live on bread and water.

Jules permitted nothing else in the room. When he was gone, Arc would sometimes appear with trays bearing cold slices of dried sausages, roast meats, pickled boiled eggs and pungent cheeses, mint jellies, cherries and strawberries coming, frail

121

and succulent, into season. A kettle of hot tea, sometimes, to soothe me and the baby.

Arc said nothing in explanation except, "Your friends have sent me with something for the baby," and so it never occurred to me that it might be improper to eat.

When Jules was at home and awake, we would talk endlessly of our sins, as he saw them. "Lust and anger lead to death," he explained, and though he was patient and soft-voiced, I railed against him.

"Your guilt over your brother leads to death," I would retort, and the debates raged from there.

"Repentance is life."

"Repentance is death! Look at you. Aging before my eyes. An old man, bent and pitiful." I uncovered my firm, rounding belly beneath his dry hand, limp with weariness. "This is life. I am life, bearing life."

"You are blasphemy. Sin is death."

"Your god is death, if he wants this from you."

Sometimes, such arguments brought a spell of clear-headedness to Jules. He would break out of his stupor and look at me, as though I had been gone and just returned, and he was glad to see me.

These bursts of recognition were followed by tender caresses and promises of normal life to come. "Your new day dress will be done by the end of Lent, Aurelie, and then we will go out together on the town, as you've wanted. We may not be able to buy nice things, only window shop, and for that I am truly sorry. But I know you will forgive me and know that I love you and am doing all I can."

"Of course, Jules. You are so kind."

But more often, the battle of words like "hell" and "hope," "sin" and "salvation" only left us scorched and withered, turning away from each other like Jules's own bitter parents, forced to endure each other's company too long. I watched him pick at his dry bread, grudging me the fatter slice that made me miserable with thirst, and wished he would go away until his Lent was done. *If only it were safe to run away to unknown "friends."*

But each night, Jules reached for me, seized me so that his thinning fingers dug into my breaking skin, and pulled me close as his dry mouth searched out mine, his breath gasped and came in raking pants, his body moved like fluid against mine, running to wetness, blood and birth waters.

And he shoved me away with a wild cry like a crazy man.

I began to sleep in my chair.

My legs ached and swelled. The ankles grew thick and stiff. The arches of my feet flattened like pillows. I couldn't walk across the room without pain.

And Jules, waking morning after morning to find me propped in the chair with my neck arched and my mouth open, snoring and gagging on dried saliva in my throat, began to stay away again.

The first night, I did not go to the bed, for fear he would return and begin his ritual seizing and flinging away that had so worn my heart and nerves to shreds. But the second night, and each long, lonely, peaceful night afterward, I slept in bed and dreamed disjointed memories of home.

The courtyard. The flowers. The hanging moss and vines parted to reveal the fountain where water splashed, clear and fresh, and I cupped it in my hands to wet my face, and my eyes were washed free of the pain that had kept me from seeing that, through the open glass doors of the library, up the winding stairway all the way to the suffocating attic, there lay Jules's withered grandmother in Franchot's arms.

They both glowed white as if lit from inside by Christmas candles, their pale sunless skin, his white nightgown, and the white sheet wound around her like a shroud, except where his lips touched her. He raised her limp body draped across both his arms like a shriveled bride as he kissed her forehead, her eyes, her cheeks, her lips, her throat, and each time his face lifted and moved the dark smears of burgundy blood splattered further across it like a spreading mask and trickled jaggedly down her breasts to drip from her fingertips.

Waking in a sweat from these nightmares, I forced myself out of bed to sit, with my laden trays and silver-handled brush and view of the deserted courtyard, to light the lantern and read Jules's poetic renderings of our secrets and silences. It was my only escape from the terrible dreams. *But they are nothing but meaningless dreams. What could they mean?*

And how could Jules have betrayed our pain, our groping toward each other in anguish and tenderness, for money? As I read, I wondered if he'd ever truly loved me.

Silence is the bond

That tells me you hear
What I cannot say
For fear of my own madness
When I look into my mind
And strive to grasp God,
Infinity and you.

I would read, but I would never memorize these poems. I hated them. *When did we lose the simplicity of our first falling in love?*

Though I ate well from Arc's tray while Jules was gone, I never saw Else again. I sent her messages of friendship to which her husband never brought replies.

The inn began to fill with a different kind of visitor. These were family people, all French and Creole, here to visit relatives and neglected gravesites for the Feast of the Resurrection.

The dead don't rise, for they have not fallen. Only those who fear to live have failed and thereby fallen. I could have written my own poems, if Jules would have left me a pencil.

Jules returned after Mass on Easter Sunday, cadaverously thin. He stared and waited to be invited in, like a stranger. His clothes were washed but frayed at the collar and button holes.

He brought me the dress, held out bare on his arms like a peace offering.

No wonder we had gone without money since its inception. It was made of the most costly fabrics. I fingered the sheer voile, the slippery silk, the tucked lace and fine embroidery that edged the high bodice, from where would cascade yards of space for the baby to grow.

125

"Lavender," Jules explained the colors, "and roses, for spring and summer and how deeply I love you." Yet, "How you've filled out. Whoever pays for our room has also paid dearly for you to dine like a queen."

I looked up at Jules, aghast, from where I bathed beyond the open screen. "You knew? You knew that someone has been paying for our room?"

"Of course," was all he said.

And as he helped me into the strangely fashioned dress-"This is the height of fashion in Europe, Aurelie, you must understand"-I wondered, with the weighty return of the old sadness, if he no longer loved me. He had left so that someone else might pay to room and feed me.

He had only paid to dress me and parade me, obviously pregnant, about the town. I was, after all, like all those other women of the inn. Something men might use to show other men that they were, truly, men.

When I was dressed, I tied the abandoned silk scarf about my hair, turban-style, and we went down into the courtyard.

But after all, once we had descended, Jules asked if we shouldn't stop and rest at our old wrought iron table, though there was no coffee or tea to sip, but only sunshine, blessed spring, and memories of all we had survived.

I looked at his veined, pale hands, resting across the table from me, and watched how the spring breeze tossed his dried, fading hair, and thought how we had aged so suddenly.

He rose and came to me and untied my turban, balling it in his hands. Then he shot out his hand to me and said, "We have enjoyed the air. Let us return to our room."

And, alone once more, he tore the dress a little in his hurry to get it off me.

But then he was all gentleness, until the rapture swept us together in its fist and crushed us into one again. The one we resented and fought against. The only one in which we existed.

"I will never leave you again," he breathed, and slept as though he had not slept in a long time.

I gathered the strange, lovely dress and spread it on the bed. Then I shook out a chemise but put it, too, aside, and went to sit nude, as I liked best, at the window to watch the fading sunset. How would we eat tonight?

And just as I thought that I should wash and dress and wait to see if Jules would take me with him into the city, to find food, he rose and came from the bed and stood behind me at the window. He said, "Someone is coming."

He meant for me to come away from the window. Or at least to turn so that the chair came between me and the person who walked in the darkness and could not see me, anyway.

Jules still loves me, I thought with relief.

Despite the hunger and the lifeless eyes, fasting on bread and water and staring through me, because I no longer mattered, and despite his leaving me to be cared for by some other person, and even despite his brother's sword raised above my neck in the darkness and the terror and the loss of his brother that could not be repaired or taken back.

He loved me and wanted me to hide myself from someone who was coming.

CHAPTER SIX
AFRAID

I moved from the window, rose from my seat, and backed toward the bed after pulling the drapes closed on the still figure outside. He stood at a distance, watching me as I shut him out.

"How strange," I said quietly, as if to myself.

But Jules answered, "I have left you too long alone. He must be a visitor at the inn who wonders if you're approachable. I will have to make my presence felt around here."

I heard, but I wasn't sure. The stillness of the man outside, his silhouette aimed at me, at my eyes, lingered in my mind. *He seems to be warning me of something. But of what?*

"I'm ready to take you out on the town now," Jules said. "Let's dress."

This time, the fashionable gown slid onto my body and clung with the full feel of its costliness. It glittered even in the near-darkness of the dimmed lamplight, necessary now as Jules's eyes had become sensitive to bright light, and he couldn't bear it.

When I was fully dressed, the lovely silk scarf shimmered about my braided and pinned hair, and the gown cascaded in all its wealth. Though I had neither needle nor thread to repair the tear he had made, I begged Jules not to insist on my covering the dress's splendor with the cloak. "The baby and I keep each other more than warm enough," I assured him with a laugh. "Please let me feel beautiful."

He strained at a pale smile. He had developed a constant chill and so swept his own cloak about him, shading his eyes from torch and lantern flames with the brim of his hat.

We left the room and found no one on the gallery. We crossed the courtyard with our steps ringing out on the cobblestones and came under the glittering chandelier of the foyer. The innkeeper at the front desk looked up, waved as if he were pleased to see us going out together, and wished us a good evening. And then we were out onto the street.

I had not been there since the moment Jules brought me to the inn, at midnight on the eve of All Saints' Day.

The streets seemed dark and vast between the spaced fires of the streetlamps. The river shushed the big boats rocking and knocking at its docks. Starlight caught in the black ripples so that sky and river were spangled with light.

And the street before me roared with the rattle of carriage wheels and the squeak of carriage hinges, the musical clop of horses' hooves and the rush of walkers coming on in clusters, now this way, bumping past us, now that way, circling into the gutter to avoid us. Some of them raised their eyes to see who we were, standing so still and blocking their way on the *banquette*.

I turned to Jules to say, "It's wonderful." But he was already taking my hand, pulling me behind him, saying, "Come on. Let's not stand here, waiting to be seen."

Were we still in hiding? Heavy with the baby that pressed upward into my ribs and downward, spreading apart my hipbones, it seemed hard to believe.

I rushed off behind Jules, laughing to myself with the joy of freedom, smiling as I stared into the eyes of passing strangers. "Happy Feast of the Resurrection," a man's voice said to me as I passed a noisy, dark room whose laughter and lively music spilled out at our feet in the street.

"Back to life," I cried out, too, to no one in particular, but Jules turned and frowned at me as though I had been flirting with an unseen speaker. A woman leaned from a balcony and dropped a posy on my head. "He is come again, *cherie*!"

We walked into darkness and past large glass windows where ladies' clothes, men's suits, delicate shoes, shining weapons, and intricately carved furniture were all on display. Jules took me further from the river, deep into the city, so that we might pass his bookseller's shop. He paused there and frowned when he saw that his book was not yet displayed, but "Never mind," he said as he pulled me on, determined to enjoy our evening out.

I kept my face turned upward toward the balconies where, I discovered, freewomen were going about their very ordinary, very enviable lives. There was a freewoman beating the dust from a small carpet slung over the balcony railing, and another visible through a balcony door thrown wide on the spring evening breeze, bathing her golden child in a copper basin. There were two freewomen, their plain, colorful cotton scarves tied snugly about

131

their heads, leaning over the railings of their neighboring balconies to chat and laugh and share a glowing cheroot. The smoke wreathed their heads like haloes or crowns.

"They are so happy," I told Jules. "Look at them. Some day, you will come home to me in such a place." Jules glowered up at the gossiping women, and one of them turned to look silently, unsmilingly, down on him.

"Let's head back and find a cafe," he said to me.

We doubled back, dropping *sous* to begging musicians, toward the cathedral. "May I go in and pray?" I asked.

"Must you?" Jules said in such a contemptuous way that I shook my head no.

He stopped and swept his cloak about me, to hold me close. "Forgive me, *chere*," he said. "It's just that my god has not been on our side."

"Maybe all that will change, Jules." I couldn't help feeling hopeful, with all this fresh air, the energy of walking, and such happiness.

Jules said nothing then. But as he took my hand and we continued to walk, he muttered so that I could hardly hear it, "I am ill at ease in my mind."

We stopped at the park and sat outside the gates on wrought iron benches. I breathed heavily.

"Does the baby cause you strain?" Jules asked, and I realized how little we had ever spoken of it.

Instead of answering more than, "I can't be sure. I don't know what is fretting and what is the baby," I asked a question of my own: "Where have you been all this time?"

He turned from me. There in the dark waved the green leaves of low-bending trees just beyond that dearly missed angle of cheek and jaw that were unique to Jules, and the quiet of his voice, heavy with regret. "I went to a boarding house for gentlemen I'd visited before, playing cards with friends."

There was something there I shouldn't touch. For the sake of my own happiness. So I let the silence between us settle.

"Look," Jules said after a while. He took my hand and raised it close enough for me to feel his breath from between his lips, but he did not quite kiss it in public. "There is a cafe just across the square."

We rose together and entered the noisy tavern. We found corner seats at a tiny wooden table only large enough for two.

The coffee and pastries cheered us, though I had to tease and feed Jules with my fingers.

"We will dine out often," I chattered. "I want to get to know the city. I will go out to shop every morning with my covered basket over my arm, as I used to see *Tante* Clothilde do." I tittered. "No. She carried her basket on her head, like an old-fashioned African. I suppose the fashionable young freewomen of the city don't do that, do they? I shall have to learn from women such as those we saw on the balconies how to be fashionable."

Jules said nothing.

We left our crumbs and dessert plates on the table and wandered out to the edge of the black, rippling river, where we held hands as we stared into its depths.

"We could die here together," Jules said when he spoke at last, off-handedly as if he were only reflecting on the moving water. "You, I and the baby."

"More talk of dying, Jules?"

"Don't you love me enough to die for me?"

"Do you love me enough to live with me?"

"Is this living? What we're doing, hunted down like wild dogs?"

"What makes you think that dying would be any better?"

"I have to believe in something. Death is all that's left."

"Believe in me and our baby, Jules. You have us." I squeezed his thin hand.

He tried to rally. "If it were a boy, would you name it Julien, for me?"

"Certainly. And Juliette if it is a girl."

"No. Fanchon. I like Fanchon."

"Fanchon it is. Or Julien. I love you."

"I love you enough to die for you, Aurelie. I wish you felt the same." Finally, Jules looked at me.

For a heartbeat's seconds of time, I was afraid that, as ferociously as his fingers dug into the fine bones at the back of my hand, as wildly as his distended eyes stared into mine, he would indeed pull me into the black depths of the river.

"Don't, Jules," I began to beg, twisting at my hand to free it. "I want to live. I believe in us. We'll be like those women, with a home of our own, and

I'll be bathing our baby, catching the evening breeze to cool off the kitchen. You'll see. We'll be happy."

I didn't get my hand back. But the demon in Jules's eyes suddenly subsided.

Jules raised my hand to his head, as if it ached. "You kill me with your faith. I cannot match it." He breathed shakily, as if he'd been running. "Come. I suppose we'd better get back to the inn."

Neither of us wanted to. We dawdled in those last moments of our evening, pretending as well as we could to be an unworried couple, strolling back to the inn through the city at the end of Easter Day.

When we entered the inn, we saw that the innkeeper had deserted his station at the front desk. "It's the dead of night. Anyone could wander through here," Jules remarked, and frowned.

I clung more tightly to his arm as we went down the hallway that let out onto our courtyard. We paused together before stepping out on the cobblestones. "What is it?" I asked, only knowing that, whatever it was, I felt it too. Something was not as it should be.

Jules wrapped his own hand over mine, tightening my grip on his arm, and started out into the torchlit space.

We heard a shuffle, as of running feet, and the muffled cry of a man's voice.

Jules shoved me before him and pushed me, running, up the stairs that led to our room. We clattered down the gallery, my open-heeled slippers clacking and sliding from my feet.

"Jules!" I cried out.

"Silence!" he answered as a shadow billowed up like smoke before our door and took on the form of a man.

Jules threw me behind him and held on with one arm. He grabbed at his waist for his brother's sword, but not finding it, he turned with a vicious high kick at the man's arm and shouted threats at the shape as it retreated before him.

Jules slammed my body against our door and braced it with his own as he worked furiously at the lock with his key.

Only then did I hear the heavy footfalls of men running behind us, and the shadow that had withdrawn into the shadows further down the corridor now took courage and returned.

We were caught between men who converged on us.

Jules bellowed triumphantly as our door swung in, spilling me into the room so that I fell and tripped him up as he rushed in behind me. The men had surged forward and now blocked the door, hesitating as if to see what Jules would do.

Jules leapt over me, giving up the door, and flung himself at the wardrobe. He yanked open the door. For a moment, I had the terrible idea that he wanted to hide away inside while these men had their way with me.

But no. He had forgotten that he had thrown his brother's sword into the river. He scrabbled in the wardrobe's darkness, trying to find his weapon.

Someone's hands gripped me and hauled me to my feet. Other men had leaped around me and now surrounded Jules at the wardrobe.

He turned on them, his eyes wild, his hair standing up and back from his head. He bared his teeth like a cornered dog.

"It is no use!" a man near him said and seized Jules's arm. Jules clenched his hand into a fist and rammed the man's face. The man's head spun, and his blood sprayed me.

"Run, Aurelie!" shouted Jules, and I tried.

But too many hands held me. I only twisted and yanked painfully at the sockets of my own arms.

More shouting. The men shouted to each other, and Jules berated the men closest to him as cowards. "Give me a weapon and a chance at a fair fight. I will take you all on!"

A handkerchief was slid between my face and the hand that clamped my mouth shut on my cries for help. A choking smell welled up from the damp linen. I struggled, writhing to get away and save my baby's life. Surely we would be smothered. This fool was killing us.

Suddenly my body gave up, though my mind fought on. I sagged and saw the room darken around me.

"Jules!" I tried to call out.

Fighting with two men who tried to hold him, Jules turned horrified eyes to me.

"Aurelie!" I heard him call, and his voice raged on, muffled but louder than the other men's, fading from me as I entered the soothing nothingness, cradled in something like sleep.

From which I finally woke with a splitting pain behind both my eyes.

There was light. Too much light. And something stiff and narrow held me up off the floor. I ached in every inch of my body.

I tried to sit up.

Vomit sprayed from my mouth as I bent forward over the pain in my belly. Briefly, my mind panicked for the ruined new gown Jules had given me. I thought of the park. The river. The posy a woman had thrown on my head like a wreath.

But as my eyes got used to the terrible brightness, I realized I was no longer out on the city but somewhere else, wearing something else. A clean white cotton gown, a chemise to be worn by enslaved girls and covered with a rough cotton skirt, for housework.

My vomit stuck to it and plastered it to my panting chest.

"Ah, not again," a woman's voice chided. Strong, thin, fine brown hands pressed hot wet rags to my chest and took them away, returned them clean and dripping and swiped them over my mouth and face. "Did the fools want to kill you, too?" the woman's voice said with a chuckle.

"Kill?" I repeated, my tongue thick and lazy. "They killed Jules?"

"Ah." The woman took away her cloths and plopped them into water. "Jules, is it? Save your worry. He'll fare far better than you ever will, *ma petite.*"

"Where is Jules, *Madame*?" I squinted in the direction of the teasing voice.

"Better ask where *you* are, *mon enfant*," she went on. "Here. Let me look at your eyes."

138

The fingers returned and gripped my chin, raised my face. I cried out as the light of the sun that ripped through her shack's windows blinded me.

"It's the stuff they used to knock you out," she said. "Bad for the brain. I told them so. Four men against a pregnant girl and a starving boy? If anyone listened to a negress, their reputations would be mud today." She laughed with a light heart.

Then she propped me up and began to work the soiled nightgown off of me. As my eyes adjusted to the light, I looked around.

I was in a small shack. Weatherworn boards made up the walls, stuffed with rags and lined with lengths of pretty cloth, aged gowns, and sheets of the city's newspaper. Bundles of herbs hung drying from the ceiling. A few skins cured on the hearth of the small stone fireplace. More skins littered the floor like throw rugs. A rough iron kettle of something simmered in the fireplace and sent fragrant steam into the room.

I had the only bed. It was a cot up off the floor. Across from it and the fireplace, woven straw pallets lay under a huge quilt of skins, thrown back as though a sleeper had just risen. Another sleeper remained, glossy long hair sleek with firelight.

"Where is this place?" I asked.

"Out in the middle of nowhere," the woman answered with another chuckle. "Save your questions and let me put your mind at ease. I'm going to treat you. When you're better, your people will come and take you to your new home."

I felt woozy. I wanted to question her more closely. But I was struggling to follow the little she had already told me.

As she worked a clean chemise over my head and down my body, I said at last, "But nothing was wrong with me. I want to go back to Jules." Then I clapped a hand over my mouth. Was his name still a secret? Were we still in hiding?

"Now, now, *ma petite*. Of that one thing I'm sure. There'll be no going back to *Monsieur* Jules."

"What?" I struggled away from her, tried to look into her face. Who was she? I didn't seem to know her. And what did she mean about a "new home"?

"Let's get this straight, *ma chere*. You're here to lose the sickness which his family doesn't want, and then to be sent, healthy and clean, to your new owner."

"Sickness?"

"So I've been told. No diseases. No problems. Particularly, no babies. You'll be almost good as new, *petite*."

Now I fought to get up from the cot. My baby was in danger. I couldn't think why or what had happened, but surely I could get away, sleep off this heaviness, and set out to find Jules again.

Or maybe I was dreaming.

That must be it! I was ill and dreaming.

I broke from the woman's arms, and she called out someone else's name. I stumbled and lurched to the tiny open door, meaning to break through it to the searing sunlight beyond. But a large copper-colored man threw off the skins and rose from the

140

floor, blocking the light mercifully from my eyes, and as I fell into his arms, I reminded myself, "It is only a strange dream."

I kept waking into this horrible dream. The chuckling woman sometimes woke me in sunlight, pouring warm lumpy soups into my mouth, to work down my throat. I sometimes woke on my own in the hearth-lit darkness to find her yelling at the copper-skinned bear of a man, or stirring something over her fire, or washing my body with slow, smooth strokes.

One night, I woke screaming in pain.

My stomach muscles worked like iron bands, squeezing everything out of me in a relentless rhythm that worked its way down from my ribs to my bowels. *Squeezing everything out of me.*

The cot and my gown and my spread legs were covered in feces and ooze and blood, my cramping legs bathed in urine. I clutched at my middle, resisting the rhythmic squeeze, and gasped out my cries for help. For pity. For Jules. For his god.

A hand took my face, covering my mouth, and shoved me back onto the cot. Another hand covered my eyes.

More hands cupped the remains of my insides, squeezing and pressing them downward, outward, to gush from between my legs and leave me empty, dying.

"No!" I screamed. I was in too much pain to fight. My lower back felt broken in two. I lay helplessly spread, one leg to each side of the cot, feeling the pressing hands ease the life and the guts

141

and the lifeblood out of me, helping the squeezes that emptied my insides.

This could not be borne. I begged for mercy.

Voices beyond the hand that covered my eyes spoke to each other in a language I could not understand. Something warm and green-smelling dribbled between my lips. Acrid smoke was puffed into my nose.

And then, though I felt the squeezes, they drifted away. Or I did.

I have left my body behind. This feels so good.

When next I came to, the roar of my own screams had died. The hand was gone from before my eyes.

Whimpering, I looked cautiously around. Where were my tormentors? What were they doing now? Why wouldn't this nightmare dream end?

The chuckling woman stood to one side of me, between me and the fire. She held something bloody, curled and small in both her hands, and she smiled at it. She raised it high.

She was speaking to it. The strange language I had heard was hers. She was speaking it to the bloody thing.

It looked like a skinned kitten. It hung limp and helpless, but it frightened me. The whole room smelled of bodily wastes, fear, and blood.

I murmured to her, to anyone who might hear, "Help me. Please."

The woman turned to me. I tried to shrink from the blast of her eyes, but she turned a smile of real warmth toward me, and I bathed in its kindness.

She said, "Ah, *chere petite*, tonight is a night of power. They take life from you, and you take life from them. What you wish tonight, must come true. Tell nana what you wish."

She advanced on me with the bloody thing. To stop her, I blurted, "I wish that Jules would always love me and will come back for me. Always!"

She laughed, "Ah, too easy!" But she muttered to the skinless thing and kissed it, and still muttering in that language, so that I caught snatches of sound that made sense, but I could make no sense of all of it together, she continued to come to me. I could not move to escape.

She lowered the thing to my face. "Kiss it and send it to heaven with your wish, *petite*," and even as my lips neared the terrible thing, I saw and knew what it was, but this could not be.

A tiny, miserable human being, its eyes shut so tightly its whole face was a fist of creased folds, its bulbous body dangling bent limbs, splayed toes, so fine I could see through them to white shadows of bone. And covered with blood, this pale, tiny hanging thing.

I had the terrified thought that if I looked long at it, I would kill the baby within me. So I closed my eyes and kissed the hot, cooling, smooth head.

The woman shouted, "Say it! Say your wish, little girl-*fillette!*"

I moved my lips against the sweet-smelling, blood-sticky skin of the tiny thing in her hands. "I wish Jules will always love me. More than life. More than anything. And that his love will always drive him back to me. Carry my wish to heaven."

My voice trembled and broke into weeping. I could not tell why.

I fell asleep still weeping, listening to the woman's voice rise and shake with the power of her prayers, licking at the taste of blood and the sticky paste of the tiny baby's skin still stuck to my lips, trying to push it from my mouth with my dry tongue.

Would I never wake from this hellish dream?

I opened my eyes again to find that the room was full of softer daylight. I felt weak, drained, empty. I doubted that any blood was left to pump sluggishly through my body. The madwoman had squeezed it all out of me.

As I stared around her sunlit, silent room, waiting to drift back to deeper sleep, the coppery man stuck his head in at the ever-open door. He stared at me, and angry, hopeless, I returned his stare.

The curtain of his river of black hair swung as he turned from me and shouted something back outside, over his shoulder.

I found myself drifting into other dreams.

Women on balconies, chatting and passing around their husbands' cigars, bathing their children and tossing the water down onto the heads of passing Frenchmen. "Take that, you swine!"

Laughter. I woke this time to the familiar sound of *Tante* Clothilde's laughter. And I sat up, knowing that, now, I could no longer be dreaming.

She was there in front of me, leaning in the doorway, chatting with another of the African women who was enslaved at Jules's parents' place.

The other woman noticed my rising from my old cot and gasped, "Clothilde, look."

Tante Clothilde, my caregiver and my life, turned, shocked, to look at me, and then left the doorway to come gather me into her arms. "Oh, *mon enfant,* my child, what have these fools done?" she asked as she knelt beside me. "At least you are alive."

I shuddered. My jaw trembled. "*Tante* Clothilde, how did I come here? What has happened? I have been dreaming the most horrid dreams, and I know nothing."

"Oh, *ma chere.*" She hid her head low down on my breast.

I gasped and pulled back. "*Tante!* What are you doing?" She, the strong one, cowering against my weak bosom?

I was the child who needed her to tell me what was what, what was going on. It was not my place to comfort her.

But I had missed her. I slid my arms around her shaking shoulders. "What they have done," *Tante* Clothilde said. "I could never have imagined it, never have warned you. They have no scruples and no conscience. They have killed your child."

"What?" I pushed *Tante* Clothilde away and pulled back the covers so that I might look at my weak, flattened body. "Who? Why?" I ran shaking hands up and down the shrunken breasts, the gurgling, hanging tummy. "How has this happened?" My frantic hands dug handfuls of my sagging skin to hold out and search, as though the baby were lost in a fold of it.

145

"They were relentless." *Tante* Clothilde raised her face to me. Tears washed it. "They would not have your child born. They will have you no longer than it takes me to heal you and send you on to your new owner."

"New owner?" I released my stomach and tried to work my way to my feet, to edge past *Tante* Clothilde's kneeling body. "Where is Jules?" I demanded. "He will want to hear of this."

"He knows, *ma chere.*"

"He knows?" I rose, shaking, and fell back to sit on the cot. I said, "He cannot know. He would not let this happen. I want my baby. Who has it?"

The woman who had been at the door now came in. "Aurelie," she said, "calmly, now. What is done is done."

Tante Clothilde stared up at me, sobbing.

I said, "You are lying. Jules does not know. And someone has stolen my baby. Who? How did they find us? Whoever found us took the baby."

"No," *Tante* Clothilde said. "The baby is dead. They have killed it."

"No!"

"Yes, *ma chere,*" both women crooned, their voices overlapping in waves like song.

"No, no, no!" I beat my fists on my cramping, weak thighs, forcing them to help me rise. *I must get out of there. Find Jules. Tell him.* Wake at last in our room at the inn, listless from boredom and reading his tedious poetry.

I had gotten to the door of *Tante* Clothilde's room before she and the other woman took my efforts seriously enough to reach, grab, and hold

146

me. I stretched my hands past them and shouted out into the courtyard, "Jules! Jules, help me. Where are you? It's Aurelie. Help me!"

The women kept crooning as they covered my mouth and pulled me back to the cot, "No, no, *petite,* it is the opium and the herbs. Together they have addled your mind. Come away from the door. The *Madame* will hear. The *Monsieur* will hear. Hush. *Monsieur* Jules will not come again. Stop calling out. It is over now."

I scratched and struggled and fought.

The other woman slid a rag full of the choking stuff onto my face. And again, even as I resisted the gagging and the sudden fear of death, I succumbed and fell limp in their arms.

Someone screamed in my sleep.

There was the limp thing, the tiny bloody baby, curled in with its bent limbs, hanging and drawing the life from my own womb as I kissed it and stupidly sent my wishes to heaven. And there was the evil woman, chuckling as she helped me make a wish that didn't need wishing. *"Too easy."*

And there, as I forced my eyelids to open again on the room in which I'd grown up with *Tante* Clothilde, was my beloved aunt, a bloody rag pressed to her eye.

She rolled on her own cot, toward me, away from me, moaning and shuddering. Her husband sat in the flickering lamplight muttering, "*O, Dieu! Dieu! Que le diable les punisse! Qu'ils aillent brûler dans l'enfer!*" And his large hands shook as he plucked, without effect, at the spreading red of *Tante* Clothilde's rag.

Did he want to take it from her? He seemed unsure. Women crowded into the room around him, shutting me out from *Tante* Clothilde's suffering.

But, after all, it was only one more nightmare. If I slept enough, if I gave in to the ache in my head and in my groin and passed out, I should eventually awaken in the inn.

I was on my side, gagging. Thin bitter streams swam up my throat and trickled from my mouth. "She has nothing left to throw up," someone said.

"Really, even if she fights, we should not use that knockout stuff on her. It will kill her."

"She hasn't eaten."

"Neither can Clothilde. This business will finish them both."

"It is a bad business."

"A very bad business."

I woke to feel my head supported on a woman's breast. Did I know her? It seemed I may have known her long ago.

She said, "Please, *petite*, you must eat. You must get strong. Open your lips. Only a little stew. Smell it. It is good for you."

My eyes swam open and onto her face. "Who are you?"

"Ah! You are awake. Please, Aurelie, you must eat."

I touched her hand and helped her guide spoonful after spoonful of the thick brew, rank with stewed dead things, to my open mouth. I shuddered and swallowed until my thick tongue had rammed it all down my throat.

148

She smiled and showed me the emptied wooden bowl. "How pleased our owner will be to hear that you are getting well," she said. "He has given you so little time."

"Time? No. Where is *Tante* Clothilde? You said you would tell me." *Didn't she?* I glared at this almost-stranger. "Where is *Monsieur* Jules? I want to know."

"Yes, Aurelie." The woman looked away from me. Stood, gathering up her bowl and spoon and sundry wet rags with which she must have tried to bathe me before discarding them on the splintered wood floor. "Clothilde has been sold. Even with that wound-"

"What wound?"

"Her eye, *petite*. I thought you had been told."

"What happened to her eye?"

"It was an accident. When the mistress whipped her-"

"Whipped her? *Tante* Clothilde is never whipped. Our owner does not allow it."

"It seems this time he could not prevent it. The mistress found out that Clothilde is your mother-"

"My mother? What are you saying? My mother has been dead all my life!"

"No." Very gently, "That was a lie our owner told to protect you both when he brought you here. We all knew the truth."

"What truth?"

"That Clothilde is your mother. See how tenderly she raised you? You were the only child allowed to her. Our owner aborted her other babies, after she came to live among us. That is how he knew the swamp witch could-" But she broke off with a half-hearted gesture at my thin middle.

I panicked. "Could what? What babies? What swamp witch?" But already the woman's shrill laughter as she raised the curled-up skinned thing to the ceiling shot through my mind before I could block it.

"But did you know none of this? Surely, growing up with your own mother, in her own room, you began to understand-"

"I understand nothing. You are telling me nothing. Where is my mo-*Tante* Clothilde, and where is *Monsieur* Jules? Why has he not come for me? I must go to him." I shook as if with fever as I tried to rise.

"No, no." The woman held out her free hand toward me, as if she would hold me down.

But, after all, there was no need. I could not stand.

She said, "You are still weak. You have lost much blood, *ma chere*. And while we tried to tend your *Tante* Clothilde, I'm afraid we may have neglected you. You slept so soundly. And we knew we would not have her with us much longer." The woman's lip trembled and a thin trickle lit her face. She shrugged and shook her head. "It has been a sad business."

"I don't believe you. And I want to speak to *Monsieur* Jules. He won't let people threaten my baby. You are not feeding me as you should. I have lived on bread and water and gotten thin. That is all. But you are making me afraid."

The woman turned back toward me and *Tante* Clothilde's empty, rust-stained cot. "Oh, but *do* be afraid, *ma chere*. It would be very wise of you to be afraid."

CHAPTER SEVEN
AFTER ALL

Our owner came into the servants' quarters to judge my progress for himself.

"This will never do," he told the woman who cared for me, now that *Tante* Clothilde, whom I must come to think of as my lost mother, was gone. "The man remembers a beautiful girl. Look at her."

He himself, however, hesitated to look at me.

I watched him hold himself away from the walls, from the woman, and from the very air we breathed in *Tante* Clothilde's shack, watched him finally cast his eyes with open disgust up and down my wrung-out body, avoiding my eyes with their challenge, *Don't you dare look at me.* I wondered how I had ever come up with the idea that he might be my father.

Surely the mistress had put such an idea into my head, with her eternal efforts to drive a wedge between Jules and me. I had no other reason to think such a stomach-wrenching thought. *I hate that man.* Tante *Clothilde's husband was right. May our owners burn in hell, starting with this one.*

Somehow, to have been fathered and abandoned by a face never seen was less personal than to sit on the little cot, bleeding away the remains of my own child while my father sneered and refused to look with pity on my distress.

No, he could not be my father. *Tante* Clothilde would never have encouraged me to plan a future with Jules if she had known Jules is my brother.

Would she?

But if she did, why did she?

Our owner said, "Have you ceased yet to give her these drugs? We will never be quit of her if she remains in this appalling stupor. I want her head cleared, I want her fed, and I want her out of my wife's and my son's lives."

"Yes, sir. What if she should—"

"See that she doesn't. Or I shall see that she doesn't. Is that clear? It is my wife's idea to salvage some pride by donating the wretch to the poor fool who paid for her room and board. Myself, I would just as soon ... "

His voice faded with the intensity of his contemplation.

Then he erupted afresh. "One takes pity on them. One acts mercifully toward them, bringing them into one's own home to mingle with one's own family, with one's own children. And how do they repay such generosity of spirit? Plotting and undermining, working every day to destroy the moral fabric of those whom I hold most dear!" He gnashed his teeth.

He turned in his fury toward me, but he still would not allow his eyes to rest on my eyes. "That miserable black whore was given the honor of cooking every meal my own wife and children would eat for the next fifteen years, after I brought her here, and what did she do with a gentleman's trust? Trained her half-breed cur to seduce my sons and drive a wedge between them, drive them mad with lust over the curse that deforms her body into something man and beast have never seen in the

153

history of the world. Brother against brother, seduced by their sin-stained sister!" He shrieked, an inhuman cry of pain. "These half-breeds and their viciously conniving negress mothers will be the death of the French Empire! They spurn all concepts of morality and decency. They treasure nothing but chaos and evil."

He turned on his heel and walked briskly from my and *Tante* Clothilde's old room, calling back to the woman, "No more drugs. She's as vacant-eyed and underfed as an opium addict. Get her sober and get her out of my home." We heard him stop again at the front door of the quarters. "And one of you negresses find that damned wounded part of Clothilde's! We don't need my son stumbling upon it in the courtyard, when he returns from the sanitarium."

"Do you mean the eye, *Monsieur*?" the woman called after him, but he was hurrying away and seemed not to hear her.

"Ha," she said and turned back to me once he was gone. She tried to ease me under my thin quilt again. "Why doesn't he send his wife to find the eye? It is she who ripped it out."

Another woman entered the room, muttering, "And gave Clothilde another seventeen good strokes of the whip after the eye was gone." This second woman, an old one whose face also stirred my sluggish mind with dim memories, spat after our owner's disappearing form. "Bah. Moral? Decent? He took in Clothilde and Clothilde's half-breed bastard? Bah." She spat again.

"Now, Ange-Marie," the other woman said, and the name raised a lively picture in my mind of rolling up a mat to uncover a splash of sunlight through an upstairs window, Ange-Marie chatting brightly as if a woman didn't lie dying on the bed right next to us ...

Ange-Marie now shouted, "Clothilde is gone! We are all in danger. He has gone mad. As mad as his lunatic murdering sons."

"Hush, I tell you."

"I have hushed, and what good has it done? What of his promises never to sell Aurelie from Clothilde? Did Clothilde have Aurelie alone? Brother and sister. Bah! It is 'brother and sister' when *that* will get our owner what *he* wants. A little royal French bastard as a wife for his son, maybe. But is it always 'brother and sister'?"

"Ha," the other woman laughed bitterly. "When it comes to what our owner wants, there is no brother and sister, if that would get in his way. But truly. How would it have hurt him to give his *mulatta* daughter a little house? And her own mother her freedom, too, maybe, to live with her there? Had he not promised as much when Aurelie was born?"

"Promised and then broke those promises as soon as his wife allowed Clothilde to be brought here, where it was cheaper to keep her. I have not forgotten, Celeste. It was our owner who forced Clothilde to turn her daughter toward his sons. It was their only hope to get out of here. That is what I say."

155

"Don't I know as well as you that there is no brother and sister and no mother and no father, for that matter, when it comes to what our owner wants for himself?"

"I remember."

"Of course you do. That same boy who drank from your breast, the very ones who drank from mine, you and I are the very first women they throw on the floor when they are ready to learn how to become men."

Ange-Marie wiped thick running tears from her high cheekbones, her thin lips and tiny chin with skinny, shaking hands. "Bah." But she had no more phlegm to hurtle to the floor. "Clothilde and Aurelie were my only hope for his honor. And my future." Her voice shook with age and rage. I watched her hold out her trembling, twisted hands toward Celeste. "Look at my hands. What will become of me in two or three more years? He will turn me out in the streets to beg and die in the cold, if no one else will take me in for free. Oh, Celeste. Probably wild birds have found Clothilde's eye and eaten it by now."

Celeste left me and embraced the older woman. "If he puts you out, Ange-Marie, I will sneak you scraps and blankets. You will neither starve nor freeze to death." As she said this, I had a quick memory of her carrying a bucket and smiling down at me, teasing me for a bite of buttered bread when I was small and still allowed to follow *Tante* Clothilde about the kitchen.

My mind would not hold the thoughts I wanted. Since that night-*How long ago?*-that I was snatched from Jules at the inn, thoughts flitted through my head-or stayed and hammered themselves into my mind and my heart.

And then the stream of memories, jerking to a stop at all the most horrible spots, would start again.

In the next few days, the world around me suddenly became clearer than the world in my head, in stabbing bright moments of despair.

The walls of my and *Tante* Clothilde's little room stood out in sharp dull woody colors. Their splinters and whorls became so absorbing that I found myself lost in them, remembering the passage of time only because I remarked to myself the patterns of shadow and the graying dullness on the wall that were signs of the advent of twilight.

I would find myself suddenly wide-eyed in a spat with Celeste, stupidly, over whether or not I would eat a strengthening stew loaded with stolen bits of tender snails, oysters, crab, and shallots that she had labored to prepare for me. I would stop. Stutter. Stare. Backtrack, looking for an appropriate apology and explanation for my ingratitude, when there was none.

Or I would find myself wandering the courtyard in the middle of the night, wringing my hands and wailing, describing to the blossoming magnolias and the moonlight caught in cascades of fountain droplets what it was to watch one's baby come bloody and dead through the world on its way to heaven, ignored by the household as though I were sleeping in my cot.

Unpunished, as though I were a crazy woman, and nothing could be done with me.

One night, I came to and found myself frantically wrenching vines about my neck, crying because I could not knot them, they were so thick with the warming weather, and I was in a hurry to jump from the second-floor gallery and hang myself before the sadness of Jules's empty room overtook me and drove me out of my mind.

I came to with the vines about my neck, unwinding, and my fingers scrabbling at them, to keep them tight as I threw a leg over the gallery railing and leaned into the sweet waterlit darkness of the courtyard below.

I fell back from the gallery railing, screaming and tearing at the limp mossy vines that, after all, fell away helplessly before my panicked will to live a little longer.

And still no one came. No one looked up at me from the courtyard cobbles. No one opened a window and shouted at me to get off the gallery, get back to the quarters.

Has such raving from me become routine?

I crept slowly through Jules's room, feeling my way along the walls, afraid to look at anything but the barely starlit edge of the doorframe that would let me out to the steeply falling safety of the stairway.

When I reached the doorway, I slid down its solid frame to the floor. From there, I crawled on all fours-testing the parquet for sudden drops-until I reached the solid resistance of the banisters that announced the stairway's grand sweep to the ground floor.

After weeping, terrified, at the head of the stairs, calling out uselessly for anyone to come and help me descend without falling, hurtling to a painful death at the stairs' end, I worked my way around to sitting on the top step. In this way, clinging with both hands and trembling so that my tear-wet hands often slipped and had to be wrapped carefully about the rails again, I managed to slide slowly from one step down to the next, gasping with fear when it seemed that there was no next step, and I must fall to my death.

But I reached the bottom of the steps and sat, feeling the floor and patting the marble of the foyer with love and joy for this new chance to live and remember my pain in safety. I crawled on all fours until I had crossed the foyer, the empty kitchen, and then crossed the threshold to the courtyard.

Where at last I stood, leaving the kitchen doorway to our owner's threatening hell house gaping open.

I pushed myself off from the doorway and ran, sobbing with relief from my terror and the fear that the vines were grown not only for beauty and a surrender to the stubborn creeping of nature in the colonies, but also with the new fear that someone had planted them just here in this courtyard with the knowledge that, someday, a distressed girl would see in them a way to end her misery.

I reached the void of my and *Tante* Clothilde's room, where there was no longer a heart that loved me beating back the stillness, and I threw myself onto my cot. Then I leaped from it, crying out in fear at its height from the safety of the floor. I crawled under it and worked my way painfully between the spindly legs.

And even then I remembered the distance that Ange-Marie's spit had to fall, arcing futilely behind our owner, trickling between the floorboards to leak to the solid earth below.

I had never crawled below the quarters, even as a small child. Were there rats?

My awareness of the world around me blanked again and receded, only to come screaming back to the front of my mind in confusion and terror when Celeste and Ange-Marie discovered me trapped in the crawlspace beneath the quarters, in the morning.

It took all three servant women to coax me out, but only after they sent for *Monsieur* to come from his office and order his wife from the courtyard. For, as long as she shrieked there, I cowered further in terror from her and everyone, begging to keep my eyes.

Our owner appeared caught between his wife's bellows of outrage, her arms pinned to her sides in his embrace as he pulled her from the courtyard, and my shrieks of terror as my legs were seized by Celeste and Yseult, the mistress's own maid and seamstress, so that I could be dragged on my back into sunlight.

Strong arms of two women held me seated at the fountain's edge, and all around me voices raged. "She is mad! Let the man come and see that there is nothing for it but to have the colony's authority put her out of her misery." This was *Monsieur*, returned to the courtyard without his wife.

Ange-Marie doused my uncovered head with fountain water, cooing to me that everything would soon be all right, and I had nothing to fear. Soaking wet, I shivered, despite the moist heat of spring, and looked pleadingly at the women holding me. "Celeste, why couldn't I have been like you? Or like you, Yseult? Faithful husbands, good African men crawling in through the windows-"

"Hush, *enfant. Maitre*, she does not know what she is saying."

"Maybe a good slap?" This, of course, from Yseult, who had always been above the rest of us, as she was married to a freeman and had a house of her own to go to at Christmas Eve.

I turned to her to win her sympathy by showing that I did, indeed, understand. "*Chere* Yseult, I know you have walked out of this compound with your head held high on holidays, to spend in your own home. I only meant that I would rather have aspired to the evenings of love and hiding that all the women-"

I was slapped at last. I went on. "-enjoyed, knowing that the risk was small, if they were found out. And I? Why did *ma chere Tante* Clothilde see fit to raise me to want something other than what contented all of you? You, Celeste, with your faithful husband, and you, *Grandmere* Ange-Marie, with your boyfriends, each sweeter than the next, bringing little gifts even to me, and you, *chere Madame* Yseult, with a husband who waited faithfully, and when he could not wait-"

Again I was slapped, and as Yseult barked at the *Monsieur* in her mistress's acid tone, "*Maitre*,

161

will you suffer her to rant at us?" he sighed and restrained her hand, saying, "Will we punish her for speaking the truth in her madness? Enough. It sickens me. Send for the man whose charity to my son has earned him the curse of this wretched girl's presence in his home. It is for him to decide what must be done with her, now that she is ... as she is. I can take no more."

Fearing to slip into the tempting world of memory where nothing got worse but only repeated the seductive hopelessness of familiar moments, so much kinder than the rapidly worsening days that I must live, now that all was said and done, I clutched at awareness.

And at last I came to in a sleeveless camisole and underskirt. The cool white was stiffly ruffled at the low neck so that it scratched. I reached to loosen the bow that tied it shut, for it was too small and the skirt too short, and it was odd that I should be so undressed in the very parlor of the *Monsieur's* house, before a gentleman who was a stranger.

He gripped a cane and paced back and forth, just beyond the *Monsieur's* supplicating reach. The man with the cane rebuked my owner. "I have not forgotten, if you have, sir, this girl's origins. Should they not have earned her a small measure of your consideration?"

"A small measure? Sir, I have been long-suffering."

"And merciful to the point that the girl has been brought to this impasse? Sir, may I remind you that even if the Americans buy our land and shoot our mulatto children down in the gutters like rats, we

162

remain French, not English, and certainly not American. We do not do such things to our own flesh and blood." The stranger gestured with his cane toward me, and I drew back, fearing-but I could not have named exactly what I feared from him. I was sure I did not know him.

But when I cried out and grasped at Ange-Marie, who held me on her thin lap, he turned toward me.

Recognition. This was the stranger at the window of the inn.

"You!" I screamed and clawed to get away from Ange-Marie, who was too small and frail to hold me in my frenzy. "You found us out and brought this upon us."

The stranger said, "*Mon Dieu,*" and backed away. He dropped his fine cane to gesture at me with his hands that I was safe and had nothing to fear, as though I were a skittish horse in the street. "No, *ma petite,* I did not bring this on you. Only let me explain my presence at the inn, and you will see."

I ripped at Ange-Marie's hands. She called out to Celeste, who must have been in the room, for soon she was upon me and grabbed my wrists in her larger, stronger hands, urging me, "*Chut, mon ange, penses à ta mere.* This is not the end of what dear Clothilde wanted for you, but only a new beginning."

"Yes," the man urged Celeste. "Tell her that I am her friend and will restore her-no, *introduce* her-to the kind of life her close connection to this house should have made her due. Explain that her problems end when she leaves this house with me today."

Jules's father reasoned with the man. "*Mon ami,* calm yourself and look at what is before you. The girl is mad. There is nothing that can be done for her. It is not your duty to carry out a promise made when she was virginal and innocent. You are remembering a child-"

"A child who was abominably treated," the man finally turned and thundered at my owner. "What do we French do with our own children, *Monsieur,* after we have had the pleasure of their mothers? It is not *my* duty that I am honoring here today, *Monsieur.* It is your own."

He had retrieved his cane and jabbed it in the air toward our owner, who stood his ground, eyes wide.

Then my owner's eyes narrowed like the mistress's. "Very well," he said. "You forget that the Americans have laws against the way you speak. You cannot name this girl's parentage nor acknowledge it. It is now against the law. I have only sought to advise you, as a father might have done. I see my advice is misunderstood."

The stranger was not to be calmed. He roared on, "I see what your fathering has done."

"Monsieur!"

"One son slain in suspicious circumstances-"

"I will not tolerate-"

"And the next son driven mad by your pretentious aspirations."

"-this insolence in my own home, *Monsieur*!"

"Your daughter and I are leaving!" The man with the cane started for the door. He was raising the cane, to point it at me and Celeste, when our owner shook off his rigid stance and chased after the man's heels.

"The girl is not payment of my debt to you, *Monsieur*. I will reimburse you for all that you have advanced to the inn, in my son's interests. Wait. This very day, I will write out a draft-" Our owner fumbled at his pockets.

The man wheeled on him. "And this very day, you will see me set it alight in your fireplace. Will you not understand? She should not have been for sale. She was your *daughter*. Are we Americans, for God's sake?"

My owner and father produced a handkerchief and mopped his brow. He tried a friendly chuckle. "For such a young man, Roger, you are shockingly old-fashioned."

The man turned again. "Old-fashioned? No. I try only to cling to my ideals, despite the decays of Americanism and Enlightenment greed that I see, corrupting everyone and everything I have been raised to value. If slavery is just, then it is only just when we do not allow it to devalue *us*, *Monsieur*. If I value myself as a gentleman of honor, then I must treat honorably my own children, however they were brought into the world."

"This from a man who never married."

"This from a man so awed by the responsibilities of marriage, that he would not undertake them lightly!"

Our owner seemed suddenly struck by the realization that his handkerchief was in his hand, mere inches from the other man's face, like a gauntlet about to be thrown down.

He lowered it and stared at it with his jaw hanging. "What was I about to do? No." He looked at the other man, who continued to stand his ground. "*Mon ami*," my owner pleaded, finally remembering himself, "these are the heated and thoughtless words that bring good friends to shoot each other in cold blood."

"I assure you, *Monsieur*. I have selected my words with the utmost care. I have had six months to ponder what I would say to you. Let me assure you that we are no longer friends."

While my owner stuttered, the other man gestured again toward me and Celeste. I felt her jerk backward with me against the *chaise longue* where I was held. All three women held our breaths. Clearly, even our owner could not protect us from this strange man, who now said, "I will take that one with me and the girl. I will pay you her rent. I will send it round. I need her as a familiar face to calm your daughter in her new surroundings."

Our owner sputtered, "Celeste? This is impossible. My wife will be left with only her personal maid and the old crone too useless to do anything but tend my own mother." There must have been something about this last phrase that embarrassed my owner, for he stopped his argument and reddened.

Now, oddly enough, it was the stranger who smiled, tight and thin. "Rest assured that I would have preferred the loan of your daughter's mother. Only, she seems to have been precipitously sold. Correct me if I am wrong, and rent her to me in Celeste's stead. No? Well, then. You hardly expect me to take the girl away in conditions which must only finish the job of driving her out of her mind, after paying your son's debts so well to earn her."

"I can pay you back, *Monsieur*!"

"I know your circumstances, *Monsieur*. I will not have your son's wife pay for his mistress's abduction and mistreatment. I have told you my views about the honor due a marriage. Even your son's not quite mutually agreed upon marriage."

"If I tell you this girl was not abducted-"

"You will ask me to judge between the passions of a spoiled boy and a girl who had no reason to hope she might escape her unjust condition."

"*Monsieur*, we have always been friends. Will you not relent? These accusations have become intolerable."

"Then I urge you to cease to arrest my departure. I have stated that I am going and taking your daughter and the woman who seems to have a way with her. I shall pay for this second woman's rental. I take it your daughter has no clothes to bring with her."

Surprising Celeste, I broke from her and Ange-Marie and stood. "I do have it, *Monsieur*," I said. "The most beautiful dress, with room for the baby to grow."

"Oh, *mon Dieu*," the man said again as Celeste and Ange-Marie rose to hush and hold me. The man said to my owner, "That cursed dress that allowed

167

you to finally track down your son. The only debt his creditors finally approached you to pay. I take it you still have the dress she mentions?"

"It was given to the woman who performed the services-ahem-yes, the necessary services of which you are only too aware."

"You gave the dress to the swamp witch?" Now the man with the cane would not be detained but strode from the parlor laughing back, "Let us hope she does not use it to curse the boy who had it made, or better yet curse his father, who paid for it!"

Ange-Marie muttered into my ear, "Or to bless the wronged girl who wore it, *ma petite*. Let us hope the swamp witch uses your dress to bless you."

I rushed to explain, "She made me kiss a baby. But I think it was dead." Then I gasped and shoved my fingers into my mouth, biting down on them as the memory overtook me.

And as I fell away from awareness of them, I heard Celeste explain to the strange man, "*Monsieur,* she has these fits. It is the drugs that have been put into her."

And our owner said, "She's had nothing that ladies and gentlemen don't take every day."

I came to briefly in the gentleman's carriage. "Look, *Monsieur,* she is opening her eyes!" said Celeste, eager to please and perhaps be bought, too, no doubt.

His face, stern and a little lined down the long cheeks, turned toward me. He gave a slight nod. "Sleep," he said to me. "You might as well awaken in your new home, after you have slept enough."

Perhaps because he urged me to sleep, I fought the memories that had barely receded and wanted to sweep over me again. Instead, I sat up straight, straining the tight camisole against my tender chest, and fought to loosen the laces enough to lean forward and see through the uncovered window. The streets were so narrow for the carriage that it seemed we must knock people aside as they emerged from doorways.

I had never been in a carriage. One rocked, miles above the solid ground, encased in a dark world of stiff benches and knees pressed to the knees of a brooding stranger. The ride was heady and frightening.

But my head cleared suddenly, and I knew this man was no stranger. This was, wasn't it, the dinner guest who had long ago told me my eyes were enchanting?

I turned to him quickly and said, "My eyes are not enchanting now," and was about to turn back to the window, for there, surely, was a freewoman, leading a small child by the hand and carrying a covered basket of her shopping, when the man said, "Let me be the judge of your eyes, if you please."

This caught my attention, and I turned fully to him, to see what I had missed. But out of the corner of my eye, I saw that the woman had gone by, and I turned too late crying out, "Oh, you have made me miss her. And she was so beautiful, too."

"Who, Aurelie?" asked Celeste when the man didn't.

"The freewoman." I began to describe her turban and gown and basket. But it pained me to speak of the child, so I left him out.

For no reason, the man said, "I saw her, and she was not half so beautiful as you. What made you think she was especially beautiful, Aurelie?"

I said peevishly, "Did you hear nothing I just said about her, *Monsieur*?"

And he answered, apparently determined not to listen to me, for everyone had convinced him I was crazy, "Perhaps, after all, you are not much changed. Please call me Roger, Aurelie."

Face to the window, I said, "I cannot. Have you not bought me? I thought I understood that, *Monsieur*. Or would you prefer *Maitre*?" *Jules at the fountain on that long ago night.*

The man said, "Celeste, please call me Roger and teach your charge to do the same. Do you sincerely believe we are witnessing the effects of the drugs?"

Celeste said, "I have known her all her life. I was nothing but a big girl when Clothilde came to us with her. I used to care for her while Clothilde cooked. Her mind was always sound, *Monsieur* ... Roger." This last she said loudly, turning to me.

I looked at her.

She turned back to the man. "I believe everyone wishes to hide how much of their hashish and their opium and their wild grass and their wild mushrooms they actually put into her, *Monsieur*," loudly, turning to me again, "Roger." She turned back to him.

I glared at Celeste's back. She was surely up to something. But, torn as I was with the beauty of the passing streets and the hope of catching glimpses of freewomen upon them, I could not be sure what. Celeste went on to the man, "I suspect that little damage will remain, once she is away from the old house and its memories. I have not seen her face so happy since she was returned to us, as she is at this moment."

I laughed out loud. "How can I not be happy, Celeste?" I cried too loudly for the close carriage. The shriek of my voice hurt my own ears. *But never mind*. I went on. "Look at all the beautiful women, every one of them free. That one, sweeping out the front of her own shop, surely, just as I wanted for my-"

I gasped. For my child was dead. There would be no shop for her, no education and no marriage to a freeman. *Now I understand.*

I grabbed my face and began to sob.

Celeste's arms went around me. "Of course, you are right, *ma chere*. Look at the pretty women, every one of them free. Are they not a lovely sight?"

I began to dry my eyes. "All with homes of their own ... " I began.

"Certainly, *ma chere*. With homes of their own, every one."

"And husbands. And they can go out upon the streets, holding their husbands' arms, though you hardly ever see it. I suppose they work so hard in the evenings at home. So few of them have servants. And perhaps they have little money to spend at

171

cafes. What do you think?" I looked up at her from where she had pulled me down onto her lap. Celeste wiped the frown from between my brows.

"Of course, *petite*. They probably have little money to go out upon the town."

The man spoke again. "But, if I may be permitted to interrupt, I'd like to point out that it may be you, Aurelie, who have been so rarely upon the town that you don't know what the freewomen do. It is only newly spring, after all. See all the blossoms on people's balconies. Now is the time they may begin to grace the town. The blossoms and the freewomen, I mean."

I turned my head on Celeste's lap so that I might stare at him. *He was at the inn and watched my movements. Knows that I went out too rarely to know what the freewomen do, for he has seen that I almost never left the inn.*

He had seen me trapped-*was I trapped? No. No. I was happy*-waiting for Jules. *Wasn't I? Happy?*

For it seemed to me now that sadness had only begun with the death of our baby and our plans.

CHAPTER EIGHT
WHEN THINGS ARE MADE NEW

When we arrived at *Monsieur* Roger's townhouse, a gate was opened to the side of the main door. I was hurried through it with *Monsieur*'s cloak flung over my camisole and underskirt and his arm tightly about me. I felt Celeste bump me from behind, she stayed so close.

We crossed his courtyard, with me looking back over *Monsieur*'s shoulder to see who closed the gate behind us. A curious young man with slanted, dark-lashed eyes looked away as soon as I caught him watching. I was rushed through a back entrance that went straight up steep stairs to the third floor.

"These will be your rooms, Aurelie," *Monsieur* Roger said as he threw open double glass doors to let me into a lovely sitting room.

A woman in spring colors rushed in from the bedroom beyond, smiling at *Monsieur*. She curtseyed toward me and Celeste.

"Yasmine, I'm not sure your services will be needed as lady's maid. *Mademoiselle* has brought a maid of her own. Perhaps they shall appreciate your acquainting them with the rooms we've prepared and with passing on to me any further needs of the *Mademoiselle*."

Dismissed from a job that I would have fought to keep, Yasmine only smiled and curtseyed again. "*Certainement, Monsieur*," she assured him. "*Mademoiselle*?" She offered me entrance into my new dressing room with an inviting sweep of her hand.

Yasmine was gentleness and courtesy itself. When at last she had me washed and dressed in a tasteful but simple day gown of Celeste's choosing, and had kindly braided and coiled my hair for Celeste-all the while pretending she was only showing us a new style-Yasmine quietly gathered up the pan of wash water and the soiled underclothes in which I had been brought to *Monsieur*'s home and withdrew, cautioning us only to listen for the dinner bell, as its sound carried faintly up to the third floor.

"She is a wonder," I confided to Celeste when we were alone. "Do you think she shall teach me my new duties?" I pressed my hands to my mouth and exclaimed, "And maybe you, too. Celeste, at last you can escape the scullery. What's wrong?" I rose unsteadily to my feet to aid her, my hands fluttering between pretty bottles that graced the lady's dressing table before me, uncertain which was smelling salts.

Celeste had collapsed to the bed and slid to the floor, laughing till the tears threatened to run. "Oh, *mon enfant*," she said, holding one side, "you are such a child. No, no, I shall be fine. And, in any case, you are never to fetch me a glass of your own water, *ma chere*, so put it down, or drink it yourself. Your station is now above such-"

"Signs of respect? I hope I shall never be above returning your many acts of kindness to me," I scolded and brought her the brimming glassful I'd poured from a crystal pitcher on a tray by the bed. "Why are you laughing at me?"

"Oh, no, *ma chere,* not at you. It is just that-how shall I put it?-no one shall teach you your duties except the *Monsieur* himself, of course. And I could not help but laugh that, after so many evidences of how your station has improved, you still do not see it."

"See what, Celeste?"

"Why, *Mademoiselle* Aurelie, that you have at last become the lady of a house. Just as you always dreamed to be."

Now it was my turn to sit on the floor with my mouth open. After a few sips of Celeste's water, I said, "Not *this* house. It's *his* house, Celeste."

"And you're going to be the mistress of it. Closest thing. It's what your mother wanted for you. What you wanted with-"

"Don't say his name." I struggled up from the floor so suddenly that the glass sloshed its water over the lap of my new dress. "Now look what I've done." I swiped with my free hand at the darkened patch of muslin.

Celeste hurried to get the towel Yasmine had used to bathe me. She said nothing while we worked at the dampness. And in the silence came the soft tinkling of a bell.

"The dinner bell," Celeste said, looking toward the doorway.

"And you haven't even washed or changed yet." I took the towel from her. "Do you think you should put on one of the dresses in the wardrobe where Yasmine found this one?"

175

Celeste shook her head sadly at me. "Is it all the opium we've put into you? Those dresses are all yours, Aurelie. You're *Monsieur* Roger's mistress, now. I'm your lady's maid, for the moment. If I try very hard to please you, I hope you'll persuade *Monsieur* Roger to buy me and not send me back where we came from. Our stations have changed, today. You're going to eat with *Monsieur*. I'm going to eat in the kitchen, I hope, with the other servants of high station, as a lady's maid is of the very highest station. Can you understand, *ma petite*?"

I had followed her careful speech with pained attention. I could not take it all in. "But I wanted *Tante* Clothilde in my home, and it would be small, and we would clean it ourselves. There wouldn't be servants except for *Monsieur*'s gardening-you know who I mean-and maybe his horses."

"Oh, *Mademoiselle*. If Clothilde were here, she would tell you this is better than what you and she had planned. This has all turned out for the best, *ma chere*. You will see. You must try to change your thinking. Every day, every step of the way, I will explain everything."

I thanked Celeste for her promise to help me-what else could I do with it?-and we went down the stairway very quietly. It was, after all, a back stairway for servants, narrow and steep. It trailed us down to the courtyard and abandoned us there. We stood, puzzling over the many windows of the townhouse's first floor and wondering if I was missed at the master's table, yet.

Finally, a door opened and Yasmine-all sunshine and flower-perfumed pastel cottons-spilled out of it, beckoning to us. "Oh, *Mademoiselle*, forgive me. Of course, I was late coming up to escort you to the dining room." Which we had never agreed she was to do. But her refusal to point out that I'd gotten lost and bumbled all the way out of the townhouse was the most generous act of face-saving anyone had ever offered me.

Celeste fell away as Yasmine took us through the long, narrow kitchen. And suddenly, without any warning, I was in a blood-dark and elegant dining hall.

Everything was burnished cherry, rosewood, and mahogany, with drapes and fleur-de-lis wall-cloth the color of burgundy wine. Gleaming prisms of crystal reflected the flames of the chandelier that hung from a chain of gold above our heads.

I fell back from the luxury of it. It had not occurred to me that *Monsieur* Roger might be so much wealthier than those who used to own me.

I don't know why his wealth should have struck me in the dining hall when it had not in the rooms he assigned me. Though I had heard that they were to be mine, I had not seen them as mine. I had listened without listening to Celeste's explanation and continued to think I would soon be sleeping in shed-like quarters with her.

But the rich smoldering flames of the dining hall burned the clouds in my mind away. I stood stunned at the entryway in the simple day dress Celeste had chosen for me as Yasmine announced, "*Mademoiselle, Monsieur.*"

Yasmine stood, smiling and hands folded, to one side as *Monsieur* Roger, invisible amid the dark room's leaping black and burgundy until that moment, suddenly appeared, walking toward me from some corner with his hand extended.

I faltered before him.

He stopped. "*Mademoiselle,*" he said. "Won't you join me?"

When I still said nothing, shocked at his behavior, he said, "My chef will feel you have demoted him to a simple colony cook if you do not sit with me. If you have no appetite, allow me to nibble at your plate before you send it back."

I caught my breath at the thought that what I ate could ever concern a servant who ranked so high as to be called a cook, to say nothing of a chef. I felt mocked.

I felt lost. "*Monsieur,* you are very kind. I think. But I cannot eat with you."

He drew closer, and I drew back. I bumped into Yasmine, who seemed to have moved behind me to block my escape. I said, "It would not be right, *Monsieur.*"

Monsieur's face grew still. He looked as I had seen him on the gallery outside my window at the inn. As if I had done something to offend him. "Why would it not be right for you to eat with the man with whom you live?"

I turned around and indicated Yasmine. Beyond her, invisible to me now in the entryway to the house from the distant kitchen, lurked Celeste. *They* certainly were not about to eat with this man with whom they, too, lived!

I said so.

Yasmine strangled on a sound she meant not to let escape her lips.

Monsieur moved his eyes to her. "Yasmine, you may go," he said. "Please send Celeste here to us. You heard what the *Mademoiselle* wishes."

This was not exactly what I had said. But it would do.

When Celeste arrived, flustered and anxious for no reason that I could see, for now we were together again and should feel relieved to be in familiar company, *Monsieur* escorted me to a chair.

The table itself was long. *Monsieur's* chair was at the farthest end of it. "My chair," as he called it, was at his right elbow. Celeste he allowed to stand at my other elbow, wordlessly swooping my napkin onto my lap and scooping tiny portions of unfamiliar, glistening, limp and black-edged foods onto my sparkling black-and-burgundy china plate. She poured wine the shade of dried wounds into my crystal goblet and lifted it, when I was unable to answer *Monsieur's* polite questions as fully as he wished, to my lips.

Monsieur talked, low and simply and insistently, throughout the many courses of the fragrant meal.

"*Ma chere,* what do you think of your rooms?"

I said nothing. Celeste saw my confusion and lifted the glass to my lips.

Monsieur went on. "If you like, *Mademoiselle* Aurelie, you may view other rooms in this house and see if other furnishings are more to your taste."

I lifted my head to him, frowning fiercely at the feeling that something in all this was vicious

179

teasing. Had he not bought me? Was I not owned? Was I going to be released into a home of my own, with some of his furnishings? As I opened my mouth at last, Celeste lifted the glass to my lips and said, "*Mademoiselle* was very pleased with the beauty of her rooms, *Monsieur* Roger. She has spoken of nothing else since she arrived."

Monsieur lifted an eyebrow as Celeste dropped her voice and her eyes, but without taking his gaze from me. Perhaps-I hoped-he had not heard her. "I had hoped to hear how you feel about the ... well, the wardrobe supplied to you."

The glass was coming as I said at last, "What I have seen of the gowns is lovely, *Monsieur*. They do seem unsuited for the duties I am used to, though."

Monsieur at last looked away from me to his plate.

Celeste brought the glass to my lips so brutally it clinked against my teeth and sloshed wine onto the napkin that covered the water spot. "*Monsieur,* the gowns are lovely, as *Mademoiselle* says," Celeste finished miserably, her voice trailing after the echo of mine.

Monsieur had come up with an answer. He looked at me as if he had won an argument. "You won't be performing your old duties here, *Mademoiselle.*"

"Then I won't know what is expected of me, *Monsieur.*" I rose on trembling legs made more unsteady by Celeste's hands shoving downward on my shoulders. "I think, *Monsieur,* that you have been very kind to let me eat with you. But if I may be excused now to learn my duties from that other woman, *Madame* Yasmine-"

"She is confused, *Monsieur*," Celeste cried out.

And as *Monsieur* rose, reaching for my arm, she backed away saying more calmly, "*Monsieur*, you have seen she is unwell."

I tried to pull my arm away. But he had it and would not let it go.

He used it to steer me toward a larger, lovelier stairway that curved up along a sweeping balustrade. "How beautiful," I said, gazing up at it all.

"Don't ask me if you may clean it," *Monsieur* Roger said, still moving me by my arm. And as I turned to look at him, "Forgive me, Aurelie. I've been rude. We are probably both tired." And bracing me with his grip on both my arms, he forced me up the breathtaking stairway. Celeste hurried along behind us.

When we were alone, she blistered my ears. "How could you, *mon enfant*? When our wellbeing depends upon his goodwill! Would you have us both sent back to-"

"Don't say it."

"To be sold? Or worse? Don't you understand what that household will become, now with both sons-"

"Celeste!" I pressed my palms to my ears. "I won't hear of them."

"*Ma chere*, have pity on me. Have pity on your dear mother, who sacrificed so much so that you might escape-"

181

"I won't hear! I won't hear," I cried, and now I was really crying, but I could not free my hands to wipe at the tears.

Celeste gave me both her hands, on her knees before me. "I am begging you," she said. "If you will not think of yourself, or cannot, then at least take pity on me, and listen to me and do as I say so that we may remain here."

I could not shut her voice out. I threw down my hands. Tears and spit flew. "And why should you want to remain here? Won't you miss your husband? Poor man."

Celeste smiled, her face warmed and flooded with the colors of relief. "Is that what bothers you, *enfant*? My husband?" She shook her head as if in wonderment. "I will not lose him, coming here. Why, he will ask and learn from Ange-Marie-"

"No names. I will not hear the old names." I put my fists to my heart. "They pain me here."

"-that I have come away here, with you. And he will search and find me again. And when you have that house of your own"-here Celeste grew calm and drew close to me, taking my hands in hers, slick with her tears-"that *Monsieur* will give you when you have accepted his love, why then you will ask if my husband may join us there, as your servant. *Ma chere, petite enfant.*" Celeste bent her head and began to press her lips to my hands in supplication, mumbling all the while, "Our lives are in your hands, *petite.*"

I snatched my hands from her. "What are you doing?" I crept away, circling the room with my back to the walls, trying to get away from her. "I

182

thought you came here to help me understand what is going on. To help me get my mind back-"

"Yes, of course, *Mademoiselle* Aurelie. That is what I am trying to do."

"No, look at you, Celeste. You are helping him confuse me."

"Oh, *encore!*" She started toward me, reaching to stop my aimless circling.

"Yes, more and more." I stopped, pounding my fists to my forehead. Was there no way out of my thoughts, which brought me confusion and everyone else distress? Out of my loss, which ate at me every minute, in between every hope and pleasure?

Out of this room?

As Celeste reached me, I turned and dashed for the window. It was a door that opened onto a small balcony. Celeste let out a scream and threw herself against me so that we went down to the floor.

As she held me there, wrestling and twisting to be freed of her weight, I heard footsteps running and voices at the sitting room door. Celeste raised her head and called for them to come help. And hands, warm and sure, all reached for her and for me, and we were pulled apart.

I rose, sobbing, into *Monsieur*'s arms. He nuzzled my head into his shoulder with his chin and carried me from the room with the tempting window to the downstairs parlor.

It was a soothing room, done in pale shades of willowy green like rising sap. *Monsieur* held me there, and we were alone. He said simple things over and over as his arms held me against his chest, and since I could not move, I sat still and heard.

183

"There is nothing to fear here, Aurelie. You have no need to be frightened. You are safe here with me." The words were as soothing as a lullaby. I eased and went limp against him.

But I did not sleep. I was wide awake and very aware when he rose from our seat in the parlor and carried me up to his own rooms.

I knew they were his own rooms because, on the stairs, I heard him call to someone behind him that, if Celeste was recovered, she was to attend me in his bedroom while he would sleep in his sitting room that night.

I couldn't think what need I might have of Celeste, whom I had no desire to see.

But as I lay, chilly and uncovered, on the bed, staring through my parted eyelashes at the distant form of *Monsieur* Roger in a brocade armchair, staring out the window, I thought it might be nice if she might help me unfasten the gown's many buttons and slip into bed and be warmed. Maybe she would hold me and warm me, as had *Tante* Clothilde when I was small. It was very hard to grow up.

I began to sing *Tante* Clothilde's lullaby. Maybe it would send me dreams that would take me away.

Suddenly, I missed my madness. I did not like to be here in the world after my baby had left it.

Monsieur turned his eyes from the window to watch me sing.

I don't know when Celeste came. I held *Monsieur*'s gaze with mine until his eyes were not his, black and stern, but *Tante* Clothilde's tender brown ones, and the voice singing was not my own, but also hers. And the baby, lost, was not mine, but me.

And I woke to lit candles and Celeste's struggles to work me out of the new gown with its water spot and slight wine stain, and into a gown for the night.

I could not help her but roused myself limply to lift an arm or sit up when she said so, only to have her click her tongue and say, "No, no! I *said* ... "

When she was done and the nightgown was more on me than off, she sat me up to drink a bowl of warm milk.

"To soothe you to sleep," she said.

"Here, Celeste," I insisted, holding it out to her. "You drink it. I cannot."

When she took the bowl, I crawled under the heavy, soft covers. "Celeste, please don't go away. Sleep here with me. This strange house and that strange man frighten me."

"Shh. The *Monsieur* will hear." I held out my arms.

When we woke together in the early morning, we were able to smile at each other and giggle over our survival of the night.

"We will be all right," Celeste said and waited for me to say it to her, in return. But I could not.

Yasmine had to bring me a day gown and help me wash and dress my hair. She took over my care, always pretending that she was only showing Celeste what to do.

And Celeste became my companion.

We wandered the courtyard, and she listened to my trailing memories that wound in and out of the inn and of our former home. It seemed that the endless thread of memories would never cease to pour out of me, winding about themselves and entangling my sense of the present, until one day, "What if *Tante* Clothilde goes there looking for us?" I suddenly broke the thread and asked. "You say your husband will ask and someone will tell him to come here and find you. Has he come? When will he come? And how will *Tante* Clothilde ever find us here?"

Celeste had my hands as we walked the courtyard, circling and circling, I in the neat muslins and linens that someone had thought appropriate for me, she in the blindingly white cottons that draped her figure and bound her head. She said, "My husband will find me. It will not be the first time he has had to search. But, *mon enfant*, your mother can never find you again. You must accept it"-I snatched at my hands and she snatched them back-"and remember that she wanted you to be happy. She paid with something precious to her because you are even more precious to her."

"You mean she paid with her eye and with being sold away."

"I mean she would have paid with both eyes and her tongue and with being whipped to death, if that was what it cost her to get her baby this kind of freedom and position."

"This is not freedom. Look at us. We cannot leave here."

"You have not asked *Monsieur* to let you leave here."

She pulled me back to her as I turned to go. She said, "He will not let you go until you are well."

I turned on her. "And how will he know when I am well? Who will tell him? You, Celeste? Then go and tell him. Are you my servant, or am I yours?"

Celeste had learned to let me go and bow her head and become very humble, when I turned on her. The sight of her, cowed and silent, always wrenched at me.

I gathered Celeste in my arms, against my heart. "You are crying, Celeste? If you keep on crying every time I finally stop, then we shall both spend the rest of our lives crying ourselves crazy. Come to think of it, it was not so bad being crazy."

Celeste tried to pull away and wipe at her eyes. I said, "I will not let you go."

She said, "Don't, Aurelie. You are right. It is my husband. He has not come to find me. But how can I go back, knowing what that house has become?"

That house seemed a place of unspeakable joy to me, knowing that it must shelter the man I had loved.

Celeste said, "The *Madame,* without her sons. She will rant. She will go mad with loneliness. She will hate everyone and herself. You have not seen her."

I said, "So what can we do to help your husband find you here?"

The sun sank by the time we had planned how she might sleep in the servants' quarters, taking

Yasmine's room, who should come to me, for I feared to be alone in the night.

If her husband came to the servants' quarters and did not find her there, answering his peculiar whistle, he might not think to risk his neck by speaking out, asking anyone to open a window and tell her about him.

It would be hard for me to sleep without Celeste, but I hated to tell her so and kept it to myself. I went in to dine with *Monsieur* with a very heavy heart. My head did not rise from the contemplation of my soup.

Monsieur Roger said gently, "You are saddened, Aurelie. What has happened?"

I mumbled, "Celeste misses her husband, *Monsieur*."

Monsieur Roger said something like, "Ah," and sat back from his bowl.

We had progressed in our dinners to the point that we no longer took them in my sitting room or even in *Monsieur*'s, for my comfort. We took them in the dining hall. I didn't even need Celeste at my side, to feed me and cue me and speak for me. I must have been at *Monsieur*'s place a long time, to have come so far in my ease there. But I hated to ask how long.

For I had not forgotten that, the longer I was with *Monsieur* Roger, the further I came from the perfect hope of my days with the man I still loved and would always.

Monsieur Roger said, "I have meant to ask about your plans for Celeste." And then he said no more. He did not push or argue with me. He always spoke and waited to hear what I might say.

I was grateful for his gentleness. I was unused to it, even from *Tante* Clothilde and Celeste.

Monsieur Roger said more softly, "What would you like, *Mademoiselle*? To keep Celeste, or to send her-" he searched for a word and settled on, "-back to her home?"

"I would go mad again without her, *Monsieur,*" I said, wondering when he had come so close to me at the table. His eyes were not black, as I had always thought. But in this light, all cherry rosewood, mahogany, and gold, his eyes had streaks of burning black in the earthen brown.

His gaze was still. "You would go mad without her? Then we must keep her. No more need be said." But still he waited, looking into my eyes.

At some time, someone from the kitchen came and slipped our bowls from before us, and I roused from the depths of *Monsieur* Roger's eyes, wondering how I had lost myself there, enough to say, "She misses her husband, *Monsieur*. What can be done to make her happy here with me? I need her so."

Again *Monsieur* Roger sat back and sighed. "Ah."

The conversation became distant from the two of us. We talked of whoever owned Celeste's husband, and how *Monsieur* could not afford to buy up all the various enslaved peoples who might have some distant connection to me, though he wished my happiness. "But perhaps, if we can learn from Celeste the name of her husband's owner, I might

189

approach him or her and arrange some visits, for your maid's contentment here. Would you like that?"

I think I rose from my chair and gave *Monsieur* Roger a hug that was surely straight out of my relationship with Celeste and all the women in the old quarters. I held him to my heart and my breasts and my hopes, in my happiness, and I thought I heard him make a small cry.

When I wished to pull away, to rush to the kitchen and find Celeste and tell her what *Monsieur* Roger would do, and surely she need not leave my rooms to sleep in Yasmine's tonight, his hands lingered about my waist and pulled.

I plied at his fingers, eager with my message and piqued that he clung.

Celeste abandoned my rooms anyway, that night, and I had to content myself with the silent smiles of Yasmine.

She was beautiful and kind, but she was not familiar to me, and I could not understand her. She called me *Mademoiselle,* and I could not bring myself to beg her to call me *enfant* or *cherie.*

She stretched out on a pallet she brought to be unrolled at the foot of my bed, should I need anything in the night, and I could not bring myself to ask her to crawl into the huge wasteland of the bed with me, where memories waited, watching for the loosening of the threads at the edge of my mind.

I rose in the night and slipped between Yasmine's arms on the pallet, tightening them about me, shutting out the voices, the sights, the memories. She woke a little and held me close.

"*Mademoiselle*," she crooned, "*dors, petite*. Sleep, little one."

CHAPTER NINE
SURFACE OF THE DARK WATERS

We woke to the last days of spring as they shimmered into summer, mist steaming up from the cobbles to twinkle like morning dew on the dull walls the house presented to the street.

I had awakened and slid from Yasmine's arms to go out on my small balcony and enjoy the morning. Another night was behind me, and I had survived it.

I watched the last of the morning's vendors, the stragglers desperate for another *sou*, singing out their wares as a breeze too weak to ruffle the hems of their clothes, stiff with filth, sent trash scuttling against their ankles. I breathed deeply of the rank air, heavy with the smells of the nearby river and, further off, the ever-encroaching sea. The humid breeze was promising, lifting from the city streets where other people went about their lives.

"We have the day to ourselves," Yasmine said, coming behind me. She put her hands lightly on my waist. "What shall we do with it?" She leaned forward and brushed the back of my cheek with a kiss. "Good morning, *Mademoiselle*," I heard spoken tenderly into my ear. She released me and returned to my bedroom, where I heard her trickle wash water from a pitcher into a basin and search the wardrobe for a fresh gown.

I followed her and stood before the open glass door as she slid the bleached cotton nightgown from me.

Where was Celeste, and why had she not come to me this morning to reclaim her duties as my personal maid? No need to ask Yasmine. Clearly, Celeste's husband had visited her in the night, and the promise I had gotten from *Monsieur* Roger to make arrangements with his owner meant nothing to her.

I missed her, but I would not ask about Celeste. She had left me to fend for myself through the night in the arms of a stranger whose kindness offered little comfort, in the sparkling light of day. I didn't understand Yasmine, and I resented Celeste for leaving me to her.

After all, it was day. Celeste's husband, if he had come, was surely gone by now. She could afford to spare me time. When she finally returned, brimming with contentment as she had in the old place, I would tell her how I felt about her leaving me to Yasmine.

I couldn't even turn to *Monsieur* Roger. Yasmine said he would be gone for "several weeks" to his plantation along the swamps outside the city, having "neglected" his duties there "for far too long." She added mysteriously, "Some matters simply should not be made to wait."

Sparing myself the trial of another of his tense goodbyes meant that I also could not have his intervention in the matter of getting Celeste back.

The first time he had taken a few days' brisk ride to his cane fields, he had held my fingers and waited for something I clearly wasn't going to say. When he finally let them go and turned, striding away so that the heels of his riding boots rang on the marble, I watched the snap of his coat tails and thought, *Has my poor* Tante *Clothilde been sent to cane fields?*

Now, watching Yasmine, whose steady smile troubled me, I said, "Why do people fear getting sold away?"

Yasmine spread her closed-lips smile to a grin that included the gleam of her perfect teeth, molded like rows of milk droplets glistening wet. "I imagine, *Mademoiselle,* that they fear losing loved ones and dying young in field work. Troublemakers, especially, you know. Under the rule of these new Americans, who see everyone as a troublemaker, I fear, anyone sold is sure to be sent where troublemakers have little effect, where they are driven so hard they are far too exhausted to stir up the others."

Did she not guess I was thinking of my own mother? For she continued to smile as she caressed the underthings she had laid out alongside the gown on the bed next to me. Yasmine added lightly, "Have you never seen a cane field or rice field, *Mademoiselle*? No, I imagine not. Come, let us wash you." She held out her hands as if welcoming me into her embrace instead of into my morning *toilette*.

As the soft towel dampened my skin, and I turned my head from Yasmine as if she were not intimately involved with my body, for I hated that she was, she said softly, "I saw how you looked at the city from your balcony, *Mademoiselle.* Would you like to go out in the carriage today? Visiting, maybe? *Monsieur* will be so pleased, upon his

194

return, to learn that you have taken an interest in living the life of a lady."

"Visiting?" I asked, startled.

She rose from washing my body, her face so close to mine that I leaned back at the waist, to give myself distance.

"Certainly," Yasmine said. "If you would like, you may go calling in the carriage. Visiting might make you happy, *Mademoiselle*."

I blushed furiously, naked and thinking, *Surely she doesn't mean that I may visit the old house, asking after Ange-Marie and ... the one I cannot name.*

Has my lover returned home?

Yasmine said, "If you can think of no one on whom you care to call, may I make a suggestion, *Mademoiselle?* My own daughters would be honored to receive you. They are freewomen, and you would not compromise your station by calling upon them."

She had finished washing me and turned, without looking into my face, to carefully put aside the soiled towel and select one of the perfumed ointments. Backing a little from her toward the balcony doorway, I said, "Compromise me? Why would a freewoman compromise herself, admitting me into her house?"

Yasmine looked sharply up at me, hesitated, her lips trembling in their broad smile, and finally let a laugh burst free of all that serenity.

I returned to the bed and sat, cowering in my ignorance. I picked up the scattered undergarments

195

to pretend I was studying how to begin applying them to my own body.

Yasmine's hands appeared before my lowered gaze to take the lacy cotton things from me. Her body surged into view, sitting next to mine. She took one of my hands. "Forgive me," she said, still barely restraining the tail end of her laughter. "Any freewoman would be honored to have the mistress of *Monsieur* Roger come calling upon her. You must learn to enjoy the privileges of your position, *Mademoiselle*."

"My position?" I rose, no longer hiding my desire to escape her. "I am not *Monsieur*'s mistress. He has never touched me." Suddenly, her closeness, her intimacy with my body and my mind, were no longer only embarrassing. They were threatening. *She is threatening.* I couldn't think how. But I wanted this conversation to end.

Yasmine swept into me, bearing her opened jar of ointment. "Back up no further, *Mademoiselle*," she said firmly. "You are seen from the street." And, standing so close to me that the cloth covering her body prickled at my skin and made the fine hairs stand upright, she began to spread ointment over my breasts, arms, belly, and buttocks with the cool open palm of her hand.

I trembled under her hand, catching my breath in little gasps for fear of breathing too freely, moving at all, afraid of giving her the idea that the flow of her hand, the warmth of the rub and the cool of her breath upon it, were pleasurable to me.

She continued to speak, watching her hand's flow. "You have nothing to fear from *Monsieur*. He

196

is a considerate lover. He will be kind to you. He has always been faithful to his women, and he frees their children."

I pushed her away with a little cry. "Don't speak to me of children," I spat at her and found my hand raised to strike her face.

She seemed as startled as I. We both stared at my upraised hand for a few heartbeats.

Then Yasmine raised her fragrant hand to lower mine. "Come, *Mademoiselle,*" she said. "Sit and let me lotion your legs and feet." She saw me shrink from her, shy again, and she began to reassert her superior knowledge. "The hose and heels you will wear to go calling will surely dry your skin, otherwise, and you don't want to look and feel like a woman in a cane field."

A pain pierced my chest somewhere, surely, around the area of my heart. *Tante* Clothilde was in a cane field, half blinded and unused to hard labor.

Yasmine eased me back onto the bed and ran her hands from my hips down my thighs, circled the back of the knee and plunged to the soles of my feet, and glided swiftly up toward the part between my legs. I placed a perfumed foot against her shoulder and threatened with a little pressure to kick her away.

Looking fully into my eyes, Yasmine took my other foot and swirled her hands tightly about it. "Are you afraid to be touched, *Mademoiselle?* Is this why you reject the *Monsieur*?"

I let her hold my eyes with hers as I thought of the many things I would say if only I trusted her. I had lived for my lover's touch, whether it gave me

197

pleasure or pain. Even if it had ended my life, I would have wanted to be touched by Jules. *There. I have said his name.*

Why hadn't he just ended my life instead of asking me for a consent I couldn't give? Surely he must have known what was rushing upon us, in our hiding place.

Yasmine's fingers had rushed up my thighs and now cupped and played lightly in the hair, among the tender moist folds that she gently opened. "This is all he wants," she said, "and all the feelings that go with it. He knows what is in you. Give yourself to him, and he will give you everything you want. Everything he can. I know." She had leaned forward and touched her lips to mine but continued to speak into the kiss.

I said, without moving back this time, "I don't want to hear about the *Monsieur* from you. Take your hands off of me. I was loved. I am loved. I don't want to be loved by anyone else. The *Monsieur* bought a slave, and he can tell me what work to do. But he cannot tell me that I am not in love with another man."

The hands lingered. Yasmine didn't withdraw them right away. She slid them up my belly to caress my nipples, neck, the backs of my ears, as she got off her knees and rose to stand between my open legs, easing my head finally toward her breasts. "Come away and see my daughters," she said, freeing one hand to work down the gathered neckline of her blouse.

When she pressed my cheek to the pillow of her bare breasts, bending to fit me into the cushion of

198

them, I no longer resisted but rested there, listening to the beat of her heart and thinking that no one would ever be another *Tante* Clothilde for me, and how could I stand it?

Probably feeling my tears cool and moisten the dry warmth between my cheek and her skin, Yasmine began to kiss the top of my head as she let her hand drift again down the hair to the shoulder and swirl, faintly, around the breast.

"You will not be unfaithful to your lover with me," she said. "I am only a woman, and your servant, at that. Your servant," she said, kneeling again and running her lips in bare touches down my face and neck and belly.

I stood and swung my leg over her head and walked around the bed, out of her reach. I picked up the day gown and began to work it on over my head.

Trapped inside it, unable to see, I heard Yasmine say, "Let me help you, *Mademoiselle*," and when the stiff gown had settled around my body and was being buttoned and tied, I was amazed and relieved to see that Yasmine, the distant and coolly smiling servant, had returned and taken the place of that person who wanted to take me away from the love I remembered and cherished.

She carefully studied her work with the buttons as she spoke again. "You should let me dress you in future, *Mademoiselle*. It isn't proper for a young lady of your new station to go out with little or nothing under her gown."

I picked up a lacy underskirt. "Then, next time, dress me. Otherwise, I'll dress myself as best I can.

In fact"-could I ask now?-"it is my understanding that Celeste is my personal maid. Where is she?" I sighed with relief at having finally begun to ask to have Celeste back.

Never mind her abandonment in pursuit of a husband that *Monsieur* was already bringing to her. *We are all entitled to be a little foolish about the men we love.* I should know that.

But Yasmine answered coolly, "Let me take you to meet my daughters, *Mademoiselle*. Celeste shall find herself quite in demand today. Ever since my daughters were freed, we have found ourselves short of hardworking hands, downstairs. Everyone thought it was a shame that Celeste's scullery skills should be forced upon you, when she could be better employed."

Does this woman never cease to undermine what I want?

Confused and unsure how to answer-*Does everyone but me know what a personal maid should know how to do?*-I snatched a trailing silk scarf from its peg by a gilded mirror and began to wind it about my hair.

"Let me dress your hair first, *Mademoiselle.*" Yasmine lifted the turban from my hands and draped it about her own neck. "Young ladies of your station are expected to remove their scarves when they go calling. The law is for the streets, not for the soul."

She guided me to the bed and sat me again.

But this time, she retained her cool efficiency, and her fingers and silver-handled brush flew through my hair. A thick braid coiled up and down the back of my head, rich and shining with fragrant oil, when I rose to the mirror again to watch Yasmine style the turban and pin it with a glittering jewel. "You must learn to accept the *Monsieur*'s gifts," she advised, securing the pin so that it held a loose tuck against the late spring breeze. "That will make both of you happy."

Because I wore no undergarments on my upper body, Yasmine insisted I allow myself to be draped with a shawl as fine as air curving along my shoulders, a layer of brightly dyed flowers and swinging fringe to brush the inside of my bent arms.

We descended the narrow stairs only as far as the second floor, where Yasmine had me come through a doorway to the main gallery, in its elegant sweep to the curving balustrade and grand staircase to the foyer.

Stepping down this stairway with Yasmine behind me, for the briefest moment I felt that this place, the servants and their owner could all be mine, in place of the cottage I had always dreamed I would have. I might someday feel contented, if not happy.

And as I faltered to examine the feeling, it fell away and left me descending the stairway in the house of a stranger who wanted from me the only thing I would never willingly give him. *My love.*

We went out to the carriage across the courtyard, leaving Celeste a blur of open-eyed astonishment that we passed quickly, with her bucket and rags in a hallway, calling politely, "*Mademoiselle.*"

The young man with his almond eyes outlined in solid black, who had opened the gate for us the day I arrived, opened the carriage door now and handed me into it.

As our fingers brushed away from each other, it was to him I turned and asked, "How is it that *Monsieur* left the carriage behind?"

Yasmine, flowing into the carriage behind me, came between us. "The *Monsieur* prefers to ride when the weather is mild. I told him I hoped you might wish to see the town a little, in his carriage, in his absence. And so his favorite horse was saddled for him, *Mademoiselle*."

By the time she'd finished, I had been rushed to a seat far from the carriage door, and the young man holding it had no choice but to say, "Enjoy your ride, ladies," and close it.

As the carriage jolted under the carriage house and through the gate to turn, swaying, onto the street, Yasmine scolded, "Don't allow yourself to be carried away by the groom's flirtations, *Mademoiselle*. What is a harmless entertainment for him will bring about your ruin."

"I was only civil, *Madame* Yasmine. You would have me be rude."

One eyebrow up, Yasmine said, "It is not what I would have that should concern you, *Mademoiselle*. Of all betrayals, men are most intolerant of sexual ones."

I thought of her own behavior with me this very morning and blushed violently. "Then you will keep your hands and your mouth off me, from now on," I said as sharply as I could.

Yasmine only gave a small laugh. "I am of no importance, *Mademoiselle.* I am a woman. Besides, they never consider what happens to us after a generation or two here in the colonies. How we might have changed from those women who came over in the ships." She had already turned to gaze out of the carriage's open window and now grew silent.

I was curious about her daughters. But after the morning's tense goings-on, pulling my fragile balance of feelings in wildly opposing directions, I was hesitant to draw Yasmine's attention again by questioning her.

So I, too, watched the passing streets. But, for the first time ever, I did not only look forward to the pleasure of being a part of freewomen's lives. Now that seeing them up close, sitting with them, and talking with them was so near at hand, I also feared it.

I was not one of them. I was not a freewoman. But I no longer waited for the day when I would be. Why had I survived to see the destruction of my life's only dream? Why had I agreed to this?

Bouquets of pastel flowers cascaded from pots and baskets hung along balconies, and wild moss spilled from the very walls of the tall buildings crowding the *banquettes.* Shade dripped with moss and the shyer blooms. Sunlight glittered like raindrops on the upturned faces of bolder flowers clustered at every railing and open glass doorway. Warmth rose in steamy puffs from the street and drifted from the heavy sky in humid tears, clinging to everything. It was full spring in the city. I thought of my lost love.

And too soon, we jerked to a stop before a plain double doorway.

And the curly-lashed groom was at the carriage door, opening it wide. When his long-fingered hand was unwittingly rebuffed in my hesitation, he gestured toward the doorway with an inviting sweep and bow.

And the doorway was eased open, and then opened wider.

A vision of bronzed blushes and eyes like starlight in a night sky and billows of black cloudy hair stood in the doorway, halfway hidden, halfway revealed in all her joy-filled splendor.

"*Maman*?" she was already calling, even before we had descended the carriage steps. "*C'est vraiment toi? Pourquoi tu n'as rien dit?* But why didn't you tell us you were coming?"

Laughing aloud, the girl turned back into the house and called behind her that Mother was here and had brought a visitor. The others must come quickly.

Footsteps shushed along the uncarpeted floor at the bottom of the stairway by the time I reached this living vision of coppery sunset crowned with the black of encroaching night. Could she be real? I had never seen anyone so beautiful.

That is, until I was released from her perfumed embrace and my eyes had dulled to see inside the darkened hallway behind her, and I saw her sisters.

It was impossible that people, girls who bathed and dressed and wept and slept and woke to wash again, could stand between heaven and earth yet look so ethereal.

But this is how Yasmine's daughters seemed to me.

They were like nothing I had ever known. Might my child have grown to be like them? Is this what freed Africans became? The best of both worlds?

They passed me, as though they knew and loved me, from arms to arms until I had been held and kissed by them all. And then the oldest, releasing her mother from a lingering and tender hug, parted her sisters with a sweep of her silken skirts and took my hand. "Come," she said, dimpling at me over her bared shoulder. "Let us see if we have enough lemons and little cakes to make a party."

When I rose from my seat in the modest parlor and followed them across the cramped courtyard to the humble kitchen to watch lemons being squeezed, watered, and sugared, and trays being laid, one of them came forward with an apron and tied it around my waist. She laughed to the others, "Don't tell me no, sisters. If she only watches, she'll see everything I do wrong, and our party will be spoiled."

I was pulled to the crystal pitcher to help make sure the lemonade came out right, not too sweet, but, "Definitely not too sour. Sour is worse!" I was assured.

When it was done and fragrant petals of mint and jasmine had been brought from an inner garden and sprinkled atop the sun-colored pool of

205

refreshment, my apron was untied and tossed onto a peg with the others. With me at its center, the laughing, golden-throated crowd of unhurried loveliness drifted, bearing trays, back to the parlor.

Yasmine sat where sunlight streaked across the little room from an open window to stripe the bright flounces of her skirts and bathe the face and fingers of a baby held in her arms.

"Whose is it?" I cried and stopped still. I carried nothing, which was fortunate. Because I jerked my hands up to my lips to stop the trembling of both and would have dropped a tray.

Yasmine snapped her head inelegantly toward me and spoke rapidly to her daughters. I could understand nothing.

But I was taken by both arms and turned from the room, gentle hands guiding and soft voices *tsk-tsk*ing as I was led up the narrow dark stairs to the bedroom floor.

Two sisters stretched me out on a wide, long bed that almost filled up its cramped, dully papered room. Glass doors had been thrown open upon its tiny balcony, where potted flowers hung toward the street.

I was wondering whose room this was-did one of these radiant sisters glide out onto this balcony at night to watch the milling crowds, to catch the plucked notes of a mandolin serenade rising from the street below?-when faint gasps and forcefully stifled giggles burst my reverie.

The two sisters who had brought me upstairs had by now loosened my bodice so I might breathe, in case I had been faint. And they had just discovered that I was dressed without sufficient undergarments.

So, as two more sisters entered the room, gleefully smiling as though I had not just caused a crisis, the news of my nakedness was passed gaily from bronze lips to burgundy ones until sprays of lace-edged underclothes had been spread about me.

And I had to be stood up, undressed, bathed by everyone's hands, and generously powdered and scented and dressed again, beginning with their own intimate wear.

A sister whose hair tended toward clumps of shining black ringlets dangling unevenly beyond her waist said airily, "Oh, you may keep those, *Mademoiselle*. Cream is so plain. I prefer my pink ones."

Another asked, when scarcely had the air ceased to stir, "Have you never had silk undergarments, *Mademoiselle*? You would always wear them, if you had tried them. Shall I ask my mother-"

I interrupted quickly, "I have had them, *Mesdemoiselles*. They were taken from me."

And a chorus of sighs and laments arose from the still-smiling, satin- and lawn-bedecked choir of earthly angels.

Who reduced themselves, as we talked, to only four in number. The four sisters were Emilie, Louise-Anne, Desiree, and Anais, and they made me learn this by pointing at each in turn while reciting their names. *How do they seem to be so many more? And to think, all their brothers died shortly after birth! How many children did Yasmine have? Even her daughters don't know.*

And then they asked about the house where their mother used to be mistress and spoke of rooms and routines that they most missed, since banished into freedom.

It had not occurred to me that they might not have been born free. How had they adapted to it so quickly?

For surely, they were like no one I had ever known. In my startled introduction to them, I could only account for their extraordinary charm by crediting their warmth of heart, polishing the elegance of all the best refinements they had been taught.

I questioned them about this. "How are you all so beautiful and perfect?"

And they let go their gay concern for me and reveled in their grace. "We freed women are the new standard. Didn't you know, *Mademoiselle Aurelie?*"

"Have you seen how women have taken to stealing horses' hats, to shield their skins from tanning darker in the sun?" Peals of laughter. "Or pinching their cheeks, to bring up their color?" Guffaws. "Everyone wants to look like the new breed of woman, the fruit and flower of the colonies." Self-satisfied sighs.

And they went on to praise the superiority of their upbringing-"Our father lavished affection on us, so we are more at our ease in the company of men than wealthy girls raised in convents by nuns"- and their naturally sunny temperaments-"We don't

208

have the worry of the poor women who know they will live out their lives and die enslaved, for we know the day will eventually come when we will be free"-until Yasmine came into the doorway and said she had laid a midday meal of cold sweetmeats, baguettes, and butter.

"You must have shopped, *Maman*," Louise-Anne said, "for we had nothing in the house."

Desiree chimed along in her tinkling tones, "Emilie is such a poor mistress of the house. She says her husband has never left her enough money. But we suspect she doesn't know how to budget."

When Emilie, the oldest, hunched her shoulders and hid her face in her fingers, as though she would cry, it was time for everyone-even me-to tease and caress her into smiles again.

It seemed that Emilie was newly married and-along with the recent addition to her small family of her three sisters, who had all spent their lives tending *Monsieur* Roger's house-was laboring with scant success to bear the burdens of housewifery.

"They are unused to hardship of even this mild kind, and to being corrected, I am afraid," Yasmine said to me as we seated ourselves tightly on mismatched chairs and stools about an elaborately carved cherrywood table. "My poor daughters think every little effort they make is praiseworthy in itself. This is the problem with girls who are raised knowing that someday they will be free. One hasn't the heart to force a servile attitude upon them. Nor to teach them to scrimp and save."

Yasmine, I noticed, had ceased to call me *Mademoiselle,* and soon her daughters followed her example, calling me hesitantly, "*Madame* Aurelie" and "*Madame* Roger," of all things, until I said, "I feel so at home among you all. Please indulge me, and call me Aurelie."

And they seemed to sigh as one and glance meaningfully at each other. If it was possible, their smiles became broader and sweeter and their cries of delight more songlike.

I wanted them to come home and dine with me. I begged. When this did not prevail, and Yasmine only smiled in her smug way and watched the interchange, turning her head slowly at the top of her long, curved neck, I insisted. "But you *must* come home with me, *Mesdemoiselles!* You miss the house, and I am so alone in it. I have just lost my friend, who came with me to be my maid but who now cleans the scullery, and you have made me feel that I am almost one of you, another sister. Please come home with me, and stay to sleep in your old rooms, whichever they are. We can make them feel at home, can't we, *Madame* Yasmine?" I turned to her.

She favored her daughters with a lingering look. "It must be your decision, Aurelie," she said without bothering to glance at me again, "for it is your house now."

I looked around me, stunned, at Yasmine's daughters. "My house? What nonsense, *Madame*. It is *Monsieur* Roger's house."

"A man's work is his own," Emilie said sagely. "His home is his woman's."

Overwhelmed by the wealth of misunderstanding it took for her to make that last statement, I glared and felt my discomfort mount to outrage.

What was I doing here, among these strangers who assumed I would willingly be passed from my very own lover to another man, and then blithely go visiting, instead of drowning myself in the first available basin of wash water?

I rose to my feet to denounce their unaccountable cruelty toward me.

But before I had finished beating myself away from my affection for the sisters with this last thought, I realized they had already dropped the issue of who ruled *Monsieur* Roger's house with elaborate disinterest and were now cooing over Emilie's distress that she could not come away with us.

Her husband would be home that evening. Evidently, married women weren't to go slumber-partying at their mothers' homes without previous and detailed arrangements being made with their husbands.

I sat again to listen in. Was Emilie really married? To a Frenchman? Or to a freeman?

I couldn't wait to ask, and did so as soon as we were pressed, silks to satins to linen, on the seats of the carriage, waving cheer back to Emilie's tearful farewell.

"To a freeman, of course." Anais, the youngest, and barely beyond the most sexless age of girlhood, answered with mature disdain for such a stupid question.

"I hope she'll remember to run upstairs and check on the ba-" Desiree began at the same time but was shushed by Louise-Anne, who filled in the following silence by lamenting that their carpetbag was too small to hold the extra petticoats and delicate fans and slippers they needed for dressing up to enjoy the magic ballroom. We would have to find less romantic entertainment to fill our evening.

At this, Yasmine laughed almost as gaily as her girls could. "Oh, I have no doubt that you'll find much to do," she said, and the girls leaped, chattering, into happy conversation again.

It wasn't until we were descending from the carriage behind *Monsieur* Roger's courtyard, and Louise-Anne took so long to join us that I turned back and saw her allowing the groom to gaze deeply into her eyes as his slender fingers caressed the hand he still held, that I wondered about the sisters' desire to visit me in their old home.

Yasmine, too, had turned. At the sight of the couple's intent involvement in their stolen moment, Yasmine called sharply, "Louise-Anne!"

Her daughter gave a start and snatched her fingers away. Sulking, she came to join us with her eyes dramatically cast down to her gleaming slippers.

I watched her walk past me into Desiree's protective grasp. Her younger sister hissed, "Look at you, pouting. *Maman* only wants your happiness."

What did it all mean? I studied the riot of feelings breaking my earlier contentment with these girls. Why would an enslaved mother disapprove of her free daughter's choice of an enslaved lover? Didn't Yasmine want to see Louise-Anne married?

Enslaved and free could marry, even under American rule! Couldn't they?

I thought of Yseult, the seamstress, and her proud visits on holidays to her husband's home, walking head held high through the gate. And pain clenched my gut.

I shifted my mind from there and stared after Yasmine's daughters.

They trailed dreamily through the courtyard and walked up the steps to the rear guest entrance to the townhouse. Had they been so welcoming and accepting of me, the stranger who had taken their place in the home of their birth, only so they could sneak back to their first home?

Everyone else had someone, it seemed to me. And I was only useful for so long, in the midst of such relationships.

The sisters exclaimed over the house as though they were strangers to it. They swept like air, like butterflies borne on a summer's breeze, past every servant and up and through every passageway, exclaiming, touching, remarking that nothing had changed except they, themselves.

"Everything is so grand," lamented Louise-Anne. "I feel like a visitor from the swamps."

Desiree burst into laughter. "Oh, sister. Remember that horrible family all in woolens that came to visit *Monsieur Papa*?"

Who was this *"Monsieur Papa"* whom they mentioned with so much intimate knowledge, sprinkling his name and his foibles throughout the conversation?

Anais went on about ball gowns of blue brocade and silk roses *Monsieur Papa* had evidently promised her, as we dressed in my room-their old room!-quite early for dinner, when I finally worked up the courage to ask, already dreading the answer.

They turned to me, all in various states of undress, my unwanted new clothes, stiff cottons and linens, drooping below their high breasts and gleaming golden shoulders. "Who *is* he?" Anais asked, finally showing every bit of her lack of a sophisticated age.

Louise-Anne and Desiree exchanged long, puzzled glances, blushing bronze together. "Why," Louise-Anne said gently, "he is *Monsieur* Roger, Aurelie. Didn't you know that he is our father?"

Thoughts flitted through my numbed mind, too quickly to be caught. One lingered, and I voiced it. "But I thought you were Yasmine's daughters."

Desiree smiled, relieved that this was all a trick of brief acquaintance and would soon be resolved. "But we are," she assured me warmly.

I persisted. "Do you mean to tell me," I said, "that you think *Monsieur* Roger has made your mother my maid, after having so many children with her?"

A Frenchman I had always loved, and who had always loved me, and the intense passion that had brought our baby, nestled in pain, to grow in my body, flashed through my thoughts and speared my heart on his way back into my mind's vast oblivion.

The sisters turned again toward each other, their curving arms draped with unfastened bits of my clothing. I sank to my bed and watched the full

214

blaze of the overblown sun pick out highlights of auburn and copper in the masses of their midnight curls.

Why had I been subjected to the pressure and tension of *Monsieur*'s loneliness, if the woman who had borne him-how many?-children was still here, beautiful and gracious, in his own home?

I would confront *Monsieur* Roger, when he returned. After all, if he disapproved of my question, I could only be sold into cane fields, to search for my mother.

CHAPTER TEN
SEA OF SIGHS AND WHISPERS

We lingered, disappointed with the plain clothes supplied to me, trying to think where we might find gowns suitable for pretending to have a ball.

Finally, the sisters took my hand and led me down the back stairs to the servants' entrance to *Monsieur* Roger's room. "At least we will have well-dressed escorts," they reasoned, until they caught sight of his magnificent satin sheets and gleaming brocade bedspread. These they ripped from his bed and flung about themselves as capes, covering the borrowed gentlemen's clothing and jeweled pins they carried. Then they hurried me from the room.

I had not wanted to go in there. And I had kept my eyes carefully turned from everything in *Monsieur*'s room, hoping his daughters would not assume the room was familiar to me.

Now knowing what I did about his relationship with them and with Yasmine, all my chess lessons and cozy little meals at the small table drawn up to *Monsieur* Roger's fireplace seemed like the behavior of the women at the inn.

The pain of contemplating such a fate with the man I had loved-*Would Jules have turned me out in our own home?*-crushed me in my chest as though I had been punched. I would not be a party to this any longer. I would ask-no, I would persuade-*Monsieur* Roger to return his mistress Yasmine to her earned

216

and appreciated station, and to let me wait on her, however poorly I might perform my tasks at first.

It was only right that it should be so.

As we gathered at the candlelit dining table, waited on by Celeste as well as the usual woman, I looked anxiously for Yasmine. She must not play the servant in front of her daughters.

I turned to Celeste to state loudly that Yasmine must not have heard the dinner bell. We would wait the first course for her.

Her daughters smiled and chatted and included me in their game: who would their escorts be to the magical ball?

Silly girls. My mind drifted to absorb the reality of Yasmine's position as she tried to seduce me that very morning. *She wants to be a part of her lover's new love life. I will return her to him.* If I did Yasmine this justice, surely justice would be done to me, in return. *No one must try to take the place of the man who has my love and my soul.*

Satisfied with the progress of my thoughts, I bestowed my most hostess-like smile on Yasmine as she appeared and slipped into the seat Celeste held for her.

Yasmine looked more anxious than I had ever seen her. My heart went out to her.

She snapped at the girls' innocent fantasies. I found myself in the odd position of explaining to this woman who seemed to have *Monsieur*'s entire household under her control that the men they were inventing were only a game for the evening's entertainment.

217

Yasmine was rigid with her effort-before me, for my sake-to be polite. "I understand, *Mademoiselle* Aurelie, but really. What good will it do Desiree to dream that she is in the arms of 'a pure African, so fresh from the continent that he still speaks many of their languages, tall and strong and with muscles gleaming under a tight rich skin,' to be her husband and 'her overseer' when she inherits *Monsieur* Roger's plantation? If she falls in love with this enslaved African, her life will be one of worry and grief, spent in a tiny room above a shop in the city, waiting for her 'husband' to return from his owners for one holiday a year, all because of a 'harmless dream.' Ask any number of the maids who know mixed couples! Ask how the free member of the couple is forced to live. If allowed to live!" She turned on her daughters. "Have you forgotten why you are all here instead of visiting the plantation grounds with your *Monsieur Papa*? Have you forgotten that the Americans have marched from Shreveport to the sea, killing the freed children of Frenchmen? You are not safe showing your face at a plantation, Desiree, let alone owning one!" As Yasmine ended this tirade, her chest heaved and her eyes fixed, watery and wavering, on her daughter.

Desiree looked down into her plate. There were no smiles trembling on the edge of her earth-red lips now.

I said gently, "So no Africans, unless they are already free. And no Frenchmen"-for I had seen Yasmine flinch when Anais introduced one into the game-"unless they are free to marry you, *Mesdemoiselles*. Are we agreed?"

Yasmine insisted, still discontent, on explaining to me, "I invented the magic ballroom for the girls so they would not wish to go to the Quadroon Balls, *Mademoiselle* Aurelie. You know about the Quadroon Balls?" She gave me an arched eyebrow and shake of the head.

I had no idea what she meant but felt this was no time to ask. "I have heard of them," I said, which was true.

"Oh, pffffff," Anais responded. "We know all about the Quadroon Balls, *Maman*, and really! Who would want to be sold to some wealthy Frenchman, to be his-"

"Anais!" Louise-Anne chided and slid a glance at their mother.

Anais looked confused. "Well, I just agreed-"

Desiree looked straight ahead-but at nothing in particular-as she interrupted. "There is no shame at all in being bought by a man who loves you and has no other way of being with you," she chanted. I suspected she had been taught this lesson throughout her lifetime.

Yasmine sighed. "Nothing wrong with it at all," she agreed, "except that I want better for all of you. Thanks to *Monsieur* Roger's generosity and honor, all of you will have better."

But I will not, I thought.

"Free girls go to the Quadroon Balls," Louise-Anne corrected her sisters gently.

"Yes, they go to the Quadroon Balls and lose their freedom," Yasmine quipped. "They leave there in thicker chains than the men and women in the cane fields."

"So, no Quadroon Ball in the magic ballroom," I announced, counting on my fingers. "No enslaved escorts who cannot buy their freedom, and no Frenchmen who are not in a position to break the American laws and free you and marry you. *D'accord?* Are we in agreement?"

The girls turned to me with their smiles wavering back into place.

"It is still a good game, *Mesdemoiselles,*" I insisted, "for all that."

And when Celeste passed behind my place at the table, she laid a hand lightly and briefly on my shoulder.

But I would not speak to her again that night. *It is thanks to Celeste that I am stuck, relying on Yasmine, who cannot-not, I say!-be trusted. They are all speaking in code around me.*

I turned a cool head away from Celeste.

But the game had been ruined. Though the sisters tried to smile again, they were clearly mourning the deaths of their preferred suitors. How well I knew their suffering. *Oh, the romance of the man who will run away with you, will break the law for you, will endanger himself for you! But when his recklessness endangers you, too? Then where is the romance?*

I looked at Yasmine's daughters and wondered what else we might discuss to lift this awkward silence. I turned to Yasmine.

She ate so beautifully at table despite her uneasiness, spooning up her soup in seamless curves away from her, to her lips, and back to the bowl with that slight twist of the wrist that was the sign of long and easy habit. The stories she must have, both of this place and of her life in it.

I would entice her to talk. "Yasmine, your manners at table have been an inspiration to me," I said with such a full clear voice that even the women serving broke their facade of not listening and turned toward me. "Would you tell us of your life? You must have seen balls and served at table, been served at table, many times."

She looked over at me almost shyly. When she looked with growing radiance like the rising sun upon her daughters, the stories began.

Apparently *Monsieur* Roger's first mistress had been an older woman than he, a woman full-grown when he was just a boy, lusting and admiring. As this first mistress aged, *Monsieur* Roger bought Yasmine from the gentlemen's club where he had met her.

Yasmine was careful to explain that she had been a serving girl there, not "a woman for the gentlemen's entertainment." *Monsieur* Roger had bought her virginity a full two years before he was ready to bring her home to his childless mistress.

"Her inability to have his children was a problem to the keeping of her hold on his affection," Yasmine said, and I thought I heard true sympathy in her voice. For two years, *Monsieur* Roger had wined and dined Yasmine, boarding her at the brothel where he'd found her, making love to her only there-Yasmine murmured, eyes downcast, that this was why Emilie was born there-before he made up his mind that it was time to bring her home.

And this elegant mansion was where *Monsieur* Roger and Yasmine had enjoyed their elaborate dinners and fancy balls, dressing up and dancing among the plumed officers and enslaved harlots of all races.

I bowed my head to shut out from my thoughts the women of all races at the inn. Must love between African women and European men always go into hiding among whores?

Louise-Anne, mouth agape, said, "But why didn't *Monsieur Papa* simply give his old mistress her freedom and send her on her way?"

"Oh." Anais rolled her eyes in apparent disgust at her older sister's naivete. But then she, too, turned to Yasmine to learn what impeded this most obvious solution.

"*Monsieur*'s 'old mistress,' as you say, Louise-Anne, didn't want her freedom. She threatened to kill herself if *Monsieur* Roger set her free."

Cries of "*Oh, là là!*" and "*Quelle idiote!*" rang out on all sides.

When they died down amid sprinkles of fresh laughter, Yasmine studied her plate of lamb and creamed asparagus before she said, "It can be very hard to give up the luxury to which one has become accustomed. Especially to give it up because one is no longer as young as the *maitre* would like to remember." Then she laughed and shook her head almost fondly, as if at a dear memory. "Even if the *maitre* himself is no longer quite so young, and should take pity."

"But freedom!" I heard myself protest, almost against my will. The story was enchanting. I was captivated. I was appalled.

Yasmine looked at me. "Remember, she had finished raising *Monsieur* Roger. He was a very young man when he and she left his parents' home, to set up house on their own. It was five years or more-I forget-before he inherited his parents' home, and they returned here."

"How did his parents die?" Just the kind of virginal question someone as fiery and innocent as Desiree would ask, forgetting that the story did not end with the happy homecoming of *Monsieur* Roger and his first mistress.

"Typhoid, I believe. Or yellow fever. Or cholera. I don't recall. One of the diseases that sweeps this city every summer."

Louise-Anne said before I could, "So how did she treat you, when *Monsieur Papa* brought you home?"

And Anais, shockingly mature in her thinking, for her young and inexperienced age, said, "And *why* couldn't he leave you where you two were so happy? Was someone bothering you there, at the brothel?"

"Yes, someone was bothering me there. And I assured him that I had taken steps to keep his old mistress from harming the baby and me."

"*Pauvre Maman!* Who was bothering you? And how?"

"What had you done to protect yourself and baby Emilie?"

"But did it work, *Maman*?"

223

Yasmine, flushed with reliving the days of being so passionately wanted and agonizingly protected, said, "There was another gentleman at the club who wanted me. I would find him lurking about my room, whenever I went out of it. Finally, he bribed a cleaning girl-just a child-to let him into my room, where he waited for me late one night and almost had his way with me, I was so frightened. Only, *Monsieur* Roger heard my cries and doubled back. He broke in the door. He had only gone as far as the bar in the parlor, you see. He hadn't yet left the premises."

Yasmine shook herself out of that moment of helpless terror. "It might have all ended, then and there, if *Monsieur* Roger had not feared that it was my voice he heard screaming above the others. In such a place, on the upper floors, there are always cries and calls for help."

"But this is what decided him that he had to get you out of there, *Maman*?"

"Did he thrash the man who waylaid you, *Maman*?"

"Yes, *mes cheres. Monsieur* Roger thrashed the man, and they threatened to duel, but nothing came of it, and they even remained friends, in a manner of speaking. Gentlemen are that way, you know. Eventually, I learned from *Monsieur* Roger that the gentleman took the little cleaning girl as his mistress and even brought her home to be his wife's seamstress."

With a jolt, I thought of Yseult back in the home where I had grown up, always so cold toward me, and wondered if I had just heard her story.

But I was missing Yasmine's. She said, "That very night, *Monsieur* Roger stayed with me and promised to take me home with him in the morning. For I would not let him leave me."

Louise-Anne sighed. "How gallant of *Monsieur Papa*! What did you do to stop him, *Maman*?"

Yasmine said, "When he had driven off the other man and wanted to leave, I told him to kiss the baby *adieu*, for as soon as he was gone, she and I would go through the window."

Anais, lips quivering and wet with tears that trembled and spilled from her suddenly reddened eyes, said, "You meant it."

Desiree said, "Of course she meant it. *La pauvre.*"

Louise-Anne persisted softly, "And how did the other woman treat you when you came here?"

Yasmine roused. "With great coolness, *mes cheres*. She was always polite. She avoided me. I had named my baby for her, so that she feared she could not kill my baby without harming herself."

"Emilie," the daughters gasped.

"Yes, *mes cheres*. She thought that, at Emilie's baptism, I had gotten some of her own bath water and hexed it."

"Her bath water? How?'

Yasmine shrugged. "Oh, that maybe *Monsieur* Roger had brought it to me in his absolute ignorance-you know these European men don't believe in anything until they are afraid for their own safety-and so she left baby Emilie quite alone. But when I gave birth to the first boy who died, I persuaded *Monsieur* Roger that his death was the result of the old mistress's curse. By then, she was living in the quarters behind the house with the other servants. She had taken an African lover. I might have left her alone. I knew it was not she who cursed me so that I could not bear boys, but I thought I had to blame someone, to keep *Monsieur's* suspicions at bay. If I had it to do over again-But I was younger then and had not learned pity."

I said, "Who cursed you so that you could not bear boys, *Madame* Yasmine?"

Yasmine smiled slightly and shrugged her shoulders as her plate was taken away. She said simply, "I did. At the gentlemen's club. Seeing what I saw, so young, I prayed never to bring such creatures as men into the world, never to increase their number. I took herbs in strong drink. I fasted and prayed and drank until the curse took. And every boy born dead to me, I mourned, but I could not break the curse I had given myself. If I could have, perhaps all would have turned out differently. Men want a son." Yasmine looked suddenly, softly at me.

Louise-Anne said, "But *Maman*, you would not have had *European* sons!"

"Oh," Desiree scoffed bitterly. "First a mistress goes because she can have no children. Then a mistress is driven out because she can have no sons. Who are these Frenchmen, picking women like tomatoes at the market, and what do they think they want?"

All eyes remained on Yasmine, and I yearned to tell her that she would not share the senior Emilie's fate. But reticence held me back.

226

Surely I would succeed in reinstating her to her former position, but I would enjoy my success only when I had assured it. People who bought and sold other people had a stubborn way of resisting common sense. Who knew what objections I might encounter from *Monsieur* Roger, himself?

So, for the time being, I said, "*Cheres amies,* dear friends! Tomatoes in the salad! Perhaps the chef heard you, Desiree," as the little plates were slid before us.

Always happy to laugh, the sisters obliged me with their best. Yasmine joined them.

And by the time we had finished our pudding, scorched and swimming in a thickened puddle of pungent rum, we were giddy and ready for the ball.

The girls had to lead me to the ballroom. I could not have found it.

It was grand, with frescoes painted between the moldings in the ceiling high above our heads, flickering in between the lights and shadows of our candelabra.

We dressed in the farthest darkness of the corners, emerging in turn as ladies or gentlemen, swept into or sweeping our partners into widespread arms.

There was no music, so we took turns humming snatches of tunes we had heard in the houses along the streets, or wafted from the passing taverns. Yasmine sang some exquisite arias until she left us, exhausted and weepy, to sleep in my sitting room, waiting on her own daughters throughout the night.

It was wrong, and I would fix it.

But now, somehow, the laughing sisters with their lustrous hair in coils and ropes of midnight and starlight, swaying down their backs and along their shoulders, reflecting the candle flames that lit the bottomless depths of their eyes, like butterflies, began to change.

And all about me, dancing in and out of the wavering lights, I began to see gentlemen in fancy dress, tossing back their capes, gliding on high polished boots, pureblood Africans, with a gold hoop high in one earlobe, and European cavaliers with their brushed moustaches.

I looked about me to count the pairs, one sister with another sister, surely, and found instead that there were four other couples dancing, each sister with one escort-when had Emilie arrived?-and since all the sisters were laughing and talking or holding their lips still to be kissed, who now was humming our dances? I searched around me, above our heads, expecting to find at least a small orchestra in the gallery.

But there was no one.

Except that the paintings had risen in full form from the frescoes and were swirled in strips of cloud and wisps of flowery mist, and the subjects watched us, awed and pointing at our revelry, as the moldings that framed them lifted, twirled, curled in again upon themselves, and settled into the ceilings and walls once more as balcony railings, loggias and garden gazebos.

I looked for the sisters, to point and tell them, "Look!"

And found that the pureblood African who held Desiree was more handsome and smooth-skinned than even she had described. He gazed down at her with adoration in his subdued desire. The cavalier who held Anais as he teased her out of her youthful shyness, expanding his own magnificence in the glow of her whole-hearted admiration, seemed to shift before my eyes from a Spanish admiral's uniform to a French musketeer's, then to an Italian courtier's. And who was that who held Louise-Anne? None other than Jacques, the groom, elegantly dressed in his owner's best clothes.

I had just made up my mind to make my way over toward Louise-Anne and Jacques-*I must warn them that the urgent gaze they share will surely get them into terrible trouble. I must ask how he got in here, when surely Louise-Anne had had no opportunity to sneak open a door for him*-but my own partner held me back.

My dancing partner held me too closely for me to move away from him at all, far too tightly for decency.

I turned and looked up into his face.

Surely I had been dancing with Emilie only a moment ago. But now there she was with some man-her husband?-and I was in the arms of ... impossibility.

I cried out, struggled to push away the man who held me.

But he held me closer and said, "Aurelie! How could you? Have you forgotten? So soon?"

I sobbed. "No. No, *mon amour*, I will never forget. I cannot forget. Oh, why are you here now? This cannot be!"

And I shut my eyes on the divine ghost, feeling him fade from my arms as the sisters pulled at me, turned me around, led me from the room.

I stood in the dark corridor outside the ballroom and gazed back in, terrorized and fascinated, at the gauzy curtains that billowed as if in a breeze that could not have come in through the shut windows.

I searched for signs of the man who had held me or even the men who had held the sisters, as the music still drifted about us. Soft voices, men's and children's, hummed tunes that came together, drifted into disharmony, lifted and swayed on the blue-black night air.

Louise-Anne held me close. "Let's get her upstairs to her rooms. *Maman* will know how to help her."

The journey back, surfacing from the blindingly black world of the ballroom to the firelit, busy world of the upstairs rooms, was a trek through mazes of stairs and doubts. What had I really seen? What had he really been, when he was in my arms and I in his again?

I bit back his forbidden name as the sisters and I wound our way through the house. *But my lover has followed me here. Or I have brought him to me, with the intensity of my yearning. And I must get back to him, somehow.*

We burst into the brightness of my sitting room. Yasmine roused from the *chaise* where she lounged to take me into her arms and lead me to my bed, all the while ordering her daughters to fetch a dampened towel, to call Celeste to bring coffee, to unbind my hair and unfasten my clothes.

I fell asleep gibbering about the magic of the ballroom and returned there in my sleep, suddenly coming upon its dark stillness after drifting through the tangled corridors of *Monsieur*'s house in the sisters' silky underthings. In the maze that led to the ballroom of impossibilities, the black of the windowless corridors lightened, expanded to the full moon blue of the ballroom, and I was there, standing just outside the doorway, staring in at the billowing curtains.

My lover was no longer there, if he ever had been.

So I danced alone in the ballroom throughout my dream and woke to the stillness of golden sun and the sisters' laughter.

They had slept scattered throughout my room on pallets and blankets. Our first excursion of the day was to find them all rooms. They protested that they used to sleep in my rooms, all together, and would happily stay in the sitting room with their mother.

But I assured them that their mother would not long be sleeping there, and besides, I wanted to fill *Monsieur*'s house with the lives that he and Yasmine had brought into it.

Desiree's new room had been *Monsieur* Roger's mother's, and it was done all in roses whose scent lifted off the painted walls and surrounded us as we entered. Anais claimed to want a room of her own, as well, and so she got the little bright yellow room next to Desiree's, too sunny for bad dreams. As its door was pushed open, I could have sworn I heard birdcalls twittering in all the corners from among the knickknack shelves, the mirrored vanity and wardrobe. Louise-Anne's room had been the *Monsieur*'s father's and was painted the green of a forested swamp at night. Even now, in full morning, with the windows and balcony door shut so that no light came in, one could pause and hear the squeals, growls, and splashes of the watery wild. This room, I decided, was where we would tell our stories.

We paused and had Celeste bring us hot chocolate and little crescent buttered rolls for breakfast, so that we might re-descend immediately into our magical world. No need to call for Yasmine, who had dangerous tendencies toward the destruction of fun.

We sat on the floor of Louise-Anne's room around our silver breakfast tray and began to recount and wonder about the lives of the sisters' ancestors, the people who had owned and slaved in this house before us.

And as we talked, raising spirits by the sisters' memories of them, giving them our breath to breathe and our eyes through which to gaze again upon the world they'd left, they took us over.

Anais began to cry out from the agony of the nobly born child bride who had died giving birth to *Monsieur* Roger's grandfather. Desiree counted on her two hands and named each of the brown-limbed beauties who had been raped and murdered in this very room, by that same grandfather. Louise-Anne recounted in wondrous detail the story of the seduction that had left Jacques enslaved on his own cousin's property.

"Louise-Anne, you can't want Jacques now. He is your *cousin*," Anais chided.

"*Sotte fillette*-you stupid girl! Cousins marry all the time," was the disdainful reply.

"Only among the French. They are such savages," Anais parroted the new Americans.

"Aurelie, that is not true, is it? The Americans marry their cousins all the time, too, don't they?" Desiree asked in true distress.

I had to confess that I knew nothing about the marital habits of the new Americans.

The fiery spat did not break the spell of resurrection, but it did create a space for more disruption. For now Celeste knocked on the door and asked if she should take away our tray, as it was almost time for luncheon.

We rose, fingers to our lips to hide our shock from each other that the day had gotten away from us, and we made our way to our separate rooms to dress in day gowns.

We lunched on cold cheeses and breads and bright summer fruits. I asked, "Who is tired of wearing my plain cottons and linens? Shouldn't we spend the afternoon shopping for better clothes?"

The sisters squealed with delight, clapping their hands.

I imagined their joy, soon some day, when they realized the clothes they helped me order today would be their own. Not that they lacked for fine things to wear. Certainly, their own clothes more closely resembled the silks and satins I had once owned than the lawns and muslins that subdued me now.

Yasmine protested, but only because Anais had been thoughtful enough to ask her if she'd like to "Join us and get dropped off to see Emilie and the ba-Emilie."

"Certainly," I said bravely in the face of Yasmine's strident objections, "it would have been ideal if *Monsieur* Roger could have helped me choose nice gowns. But he is not here, and your own daughters have been raised with such impeccable taste that I feel certain what they choose will please. At any rate, you see how I've been given the plainest of plain clothing."

"So you would not want to gad about the town, showing off, but prefer quiet evenings at home." If I were not mistaken, Yasmine seemed offended by my dislike of the gowns I had found here. Had she chosen them?

I insisted, "I did not come here expecting fine clothes, and these are finer than even most Frenchwomen wear. But your daughters and I would like to dress up and pretend. Surely their *Monsieur Papa* will not mind the expense?"

To my astonishment, she pleaded with me. "Then let us wait, *Madame* Roger, for his return."

But the sisters and I would not be dissuaded. And, in the end, Yasmine came away with us in the carriage.

I thought that Louise-Anne and Jacques avoided each other's eyes as if they feared to look and see what they might find there, their fingers not even touching as he handed the rest of us into the carriage. Yasmine swept from the carriage and into Emilie's house, sending the oldest daughter out to the carriage to join us in our outing.

And our pleasure was complete.

We regaled Emilie with the tales we'd learned and lived since the evening before. Her gasps and sighs refueled us, and we began to plan for the upcoming night. "How I wish I might join you," she exclaimed. "It all sounds so enchanting. And I do miss *Monsieur Papa*'s mansion. Not that I am ungrateful for the house he bought for me and my husband, you understand. Only, everything seems so poor, after having been raised with so much."

We all rushed and leaned forward and seized her fingers, to reassure Emilie that she would be most welcome to spend the next night with us, playing our games. Desiree mentioned that Emilie's husband might be away for the next few nights.

Emilie, aghast, said, "How did you know? He told me only this morning."

Desiree shrugged off the question. "It is his pattern, *chere soeur*-my dear sister. Only, you do not notice such things. Two weeks at home every night is his utmost limit."

Emilie pouted. "Maybe two weeks of him at a time is all I can bear," she retorted. "Maybe I send him away until I can stand the sight of him again."

"What does your husband do?" I asked Emilie, to break the tension.

"Do?" she asked and stared at me.

As the others took a sudden interest in the passing scenery, Desiree said, "He will be the richest freeman in the city, by the time Emilie's ba-

235

child-is old enough to need a tutor. His work assures that Emilie and her children will enjoy more wealth than most Frenchmen."

Nothing else was said. Though I didn't understand what work Emilie's husband did, I did understand that it was not to be named.

We looked forward, instead, to the dizzy rounds of fabric and Parisian fashion plates to be displayed at the tailor's.

The tailor took the sisters' word for my identity as the new *Madame* Roger and asked, with the slightest bow, if I found the first order of gowns satisfactory.

"For day wear, *Monsieur,*" I said, imitating the absent Yasmine's great grace. "And I trust you can provide us evening gowns of equal quality." I had ventured into the stilted tones of-a woman whose memory I hated.

I must speak more carefully.

But there was little need for me to do more than smile and nod agreement as the sisters took over the selection of patterns and silks and satins and laces, showering upon the tailor their abundance of rain-fresh charm.

When we left the shop, caught up in the joy of our few ready-to-wear purchases, looking forward to the claiming of those which would be tailor-made for us, we could not bear to end the outing and go home. We had the carriage park alongside the park by the cathedral, so that we might promenade, enjoying the bright day, seeing the sun into the restless river, and maybe taking our dinner at a local cafe.

Jacques, excused by the carriage driver, escorted us, and we pretended not to see as he walked a little too closely to Louise-Anne and took her elbow as she stepped down at every curb.

The river reached out to me with memories, so I could not bear to draw close to it. We turned back, and the cafe-where a last supper had been shared-took up the street, beckoning to me.

Jacques hurried for the carriage as the sisters surrounded me, fanning me and cooing reassurances.

We dined quietly at home, after all, with Yasmine feeding Emilie's child out of sight and sound in the kitchen. Blessedly, Celeste was my personal maid again that night.

She helped me dress for the night's ball wordlessly, sensing my distance, apparently, and my resentment of her. I wanted to ask if her husband had found her in the servants' quarters. But then I would throw at her that my true lover had found me at the magical ball. And, somehow, telling anyone about that seemed an ill-advised idea. *What if someone tells Roger?* So I kept my back to Celeste and confided nothing.

The sisters dressed each other and met me, holding candelabra, on the main stairway. And again the threading of the maze took place. The ghosts we had raised together followed us and swarmed about us, parting like a sea of sighs and whispers at the backs of our minds.

We could not find the ballroom.

We sat finally, spreading the silken skirts of our gowns below us on the cold marble, retreating from the lengthening dark walls where no doorway ever broke through, to talk about our predicament. "Should we try to go back?" I asked at last.

"We are trying to go back," Desiree replied miserably.

"No, silly," Anais moaned. "She means back to our rooms. She means give up. Let's not!"

"No, never!" her sisters chorused.

"So what do we do now? I've never found it, without all of you. I can't help," I said and then guiltily remembered my dream of the night before. *I came on my own. How did I find it?*

I came out of my reverie with an idea.

I had brought Celeste with me, to carry my candelabrum. I gestured to her to bend her ear close to my lips. When she did, I whispered to her my suspicion that her presence might be impeding the magic.

I told her to go back, holding high a single candle of her own. Celeste stood at the far end of the corridor, turning back to see us as if she might never see us again. The white of her chemise and skirt and apron glowed in the light that suffused the maze. When she turned her face away, I thought I heard a muffled cry.

But when she had gone, the maze melted like mist, to reveal the ballroom's doorway.

We stepped cautiously inside. It was empty, quiet and still. No movement lifted the curtains from the windows, now open to air the great room. The ceiling frescoes rose, flat and still and cold, just above our vision. The moldings did not lift and reshape themselves but curled in their frozen whiteness, as if frozen in place.

No men and children hummed sweet tunes. No partners came forward, arms inviting us to dance. Such emptiness sucked at us, tugging us into the ballroom's center, that we fought it and turned and fled, the rustle of our new gowns dying in the void we left behind us.

We rushed together through the blue glow of the black corridors, expanding and twisting to accommodate our terror. The candles of our candelabra blew out in the wind of our rush. But globules of sudden light spilled into our maze of hallways through glass doorways that appeared on all sides, leading to balconies and galleries where couples danced and music and laughter invited us to pause and peek, to linger.

But we tugged at each other's silken sleeves, ripping the lace a little in our urgency to hurry on, to ignore the seductive strains of strange music and the odd hollow echoes of joyful voices.

Our own shrieks, startled and fearful, echoed off the blue walls and glowing glass that fed us into the ever-growing maze.

Yet, sometimes when I looked back, when I hesitated and thought to myself, *But surely there is someone there, just beyond my friends' shoulders,* indeed I would see a shape, a shadow fade into the corridor's darkness.

Was it the African who had partnered Desiree? The cavalier who sought to rouse first feelings of passion in Anais? If not the African and the

European, was I being followed by-but why should I fear to find in this house of exile the man I loved?

Did I fear to find him again? Is that why there was never anyone there, when I turned?

Suddenly I wanted the mad dash to end, the maze to fade and brighten into the harsh lights of the house I knew. I wanted my rooms, and Yasmine in them, waiting to undress me and put me to bed.

And just as suddenly, we spilled into the real world.

We turned to each other, fumbling with the latch at the door to my sitting room, greedy to emerge into the flickering firelight that surely awaited us there, suspended from the small chandelier and blazing from the sconces on the walls.

Yasmine wasn't there.

We searched the sitting room, the bedroom, the dressing room, and the balcony. "Where might she have gone, when it is time to be asleep?" I demanded peevishly.

Celeste woke from Yasmine's pallet at the foot of my bed to say, "No, I have not seen Yasmine ever since she told me to attend you in your rooms. I am so glad you didn't stay lost in those hallways, *Mademoiselle.*"

We swept down the grand staircase to the sisters' rooms. Yasmine did not answer our calls, did not blink in the sudden light of our upheld candelabra.

An unwelcome thought occurred to me. We had not chosen a room for Emilie. Surely Yasmine assumed we would give her oldest daughter the

Monsieur's room, and Yasmine had gone there to await Emilie with the child.

We moved as one to the doorway of *Monsieur* Roger's rooms and stopped, feeling the heavy emptiness inside that blocked us already at the threshold. I called, "Yasmine!"

And her daughters called, "*Maman!*"

She did not answer. She was not there.

We left, straggling.

But I turned back, wondering that I had ever felt at home in Monsieur's rooms, laughing with him over the difficulty of sipping soup together at such a small table, without knocking our heads. How had Yasmine borne it?

And then I realized she had not borne it.

What had she threatened when *Monsieur* Roger meant to leave her for one more fatal night at the bordello, risking that some other man's lust might make her a common whore and no longer the *Monsieur*'s own mistress?

She had threatened to jump from the window with the baby.

Tonight, she had a baby. Her captive status, demoted to a lady's maid, was ever more clear to her as I feted and dined her daughters.

Yasmine has jumped from a window!

We would find her broken body on the courtyard cobbles.

I rushed past the sisters, milling and gesturing their confusion, singeing someone's waving lace with my candelabrum in my haste.

Why hurry? If she had done it, I could not save her.

Her daughters rushed after me, begging to know what terrible thought drove me on. Bravely, I refused to tell them. And so, of course, they guessed.

I could not protect them.

We erupted into the courtyard, a cluster of flower-colored silk and wavering candle flames, our hands to our throats, panting and crying out, "Yasmine!" "*Maman!*"

Only the tinkle of the central fountain answered.

But then a door to the servants' quarters was flung wide. A figure in bright clean cotton hesitated at the top of the steps and then descended. We drew back as if from a ghost.

But, "What is it?" Yasmine demanded with what was becoming habitual peeve.

And we collapsed against each other at last, laughing.

CHAPTER ELEVEN
ROARING, WEEPING, RAGING PIT

Yasmine clicked her tongue at our stories of her suicide and what she called the "phantom ballroom."

"There is no magic ballroom in this house! There never has been. The magic ballroom is a game, not a place," she insisted.

Her daughters believed her and hung their heads when she said, "This is what happens when young women are left alone to entertain themselves. I should have stayed with you. I should have left Emilie at home, to mind her baby and wait for her husband's return."

But I resisted these arguments.

Of course there was a magic ballroom. We had danced in its splendor. We had fled its clutching emptiness. We might not understand it or what happened in it-how did it bring to us the men of our dreams?-but we needn't doubt that it existed.

Maybe we had not been welcomed into the magic ballroom the second night because we had a married woman with us, Emilie. And if she did not wish for her husband, but would have no one else, the magic ballroom might have rejected her and confused us, to keep her away.

My thoughts began to run wild. *Maybe the escort the magic ballroom has waiting for Emilie did not think she was ready to meet him in person, for she was certainly there in spirit, the first night.*

I became suspicious. *Maybe it was only Emilie who had been frightened at the stillness and started our shrieking flight back down the corridors. Maybe we can go back, without Emilie.*

But Yasmine took it upon herself to take over our entertainments.

She did not come with us. She preferred to stay behind, run the household, and tend Emilie's child in the servants' quarters, "where his presence will not disturb *Madame* Roger," she said pointedly, nodding with averted eyes toward me.

But each day she sent us off in the carriage with supplies to dine outside in the flower gardens of the square, and with strict instructions as to what parts of town never to stop or pause in, lingering.

We went one day to the levee along the river, braving the shells and boulders with our bare toes, so as not to tear up our cloth-bottom summer slippers, only climbing onto the soft grass when it was time to spread our tablecloth and refresh ourselves. We went another day all the way to the ocean's shore, shutting our eyes to the dismal city's slums and the countryside shanties until we burst through the windbreak of palms and cypresses that lined the fine white sand of the beach. We waded into the lapping water barefoot and fully clothed, fading and shredding our new silks in the scrub of salt waves and seaweed.

On another day, we were boated to an outlying island, to lunch on fresh oysters and dry bread, once we had recovered from our seasickness. We shopped, and I bought the sisters the trinkets of jewelry, lace, ribbons, and hair combs that caught their eyes. We bought perfumes to scent our hair above the daily sweat we worked up on our bodies, and cremes to soften our adventurous hands and smooth our explorers' knees and heels. We bought ointments to heal and peel away the burn of our darkening tans.

"Your husband will not recognize you when he returns," Yasmine warned Emilie, and Anais chimed in teasingly, "You will soon be as dark as he!"

Our lovely silk gowns went limp and frayed at the edges from our determination to wear them on all occasions, but "Never mind," I told my companions. For, on one of our very next outings, we picked up the new dresses, tailor-made, with imported Kashmiri shawls to protect and enhance them.

We were seated one evening at a candlelit dinner, gowned in our new silks and shawls, when *Monsieur* Roger walked in.

We heard his heavy boots ring out on the marble in the foyer before he emerged through the doorway into the dining room. We stared at each other as if in horror, then rose and curtseyed all together as he came upon us and said, "I thought I heard your voices. Yasmine's daughters, all of you, it is time to go home. Emilie, I am surprised you would risk your husband's displeasure, leaving him to wonder where you get to when he is out of town."

I said, "They were invited here as my guests, *Monsieur*," as he turned away to shrug out of his riding coat.

He turned back and flung at me, "And you are forgiven for your obvious ignorance of protocol. Yasmine, on the other hand, is another matter."

I spluttered, "But I insisted-" to his retreating back.

But, as if called, Yasmine-the only one who had not risen and curtseyed-was out of her seat and ran after *Monsieur,* arguing with him so forcefully in the foyer that her lowered voice carried back to us as though she were shouting.

"You think you have understood? You think you know what you're doing? You have understood nothing, *Monsieur.* How were you planning to win the girl over to you and to her new life here with you? She needs friends. She needs the silliness that girls give each other. She is not a grown woman, to grieve her baby until she recovers and has another. She has to be won." The contempt in Yasmine's voice added the "you fool" that even she was too cautious to say.

"Enough!" I heard *Monsieur* Roger bellow. We heard his heels grate on the marble. He must have turned around in the narrow space to confront Yasmine.

Her daughters paused, clustered about the doorway with me, unwilling to eavesdrop on their father's furious rejection of them but even more unwilling to brush past him in the foyer.

Only I could do this.

I pushed past the milling sisters and hurried up to *Monsieur* in the unlit passageway.

He and Yasmine were at each other's throats with their cutting words. "I see what you're up to!

You're not letting go. You're digging in. You're holding on to everything. To this house. To the dresses and jewels. To *me*."

"To *you*? Why should I hold on to you? I can never be free of you! I have had your children and buried half of them. I have the weight of our years together bending my back and making me old and sick. I was only unwilling to see you throw away your last chance at real happiness, after you gave my daughters their freedom." Had Yasmine lost her mind, hissing like a snake at her owner, who had not yet set her free?

"Throw away?" *Monsieur* repeated, incredulous. "I rescued the girl!"

"*Rescued*? You *betrayed* the girl and her brother to their father, don't you mean? So you could get your hands on her!"

Monsieur still carried his riding crop. He snapped it above his head like a fishing line and slashed it down across Yasmine.

She turned so that the crop tore across her shoulder. As she whipped back around to lash at *Monsieur* again with what she thought she knew about him, a pair of thin red lips pouted open in a long gash across her shoulder and arm to the elbow and vomited a line of blood into the cut sleeve.

I was near her now and threw myself onto her, knocking her backward as I wrapped my arms around her shoulders. Her fresh blood drenched the bosom of my new silk gown.

Monsieur had dropped the riding crop and reached for Yasmine, too. "Forgive me! I was maddened. This must stop, Yasmine."

But Yasmine was turned toward him now. She steadied herself against me as she spat at *Monsieur* Roger, "I was *helping* you, you fool! You could not win her. I and my daughters were winning her for you." She tapped her chest with the forefinger of her uninjured arm.

Monsieur turned to me, his eyes wide. "I did not betray you and Jules. She does not know what she is saying."

I wailed at the sound of that name. *Oh, God, so carelessly spoken.*

"I did not," *Monsieur* persisted, unaware of the reason for my cry. "You must believe me, for this is the sworn truth. It was the seamstress Jules went to for that last dress. He had not paid her, and as all the clothiers in town knew his mother, the seamstress went to her to be paid in full. I swear it, Aurelie."

I could not release Yasmine. But as I sagged with the dizziness that overcame me at hearing this beloved name, hearing these events and those awful, blessed months recalled so suddenly, brought to life again inside me, Yasmine shifted to hold me, in turn.

Monsieur Roger went on, "It was I who kept the innkeeper and the grocers from going to Jules's father months before, Aurelie, to collect payment. I paid all the debts I knew he had. I simply did not know about that last gown. I do not ask for gratitude. I only ask that you understand my self-restraint. I, who wanted you, too, who had already paid Jules's father a down payment for you and could have taken care of you, who knew what horrors lay ahead if I could not intervene as fully as

I liked, that I should have refrained from frightening you further by forcing myself upon you, demanding you-"

Monsieur Roger had edged up to me as he spoke and now seized me, as if trying to pry me from Yasmine. "I would not hurt you," he said.

When he got my hand loose from Yasmine's uninjured arm, I used the free fist to strike at him. I was frightened, swept back into that time and that place, wondering what Jules, blessed Jules would think if I let myself be touched by this insistent stranger while he was out, and all my resistance was doing me no good. I remembered cowering behind the drapes of the inn room's window, hiding from the importunate knocking at the door.

Yasmine urged me, "*Madame* Aurelie, stay here with us! Don't go back there. Oh, Roger, you fool, don't you see it in her eyes? Now look what you've done."

I roused and looked around at their faces, wide-eyed and staring. I felt the squeeze and pinch of their struggling hands, too tightly gripping me.

I was here. I was now. And Jules was not coming.

Only *Monsieur* Roger had come. "Oh, why did you have to come back now?" I cried at the *Monsieur*. "We were so happy. I was so happy." I looked miserably, yearningly toward the sisters, who still watched from the dining room doorway.

"Because of the storm," *Monsieur* said with admirable calm. "I thought you would be frightened, in the house with only the servants while the lightning and thunder-"

I surely would have challenged him, "What storm? Only today, we had to walk under parasols around the park square," but, as if my desperate glances had given them permission, Yasmine's daughters now surged forward and pried us all apart.

They took charge of their mother, leading her toward the servants' stairway. They urged me to come away to my rooms and lie down, to let them call Celeste to wash the blood from my gown. I do not doubt that they even had extra hands and attention to spare for *Monsieur* Roger, cooing to him, too, that all would soon be well.

"There is no harm done."

"We should not have stayed so long."

"We can come again, at a better time."

And as the sea surged into the sky, shivering there before cracking it apart, sending long streaks of light to burn the city as the rushing waters fell upon it, I lay in the third-floor rooms and tried to remember where and when I was.

Celeste, the hated one, nevertheless held me. I thought murderously, *She has her happiness. Her husband. Must she help that stranger at the door torture me now?* as *Monsieur,* through the closed door of my bedroom, tried to outshout the breaking thunder and the despairing wind.

The wild elements shrieked in my mind, which had at last broken free and was rampaging through the city with its havoc and its screaming chaos. Where was my revenge? Our baby was dead.

Glass rattled in the window panes. Surely it would splinter. Thunder rocked the third floor, a spindly structure of wood and brick. Celeste held me steady against its motion. She sobbed with fear into my neck.

Monsieur Roger shouted, "Don't make me break in this door! Let me help you, Aurelie. Let me comfort you. You see what Yasmine has done. She has turned you against me. You will hardly hear the storm, in my rooms."

Lifting her weeping face now and then, Celeste would say, "*Mademoiselle,* let me open the door to *Monsieur*. Surely, he will punish me for this."

And I would answer, "If you open that door, I will open the door onto the balcony, and I will jump from there. I am afraid of him, and I hate him. Don't let go of me."

I think she did not let go because she was as afraid as I to cross the fragile room alone in the whipping storm.

And now I remembered when I had hidden under the bed of the dying grandmother, alone with her in the dark tower of her third-floor room, as the sky split and spilled its months' weight of fury on our heads, until Jules had come to find me. "Don't be afraid," his voice soothed me, tender in the dark and the dust, muffled by the storm that clawed at the edges of our hiding place. Surely, when we crawled out from under the bed in the morning's calm, we must find the grandmother's body shredded by the wild and shrieking beast that was the storm, I had thought then. But, after the storm, she and we were all still alive.

Unchanged.

Maybe we would live through this, too.

251

I looked up to see if the storm was passing just as something hurtled against the panes and flung them open, flapping and slamming into the room.

In the next instant, a blast of lightning seemed to have lit the curtains at my windows and left them burning, blinding me so that I pressed my shut eyes more deeply into Celeste's skin. We screamed together as thunder seemed to rock my third-floor rooms loose from the rest of the house.

Monsieur Roger's boot had broken in my bedroom door from the balcony.

He seemed part of the flying debris, the leaves and rocks and trash and dying animals the wind hurled against my shaking window panes and walls. Only, as he came through the fragile glass, he scooped me in his arms as hard as cast iron and turned, never faltering, to run with me from the room. Celeste leapt from the bed and grabbed at *Monsieur* Roger, holding onto his shirttails and suspenders as she stumbled after us.

We fell down the long shaft of the grand stairway and were blown into the *Monsieur*'s rooms, where the doors slammed us in and we stayed.

When my shaking stilled, I looked out from under the heavy dark covers of his bed to see a fire bravely leaping at the shadows of the stormy night and a platter of bread and cheeses and a carafe of *cafe au lait* laid upon our little chess table.

Celeste sat in one of the chairs, studying the draped windows and no doubt thinking of the storm beyond, for she clutched at her shawl and shivered now and then.

I said, "Don't worry, *chere* Celeste. I am sure your husband did not venture out tonight to find you."

She looked at me gratefully and smiled. "No, surely he would not," she said hopefully. "He must have better sense than that, mustn't he?"

"Men in love do foolish things," *Monsieur* said into my ear, and I realized that he, too, must be lying upon the bed, holding me. "But I took the precaution of arranging with your husband's owners that you and he should have a lengthy visit once I returned from my plantation. He had no call to risk being hunted down as a runaway, to come into the storm."

Celeste was silent. I suspected that her husband had risked just that many times before tonight.

And suddenly I no longer hated her. How could I blame her for snatching at her happiness with both hands, just as my *Tante* Clothilde had advised me every time my life threatened to take it away?

I said, "Will that coffee calm me, *Monsieur*?"

And *Monsieur* leapt to carry me from the bed, as though I were ill, and seat me in the winged chair Celeste had just vacated.

"Coffee is very bracing," *Monsieur* said. "It will drive away pointless fears. You have nothing to fear. I am here. I will let nothing and no one hurt you."

How could he say such a thing when I had just lived again through the kidnap from the inn, on my way to waking up again at the swamp witch's shack?

No. Do not think of it. I shut the memories from me and pressed my lips to the fragile dipping curve of china and the prickling sting of the hot coffee and milk.

There must have been something besides milk in the coffee. For soon after I began to sip it, my head flopped on my spongy neck. My eyelids fluttered and fell. I felt myself carried back to the open, waiting bed.

Where, "Wicked girl!" Jules's mother raged, as she had so often in my childhood. I had not heard it in so long; but now, on the occasion of my own child's birth, it seemed only fitting that we should recall when I was little. The swamp witch held my bloody baby high, and against the stabbing, tearing light that seared the bursting black sky, my tiny baby began to squirm.

"My baby," I cried and reached for it from the blood-washed cot where the copper-skinned man held me. But no, it was Jules who pinned me down, straddling my spread legs to unbutton my bodice and expose the breasts the baby would need to suckle.

Jules positioned himself between my outspread legs, shaking with the fatigue of childbirth, and lowered himself into me. I would have closed my arms around him, but he held them pressed back into ... pillows?

I opened my eyes and found that it was *Monsieur*, not Jules, who held my hips and drove them up again and again to welcome and take in his own. I spoke, but his mouth hushed mine.

254

And I closed my eyes again. There was no use. I listened to distant cries.

Monsieur was wrong. I surely heard the storm in his room.

Celeste later told me that I passed weeks in a silent stupor, the remainder of the summer. But I was not in silence. I was in the roaring, weeping, raging pit of my memories.

Rarely, I would surface and ask myself, *What has Monsieur done to me, and why? Why couldn't he leave me to Jules? I am his slave; I could have worked ...*

Where did I find myself when I woke? Not in *Monsieur*'s rooms, thankfully. Back in my rooms, cleaned and repaired in the lull between summer storms, or sometimes in the rose room that used to be *Monsieur*'s mother's.

I sometimes thought of Desiree there and struggled to recall myself to the present. It felt like dragging through mud. I clung to Celeste to anchor me. But she was not always there.

And Yasmine was never there.

When the stupor fell from me, and *Monsieur* himself came to my rooms to see this miracle of recovery, I asked him why Yasmine had not tended me through my illness. *Monsieur* said, "I sent Yasmine away with her daughters after the storm that night."

That night. "But she was hurt, *Monsieur*. And it was not her fault. It was mine. I begged her to let me have her girls with me." I looked up at him, my hatred probably plain on my face.

255

Monsieur Roger said, "I had no idea you would take it so. I thought you wanted-that is, I thought you might have wanted-me to take care of you without her help. Knowing her former station, so recently lost."

I would have asked if he had given Yasmine her freedom, in recompense for his brutal treatment of her, but I couldn't bear to speak to him any more.

Monsieur Roger asked if he might not invite his daughters to join us for dinner, to celebrate my recovery. Would I be staying awake that long?

"I would like to see your daughters, *Monsieur,*" I said. "I would also like to see Yasmine, if I may."

Yasmine did not come.

Her daughters sat in the radiance of the silks I had bought them-or so they told me, for I did not remember-and gossiped happily about Yasmine's new marriage to a soon-to-be- freeman. Apparently, *Monsieur* had had a personal manservant before bringing me into the household. Once he believed I would be coming, he had begun to free and move out people, beginning with his bachelor-"*Very* handsome," said Louise-Anne-manservant.

Roger's daughter Emilie was already married, as I knew. Louise-Anne, Desiree, and Anais were too young, yet. So he moved them into Emilie's house.

"Why?" I asked.

Louise-Anne, smiling, said, "So you would not think of your young lover and regret coming here. So you would not think *Monsieur Papa* is too old for you to love him, when you discovered he has daughters your age and older."

256

Anais giggled. "*Monsieur Papa* had *Maman* explain it all to us. We thought it was romantic."

Louise-Anne finished explaining about the manservant all by herself. I wondered at her interest in him. Had Jacques a rival? "This former manservant," Louise-Anne explained with great relish, "had been-not exactly freed, but-released to live in the city and take over some of the business that the first Emilie's husband had established-he and Emilie were both dead, now-and that our sister Emilie's husband had, in part, taken over, over time."

"You're not telling it right," Anais interrupted again.

"You've left out too much," Desiree complained, as well.

"I've left out nothing," Louise-Anne snapped. "So, this manservant, Marcel-now our stepfather, since *Monsieur* has married him to *Maman*-has in fact had the difficult task of reestablishing old contacts and winning back the trust of those who worried that the business had passed too soon to our sister Emilie's husband. Marcel has maturity and discretion, according to *Monsieur Papa*," Louise-Anne assured me.

She went on to tell me, clearly reciting what she'd overheard her father say, that Marcel could handle even the most difficult business with secrecy and dispatch.

Monsieur Roger walked in during this recital and regarded his daughter curiously. She brightened and looked at him. "Isn't that right, *Monsieur*?" she finished.

257

Monsieur Roger looked thoughtful and said carefully, "Marcel can be trusted to wisely invest and diligently safeguard the money he has been given for the reestablishment of business with lost customers."

I said, "I do not understand, *Monsieur*."

And he replied patiently, "Ostensibly, Yasmine's dowry. He has enough capital to reestablish lost business opportunities for me."

Anais challenged her father. "Does this mean, *Monsieur Papa,* that you have spent all our remaining dowries on *Maman*? Only Emilie shall ever be married?"

Monsieur Roger regarded his youngest daughter as though he'd never seen her speak before today. "It certainly does not mean that, Anais. There shall be plenty of money for all of you to have secure lives and husbands who are well situated to take care of you."

Anais stared, straight-backed, at him. But the questions that seemed to needle her remained unasked. Perhaps she was as dumbstruck as I on the topic of business and couldn't even begin to guess the right questions.

Monsieur Roger took the opportunity to ask, "So, is this a party for girls only? Or may an old gentleman join you ladies?"

And a thought struck me. I said, "Whatever happened to the first Emilie? Did you give her a dowry for a free husband, too, *Monsieur*?"

The daughters grew silent, instantly swallowing their chatter. *Monsieur* Roger seemed to consider whether or not he wanted to answer. Then he said simply, "Yes, I did." He seemed to think a moment more before adding, "She learned to love him deeply. She was very happy with the man I chose. She came back to tell me so."

Emilie said, "I remember that, *Monsieur*. I thought she came back to beg for work and food because they were starving."

Monsieur Roger snapped, "How was I to know how hopeless it might be for a freeman to maintain legal employment, if it takes him outside the colored community? I've learned better since. None of you seem to be starving. Besides, Emilie's husband was chosen for his ability to protect her. From Europeans and Americans and freemen, and from herself. You seem to know everything. Did you know she threatened to kill herself if I set her free and sent her away? For years, she'd threatened that. I chose a man who, whether he loved her or not, would not disappoint me by letting that happen."

Desiree said, "It was her life, *Monsieur Papa*. You put her life into her keeping, when you gave her freedom. Why not let her end it, if she was tired of it?"

Monsieur Roger looked forbidding. "You know better than to ask me that, Desiree. A slaveowner has moral as well as legal responsibilities to his chattel. I am not one of those men who believe that only Europeans have souls. Freeing Emilie into a situation that would allow her to take her own life, as she'd threatened, would have been damnable, on my part. Besides, I had once loved her. Very much. I wanted her eternity to reflect the best and happiest

259

moments of her life. I wanted her buried in the part of the cemetery reserved for Christianized Africans, not thrown in the communal ditch reserved for the disposing of pagans."

I asked, shocked, "Why are pagans thrown into a ditch?"

Anais answered, "Because most freemen are too poor to afford a nice burial. Isn't that right, *Monsieur Papa*?"

Desiree said testily, "Poor or rich, once their money is taken for a decent coffin, all those of any African descent whatever are more likely to be thrown in a ditch than not, and their money pocketed. It makes me wonder who the real pagans are. The people who died, entrusting their souls to their greedy countrymen, or those who took their money and dumped their earthly remains in unhallowed ground. You tell me, *Monsieur Papa,* which of the two is demonstrating a lack of faith in his god."

Monsieur Roger said, "Slaveholding challenges one's moral fiber. It is a damnable institution. All civilized Christians experience doubt." Then he stared at his own daughter with such open resentment that I feared the sisters might never agree to come dine with me again.

So I said, "Did you give the senior Emilie the gifts and dowry set aside for her, *Monsieur*?" and he glared at me, instead.

"Food and money," his own daughter Emilie said quietly, "but not work."

Monsieur Roger growled, "In fact, I beg to differ. I put Emilie's husband in touch with wealthy

Frenchmen who needed his services, and in time we set up such a demand for him that he had to hire his own employees. Including your husband, little Emilie."

I asked, intrigued, "Oh, *Monsieur*? What services did Emilie's husband perform for wealthy Frenchmen?" I meant the original Emilie; but I might as well have been talking about the younger, as well.

"That was at the beginning of the American invasion," *Monsieur* said darkly. "Many services were needed." And, just as with the younger Emilie's husband, silence fell on the topic of the work the elder freeman did.

Finally, after I repeated my question, *Monsieur* Roger said, "Obviously a freeman must be ready to do work that no Frenchman will agree to do. Once the freeman rids himself of the limits of false pride, he may live quite well."

"Will you choose all our husbands?" Anais asked, impatient with philosophical debate.

"Certainly," *Monsieur* Roger assured her.

And the glory of Yasmine's husband's golden earring and bulging muscles faded in our awkward awareness that he had been chosen for her by the father of her children, her owner and original lover. *Take her, for I am done with her and her dying babies and weak pretty girls*, I thought to myself. *And I know that if she truly loved me as I think she did, she can never love you. So you can have what is left of her.*

When the daughters left, escorted in the carriage by Jacques-was the *Monsieur* blind, or did

261

he want to tease Louise-Anne's furtive passions?-
Monsieur Roger followed me silently to my room
and waited in my sitting room "to talk."

I wished to avoid him and pleaded melancholia.
I asked for Celeste to come hold me, as I was
feeling oddly out of touch with the world around
me. The sight of the sisters and the sound of their
infrequent but still familiar laughter had brought
back, with a rush, the thrill of the phantom
ballroom. I wanted to go in search of it.

And I did not want to have to hear whatever
Monsieur Roger now wanted to say.

But what I wanted or not did not deter him. He
crossed his legs before my cold fireplace and said,
"Aurelie, hear me. I did not mean to cause your
illness to overtake you again. I want your company,
even if you are not yet ready to share with me your
affection. I think it would be best if we make an
effort to get used to our intimacy. Inevitably, it shall
become our habit."

I said, "Is it true that none of your rooms in this
house is a ballroom, *Monsieur*? While you were
away at your plantation, I was sure your daughters
and I discovered one-empty and unused, of course-
only, one could still hear the strains of music."

"There is a room that was once a ballroom,"
Monsieur Roger said with mild surprise, "when the
colony was young and tastes were less grand. It is
too small to be considered a worthy ballroom now."

"What is it now, *Monsieur*?"

"A sort of grand salon I use as a parlor when
meeting with particularly difficult business persons

I wish to intimidate. It is a large and cold room, as a parlor."

"Will you take me to it, *Monsieur*?" I asked.

Confronted by *Monsieur*, the maze was flat and simple, cutting away its own curves to present us with the room in question before we had time to build up any expectations.

The room was the same, only smaller, chilly, and shadowed, haunted by the absence rather than the presence of its ghosts. "It's so lonely in here now." My voice echoed off the still frescoes. I spread my arms and pirouetted.

Monsieur Roger strode up behind me and took me in his arms as I stared up at the ceiling, spinning slowly beneath the staring faces, willing them to rise, shift, and resettle, or sing their strange arias to make us dance.

The *Monsieur* and I began to dance.

He steered me with only the slightest touch. He wheeled me about the room with my new silk dress swirling and clutching at our ankles before it fanned playfully away. Our arms were outstretched so that only the heated center of our palms touched.

My free hand held my skirt slightly above the floor. His free hand hovered, unwanted, afraid to touch, just above my waist.

I felt his desire for me, and how he wanted to be invited. And I recoiled from it.

Monsieur Roger began to hum a tune, familiar in its hopeful, sweet lilt. I hummed it with him. He said, startled, "Do you know it, Aurelie? Where did you learn it?"

I said, "The night I danced here with the man I love, *Monsieur*," and *Monsieur* Roger stopped and gripped my shoulders.

"Enough of that!" His voice was harsh, his face close to my face. "You are playing crazy, and I have had enough of it, Aurelie. Jules has not been here. He cannot have been."

I fell away from the *Monsieur*'s grasp and returned alone to the dance. *So now he knows. What can he do about it? Whip me? Kill me? I wish I had died.* "Why ever can Jules not be here, *Monsieur*?"

"He has not yet returned from overseas. He is still restrained in a European sanitarium."

Monsieur Roger caught up with me and took my hands. Already the room was lightening, expanding. The whispering, laughing spirits of those who'd danced and loved here before tonight flashed into sight and vanished from the corner of my eye.

Monsieur Roger said, "Perhaps it is too bad for Jules. Perhaps he has little to look forward to, after losing you. But you. You have everything ahead of you to enjoy, Aurelie. Look at me. Look at what I've offered you. No, look, I tell you, and don't turn away."

He had caught me up and spun me back into his arms, against his chest. It was hard, and the breath was knocked a little from me. I gasped and pushed at his chest to keep him away, and said, "Oh, *Monsieur*, I miss your daughters. I miss Yasmine. I want them back."

Monsieur Roger lowered his head to where I stared up at him and swallowed my words between his teeth and down his throat, sucking at my breath with the rhythms of his tongue. He pressed me backward toward the floor until pain shot up my back toward my neck. He eased me to the floor beneath him.

Not again, I wanted to beg, but he swallowed down the words, sucking them down his own throat as he drew them into his mouth between his gnawing, gnashing teeth.

My lips bled between us. I felt the sting and the flow of warmth. And the ache of the fine bones of my spine being pressed, one by one, into the icy marble floor. The buttons that closed the back of my silk gown resisted the *Monsieur*'s weight and dug into the hard stringy muscles between my shoulder blades and hips.

The *Monsieur* had bunches of my gathered skirt in his hand and jerked them up to my chin, pulling back enough only to work at his trousers and assure me, "You will get used to me, Aurelie. We will get used to each other. All will be well."

I stared at the flat, emotionless faces of the ceiling frescoes while the space in my heart and mind that made Jules's and my love sacred and special was broken into yet again.

And when the *Monsieur* grew calm again and began to cool his sweat on my face with light kisses, I waited to see the frescoes fade, the moldings writhe and the room fade away. I waited for the merciful madness to descend. But it had deserted me.

I lay there, not lost, but remembering-Jules's tenderness and his rages-and asking myself, *If he*

265

knew about this, what would he say? How would he feel about me? He can never know.

Monsieur Roger rose and dressed himself. When he was presentable, he looked down at me, still lying there stunned and spread-eagled. "No more of your theatrics, Aurelie. Get up and come to bed with me. You have not been raped. I treat you better than most girls in your position dare expect."

I continued to lie there, caught up in the urgency of my wanting to go anywhere, be anywhere in the lost moments of my life-even in the swamp witch's shack, placing my lips to the bloody body of my dead baby-anywhere but here and now. I began to weep with the effort to pull the illusive past back here to me, down upon me like a blanket, to blank out the ugly, sweaty here and now with its cold floor, the ache where the buttons pressed into tight back muscles, the sour private smell that clung wetly, hotly to me, rising from between my legs as though I'd forgotten myself and soiled myself right here in the ballroom.

Monsieur Roger tugged down my skirt with a grunt of disgust and said, "I will not carry you, Aurelie. I will not encourage this. I will send Alain for you." And he left, taking his candelabrum with him.

Alain, of course, was Celeste's husband, bought from his humble position as dairy peddler and delivery man for the family that owned him, to be trained as *Monsieur*'s new valet, now that his old one had married Yasmine, because *Monsieur* saw great promise in Alain. His courteous, straightforward manner, his many contacts about the city, his reputation for circulating widely on legitimate and legal business all recommended him highly to *Monsieur*.

I thought morosely, *Celeste wanted me in exactly this position so that she could be with her husband. She should be quite happy tonight. And I, who helped her to get everything she wanted, at my own expense? Will I ever be happy again? How I hate her.*

I rolled over and braced my face in my crossed arms above the marble, as if, like a child, I believed that if I could not see Alain when he arrived, he would not see me. But I could shut nothing out. Even in the dark, I thought I saw the glint of the marble floor between my arms.

But no, I was no longer in the dark. That was candlelight that glinted beyond the barricade my arms made.

For Celeste's husband was here.

I raised my head and blinked away the mists that clouded my vision. "Alain," I said, searching for words that would make him not treat me as what I seemed to be, a girl to be used and traded, discarded on the floor when she did not quite satisfy.

Alain's voice was kind. "*Mademoiselle,*" he said with great deference. "So I have found you. Celeste warned me that finding this room can be tricky. Large as it is, you would think it would stay in one place." He broke off his own laugh when he saw how I struggled to understand that he was joking. Then he squatted down near me, sitting

267

inelegantly on his heels like the workman he was to take my elbow and help me rise.

I startled us both when I pulled away. But I was suddenly quite ashamed to have him so close to the smell that Roger had left upon me. I rolled to the opposite side and worked my way stiffly to my feet, unassisted.

When he reached for my elbow again, I did not see his hand coming. He had a firm grip before I could flinch away. "It is no matter, *Mademoiselle*," he said between the gentle sounds one makes for a skittish horse. "You must not be ashamed of your place in the life of a Frenchman of such wealth and power as *Monsieur* Roger. Can you understand me, *Mademoiselle* Aurelie? You are a certain kind of lady now, but a lady-nearly a freewoman-nonetheless."

I hoped Alain's words and his firm grip on me as we wound our way through the blunt, short corridors meant that at least Alain did not look down upon me for what I had become. As Alain led me up the stairs beyond the second-floor landing, *Monsieur* appeared in the doorway of his room. When his stare caused Alain to hesitate, he said, "Do as the mistress of this house asks, Alain. If she wants to go to her own rooms tonight, we must indulge her," and the next flight of stairs dumped me suddenly back into the yellow light of my third-floor tower.

Long after Celeste had helped me undress and wash, I lay in the darkness of my bed, gazing through the glass door to the balcony and the tiny stars beyond, wondering at my hatred of Celeste.

Was it envy? *Might anything have turned out differently if Celeste had urged me to flee, had offered to carry notes from Jules to me, once he returned from the sanitarium? Had he ever returned?*

Maybe nothing could have happened differently than it had. Neither better nor worse, up to this point.

A terrible thought formed itself in my mind, against my will.

If Roger could tire of Emilie, the lover he'd brought with him from his parents' home, and put her in the care of another man, might Jules have ever done the same with me, the love of all his life?

Oh, surely such a comparison should not be made! I will drive myself mad with what-ifs.

But I could not guard my mind against the insidious doubt. Scenes of abandonment that had never taken place raged through my thoughts, along with the realization, *If Jules ever found out what has become of me, surely he must curse and reject me in his heart.*

I fought to keep the shreds of my lifelong vision of love between me and Jules together. *Oh, surely, we have always loved each other with a sincere love. He would never have sent me away!* Unless he thought I had been unfaithful?

This new fear that he might now think I had been willingly unfaithful made me feel as if my past life and love with Jules were in danger of being destroyed, as if he might reach into the days gone by at the inn and make them something else, the enjoyment of a wanton whore by a spoiled rich boy.

269

He must not think that I had been willing to betray him. He must treasure those days and these hopes that we would one day be together again as tenderly as did I. If only I could go to him and tell him none of this was my doing.

I rose from my bed to go find Jules in the last place where we had met and spoken to each other. The phantom ballroom.

CHAPTER TWELVE
JUST BEYOND MY VISION

I made my way down the stairways to the marble foyer of the first-floor landing and began the familiar search, candle held high, through the blue-lit corridors of the maze that grew away from me as I walked it.

Celeste had not risen as I passed her pallet. I had asked her to return to the quarters to sleep with her husband tonight, particularly if she had missed sleeping with him so she could tend me through my recent illness. But *Monsieur* Roger must have warned her against leaving me tonight, for she refused.

Her fatigue must have gotten the better of her. Either that or my own glass of soothing hot chocolate that I promised her I would leave on the vanity for vermin to drink tonight, if she did not drink it for me.

Celeste now slept senseless, as if drugged. I meant to profit by it. As I passed the shut doors of *Monsieur* Roger's rooms, I suffered a momentary guilt, wondering if Celeste's husband slept in there, ready to leap up at the slightest sound from the *Monsieur*. I pitied her all over again.

But once in the maze, I only had concern for my upcoming confrontation with Jules.

I had no doubt that I would find the ballroom and find Jules in it. I also had the uneasy feeling that, if I defended to him my innocence and my faithfulness, our meeting might become charged.

But if I would live with myself, and with what my life had been up to this point, that confrontation was vital to me. No matter what Jules said, in the end, I needed to know that he knew what I had suffered with the loss of our child and our hopes to be together forever. And so it was that, distracted by this worry, the maze landed me suddenly right in the circular middle of the dance floor I had thought was a rectangle.

I looked around me in confusion, holding my candle high. *Is this the room?*

The moldings lay still and white against the plaster. The painted angels and ladies and gentlemen stared soundlessly. Tonight, there was no sweet lifting of angelic voices in song.

But even in its stillness, the ballroom comforted me. I could feel that soon Jules must appear.

I turned and searched the curves of the ballroom, shivering in the cream-colored layers of lacy silk underclothes that I had worn to bed. The running candle wax burned as it dripped on my bare hand.

"Aurelie."

He was already here.

I turned to face him and felt my stomach squeeze and flutter as warmth flushed through me from my face to my thighs, and my nipples tightened and tingled. It was Jules.

He came forward from the pure blackness, and I watched him, wanting our old world back again.

Maybe I would say nothing about my new life with the *Monsieur*. Jules was here. He was real. I could ask him to help me run away with him again to the inn, or anywhere else he wanted to go. "I have missed you," I said as he drew nearer but not near enough to touch.

He didn't speak but continued to approach me, and I withdrew a step. *Oh no.* Was this to be the Jules of our last meeting? *Will he blame again? He was so hateful.*

Or was he as overwhelmed as I and unable to say more than my name? My own "I miss you" was so little, compared to what raged and raced through my veins and my mind.

Perhaps Jules was right to be silent.

He stopped, still out of reach. "Have you missed me?" was all he said.

"Oh, Jules, yes. Of course. You are my life. You know that." I forced myself not to back away from this apparition.

Where were his eyes? I stared into blurred shadows beneath the brows. "Jules," I began to beg, and moved as if to run into his arms.

But he stopped me with a suddenly raised hand that sent a cold wave right through me. "You have betrayed me. Our love. Everything," Jules said.

I wavered. *Already, he has condemned me? We have not even begun to talk about what we have been through!*

"No," I said. "I have not betrayed you. I would never betray you. I have been made to do things I did not want to do. But you can save me, Jules." I smiled at him, like Aurelie of the old days. Brave and in charge, like *Tante* Clothilde. Always knowing what to do. "Take me away again." I reached for him.

And just like that, Jules was no longer there.

The shadows and harsh brightness that had been his face were just not there any more. The iciness that swept past me from his space on the ballroom floor vanished like a passing breeze.

I blinked, turning, and raised my candle again to search the shadows. *Gone so soon? And on so bitter a note?* Surely this was not to be all of the long-dreaded, long-hoped-for, impossible meeting alone in the night!

"Jules," I called, and then turning to each of the fading, far-flung reaches of the ballroom, "Jules, come back. Don't go." I began to turn more slowly, the candle held out from me at arm's length to cast its wavering light into the shifting corners.

I began to comfort myself in the emptiness with a lulling song *Tante* Clothilde used to sing. I had to fend off the void of the ballroom without music, without dance, without couples sneaking with whispered words and locked gazes into a love that was uselessly forbidden, as ours had been. I had to wait for Jules to come back.

Surely, if he came again, we would be able to speak openly and kindly with each other, as when we were children. I would make him understand.

I sat, setting the candle beside me so that the ballroom's emptiness might not creep close when I was unaware, and clutched my knees. I bent my head, pressed my eyes into my knees, and continued to sing the brave little lullaby.

The children's and men's voices of that other, blessed, faraway night when we had found ourselves in each other's arms, dancing, rose around

274

me one by one, adding their voices to mine, as though to soothe me and tell me that, in the beauty of dreams and memories, I was not alone. *Anger such as Jules's comes only from protracted and unbearable pain,* I reasoned with myself. *But there can be no doubt that he loves me and holds our love sacred, still.*

I was still sitting there when Alain found me in the morning.

I woke with a start when his warm hand fell on my shoulder. I thought at first it was Jules's and clutched at it, startled to find that it was no longer cold.

My second shock was that sunlight, actual light of the ordinary day, could filter into this place, the last retreat of the kind of magic in which Jules and I had always hidden away our love and hoped for a future together. Maybe the magic ballroom was just an ordinary parlor, after all.

I scrambled away from Alain's outstretched hand and startled face and called out for Jules.

Alain did not leave me but followed me around the sharp angles of the ballroom, rectangular once again, looking up with me at the flat dull faces painted on silly posed bodies on the ceiling and at the stiff moldings, casts of leaf and artificial flower. We circled the ballroom together, Alain always a few steps behind me, reaching for me but never touching me, just as I reached for someone just beyond my touch and my vision, always almost there, but not quite.

I don't know how the *Monsieur* knew to come. But he appeared in the doorway one of the times I

275

circled by there, sending me running backwards so that I caught my bare heel on the silver of the candle holder I had left on the floor, tripped and fell, clutching the scrape.

I insisted from the floor, "He was here. I spoke to him. He doesn't understand what's happened. I have to make him understand, *Monsieur* Roger," resisting the urge to cower before the *Monsieur*'s ugly, incredulous scowl.

Alain said, "Sir, I found her like this."

A thought came to me. I leapt to my knees and scuttled quickly forward to seize *Monsieur*'s ankles and calves before he could recoil. "He will listen to you, *Monsieur*! You are a gentleman. You will tell him the truth. Tell him I had no choice, that this was all your doing. Yours and his parents."

Monsieur Roger, recovered from his terror at my change of tone and direction, now kicked at me to let him go. I held on. "Silly wench!" he bellowed. "Alain, go get your wife and see what she can do about this."

We battled until Alain and Celeste returned, *Monsieur* Roger alternately pulling from me in disgust and grabbing my shoulders to shake me, in desperation, all the while shouting at me to recall things that I did not recall, or, at least, did not recall in the way he put them to me. "Jules *cannot* come here, Aurelie. You have made it all up, damn it to hell!"

"But he *was* here. He was *right here*," slapping at the floor with the flat of my hand.

"I've told you, Aurelie, he is at a sanitarium. In Europe. He is a very sick man, and he *cannot* come here. And besides all that, you *cannot* claim that our relationship is against your will. You are my *property*. I *own* you. You *have* no will, when it comes to me. What kind of madness has Jules taught you, to drive you so out of your mind?"

"It is this place that has driven me out of my mind, *Monsieur*. It is you who have driven me out of my mind!"

The statement fell between us. As soon as the words were said, *Monsieur* Roger's face was suddenly transformed into a mask of such staring stupidity that I ceased my spittle-spraying shrieks at him and threw back my head to laugh, open-mouthed.

I laughed so hard, my mouth stretched so wide, that it forced my eyes closed. I could not see the *Monsieur*.

But I heard his voice eventually say, "You are that, Aurelie. Yes, you are out of your mind. Why did I think I could help you?" with such sober weight that the laughter choked me in my throat.

Coughing, I lowered my head and glared wide-eyed at him. "*Help* me?" I repeated. "*You* thought you could help *me*, by making me your property? Another man's freed lover? The mother of another man's child-"

"Where is this child?" *Monsieur* Roger bellowed, shedding his shock and hurt and spinning backwards, fists out and up, looking for something to strike. The change in him was so sudden that I was still falling backward when he smashed through a tall window pane and the curtain was sucked into the breezy morning, waving its fringes outside.

I gazed in fascination at the weird world beyond the broken window and lifting curtain. What had I expected to see? The street beyond the front door? The alley behind the stable? The house next door, its stained glass glinting deep colors into the bright morning?

I had not expected this, an endless blue puffed with shredding clouds as though the room were high in the sky, far above my third-floor rooms.

Monsieur Roger pulled his fist back into the ballroom and slammed it into a jagged edge of the glass that remained. This time the broken pane gave way to a roar of pain and rage that seemed to have been let in from the blackest reaches of the night sky, suddenly just beyond the torn, bloody edge of the curtain, as if this room were neither on earth nor in the heavens but hurtling with us through whatever lay at the end of falling.

I fell to the floor, my knees suddenly useless, as Roger came at me with his face twisted in pain and spattered with his own blood, oblivious to the sucking, star-filled night behind him where there still should have been early day.

And the next thing I knew, knew so well I could hold onto it, was that Yasmine was bathing my face in gentle touches of a white cloth dipped in mint-scented water.

I clutched her hand and looked around wildly for the *Monsieur*. "Where is he?" I cried, jerking my head from side to side and struggling to rise so that I might run if I spotted him. "He is going to hit me. I think this time he will surely kill me."

"It looks as if he has already hit you enough to satisfy himself. Sit down and let me wash these cuts." She pressed my shoulder with a damp hand.

I sank, my eyes still roaming. "No. No. You don't understand, *Madame* Yasmine. *Monsieur* Roger was about to hit me! I was telling him that he had forced me, but I am Jules's. I was calling on him to help me explain, and he had broken the windows onto the night-"

"Aurelie, calm yourself. You have been beaten, and you have survived it. Thank God the *Monsieur* sent for me and let me bring you here."

"Here? What do you mean? Where are we?"

"In my husband's home. Marcel. Don't you remember coming here, or the friend who brought you? For I could not go to you. Marcel doesn't wish for me to return to the *Monsieur*'s house." She said this flatly, as if it held no interest for her, and then prodded, "Who brought you here, Aurelie?"

A blurry scene, as if from a dream, flicked through my mind, trailing warmth and hope. "It was Arc," I said, "from the inn! Where we were so happy, so in love, Jules and I." I smiled up at Yasmine.

Yasmine continued to sponge at my wounds, sending minty stings zinging through my body from tiny pinpoint slices. "You should want to survive," she said. "You must tell me, when you are calm again, why you keep pushing away your chance to survive."

"Want to survive?"

Sighing, she said, "Do you remember why you were so glad to see Arc? What did he say to you at that inn you cling to with such a passion? What did he offer you?"

"Nothing."

"Oh, Aurelie. I should leave you to rest, but how can I? I have no idea how long the *Monsieur* will leave you with me-he does not trust me-nor what he will do when he takes you from me."

"Takes me from you? Again? But he has beaten me. He has told me I am crazy and sent me away. Surely he does not want me back." The thought filled me with misery.

"But surely you have been beaten before, Aurelie. Has not Arc seen you frightened and bruised, recovering from another man's jealousy and anger, *ma petite*?"

"Jealousy?" Panting with fear, as though cornered, I stared at Yasmine. What was she doing to me? How had I gotten here, and was this *Monsieur* Roger's way of finding someone to destroy what I remembered of Jules and our time at the inn, awaiting our child, hopeful about our future?

"I was going to be free! I gave Jules no cause to be jealous," I reasoned with her. "I was faithful, and we were in love. We are still in love, and he will come and free me!" My voice was ragged with sobs. "I know this. I love him, and he still loves me. He always will."

"Oh, Aurelie. Hush," Yasmine sighed. "You don't understand anything I'm saying. I'm not asking about love. I'm asking about being beaten. Didn't Arc have to feed and sit with you when you had been beaten by Jules and were frightened of his returning?"

"Witch," I screamed and pulled away from her. "How do you know these things?" The look on her face made me wonder what I had said. "Know." That was the word. The wrong word. She did not know. She was maligning, changing what had always been. Lying. "You are wrong," I said, the finger I pointed at her shaking. "He loved me. I loved him. We were always in love. All our lives. It wasn't what you say."

"I said nothing except that he beat you, Aurelie, and that you were frightened enough to ask Arc and his wife to sit and eat with you." Yasmine spoke so quietly that I found myself stilling my panting, ragged breath to hear.

Her words cut me worse than *Monsieur* Roger's glass. Had I ever so mistrusted Jules, whom I loved? Who loved me? Whose child I had carried and treasured so much so that, at its loss, I had little or nothing left to mourn the loss of my own mother?

"You weren't there," I argued weakly. "You don't know."

"No," she assured me, shaking her head. "I was not there. Only you know. I am not asking you to believe that Jules did not love you. Listen, and do not pull away," for she had gripped my sliced arm and was hurting me, tugging me back to sit before her and her bowl of wash water. "I only ask that you remember you *were* beaten, though loved. And now you are beaten, and still you are loved, though you do not love in return."

The words fell into my mind softly, like feathers drifting from a nest in a tree down to the palm of my hand, and I let them stay. "What are you saying?" I asked, when I realized she could not be through. This could not be all she wished to point out to me. I listened warily, ready to fend off whatever else she might say.

"Do you remember, Aurelie, what Arc said to you when first he met you, beaten, loved, and kept? What did he try to tell you?"

I searched and searched. It had not made sense. It had had so little to do with me and with waiting for Jules to return and the baby. And something about poetry.

I said, "I was waiting for the poetry to be sold in books. I did not want it to be. But I thought that perhaps the money would ease Jules's mind." I looked up at Yasmine sharply. "How do you know all this? How do you know Arc, and why has he told you these things about me? I trusted him."

"You were right to trust him, *petite*. He has put himself at some risk to help you, to give his wife peace of mind, and still you do not understand. What shall we do?"

"You should answer my questions, *Madame* Yasmine." I stared at her, the shape of my world changing until it had come round full circle and I realized I did not know where I stood in it. "Help me understand," I said. "I am so frightened. I think I have gone mad again."

Yasmine came slowly around the bowl and took me into her arms. She pressed my head to her chest, where I heard the soft thump of her heart and the deepest echoes of her voice. "I know Arc because he works for my husband, as well as his owner. And yes, you surely have gone mad again, *mon amie*, and with that, I am not at all sure that I can help you. But I can help you get away."

My head jerked up off her bosom. I stared into her eyes. "You can help me do what?"

"Go," she whispered. "You must tell no one what I've said, unless you want to see me killed."

"How can you help me do that?" I, too, whispered, a sudden burning in my chest from the breath held too long, needing to be released. But perhaps if I breathed too loudly just now, someone would hear, *Monsieur* Roger in his mansion, or perhaps Jules's parents, who wanted to do away with me.

"That is what Marcel and Arc and Emilie's husband and I do. One of the things we do," she whispered. "Help people get from where they are to where they or their loved ones wish them to be. Escape."

"Escape where?" I asked, breathlessly.

"Anywhere," she said more firmly. "To another owner. Then you are protected when bounty hunters come looking for you, trying to return you to the owner you've left. For the new owners have paid a lower sum for you, but still don't want to lose their money, as they have no protection for money lost in the illegal buying of escapees and refugees."

She was losing me with these details that sounded like talk around Jules's parents' table when visitors came in evening dress. I shook my head to clear it.

Yasmine said, "Or you can escape to a kind of freedom. Only, it is much harder to keep. We might get you to an island where people speak French, and you would not feel quite so lost. Or across the colony into the heart of America. Along the way, you might speak with few, for most of them speak English between here and there, I'm afraid. But once there, in the heartland, you would have a community in which to rebuild your life. Either way, though, freedom is more perilous for a young girl alone."

I repeated dumbly, "More perilous?" remembering the American woman at the inn who had followed me and berated me.

Yasmine smiled. "I think you might be safer with another slaveholder who won't want to lose his money by killing you, as *Monsieur* Roger can afford to do."

My heart leapt at her words. "You could get me back to Jules!"

Yasmine's steady eyes held mine, but she said nothing.

When I, too, stared without saying anything, she shook her head. "You just won't understand, will you, Aurelie? Your *Monsieur* Jules is not here. If you wait for him to return, who knows what condition you will be in? Look at you. You are not learning to make the best of your situation."

"But if I wait for him, you could get us away together?" I insisted as the room clarified around me, the slivers of green and gold and black in Yasmine's eyes becoming sharply outlined in jagged strokes. The world was coming back to me. Hope would make me sane. I could feel it.

Yasmine said evenly, "It isn't I who help people escape, *Mademoiselle* Aurelie. The man who does it doesn't trust Frenchmen very much. I'm not at all sure he would help Jules escape with you."

"Who is this man?" I persisted. "Perhaps I can talk with him." My mind continued to sharpen more quickly than I could keep pace with its rapid thoughts. "Is it Arc?" I asked with sudden insight. "Is he the one who helps people escape?"

"How you throw around other people's names! No, it is not Arc. He only does what this man tells him to do, including fetching you today from the home of the man who was beating you to death. African and European men alike do what this man wants them to do, because they do not always know that what they are doing is his idea. They think they are deciding. They think they are acting to please someone they love, or someone who owns them. Arc is nothing but a man who thinks he took an interest in you because his wife wept for you."

Yasmine leaned close to me and seized my arms in a grip that pinched. I felt my fists swell with the stopped blood. She yanked me close. "See here, *Mademoiselle*," she hissed. "It is time you learned that some people want to live in comfort, without fear, and even if they help you, those people don't want you blabbing. Craziness is no excuse."

Yasmine sat back from me. "I don't want to die for a bunch of strangers who want to go from one danger to another. But I am risking my life talking to you because I know you, and I would have loved you if things had been different. But because I know you, I know you cannot be trusted. You think your craziness excuses all things. It does not, *Mademoiselle* Aurelie."

Suddenly, Yasmine released one of my wrists and used her free hand to soundly slap my face. It stung. I stared at her, dumfounded. What had I said to deserve that? My ears kept up a steady, dizzying hum as she continued to speak.

"Remember this, *petite*. Should you confide in anyone, even my own daughters, or excuse yourself in a moment of madness to blab to anyone, even Celeste, someone will find you and kill you for it, and there will be nothing I can do to prevent it. And there will be your *Monsieur* Jules, back from his travels and waiting for you, watching for you, wishing to escape with you. But you will be a crumpled body in an alley, being eaten by rats and wild dogs before you can be found and dumped in a pagans' burial ditch."

I said, "But *Monsieur* Roger would never have me dumped in a pagans' pit. He would have me buried in the ground consecrated for enslaved Christians."

Yasmine laughed. "So be it, *petite*. I will do everything I can for you because I love you. Yes, I do. God pity me, for Marcel will not. And when you are off on an island where African men rule and African women wear jewels and attend balls to find husbands, not lifelong lovers, remember that I did this for you. For you."

Yasmine, holding both my wrists again, pulled me closer. Our noses touched. She said, "And would you even care if any little thing went awry, and I was killed for you? Maimed, for you? Bah! You don't even think of your own half-blinded mother, *Mademoiselle* Aurelie."

She shoved me away and rising, knocked the bowl of bloodied mint water to the stone floor. She turned and stared at it, surprised, but left it there as she turned back to me. "Three months nursing you through illness and madness, and not once did you call for your *Tante* Clothilde. But your *Monsieur* Jules? Bah," she spat. And as Yasmine left the room, rushing so that her skirt pulled the chair she had leapt from, it toppled.

I sat up and kicked at the spilled water with the cloth slippers someone had slipped onto my feet before bringing me here. I recognized them from the wardrobe at *Monsieur* Roger's. I watched the bloody water seep and dry into the stones, unable to edge it further to wash away Yasmine's phlegm.

Was I to be blamed for having placed all my hope in Jules, all my life?

If it was wrong to call out for him when I had also lost my mother and child, then surely it was only fair to remember that it was that same mother who had taught me to believe that Jules would be my salvation, someday.

Yasmine returned with me to *Monsieur* Roger's when his carriage came that night to fetch me.

I asked her anxiously, "Didn't you say your husband does not want you to go there?" But she was well past speaking with me.

She turned her head away and said nothing until we arrived, rattling to a stop before the rear door that opened across from the stables.

As we descended the carriage steps and ascended the few steps to the mansion's back doorway, Yasmine murmured to me, "Say nothing. If you can, keep your eyes down and only look up to smile at him. He is still your owner, and you have been an unforgivable fool."

Alain opened the back door and, smiling and sweeping us a bow as though we were guests calling at the front entrance, ushered us into the *Monsieur*'s sitting room. As our eyes fell upon him, brooding in a chair by a small table set with a chess game, I urged a smile to tremble its way across my lips.

How I hate this man.

Yasmine said, "It was wise of you to send for me, *Monsieur*. My husband has excused me to stay and help you with the *Mademoiselle*."

Monsieur Roger interrupted. "I still own your husband, Yasmine. Spare me speeches. Tell me, how is she? Is there hope for her senses?"

Yasmine said simply, "There is always hope, *Monsieur*. At least, this is what the priests tell me."

Monsieur Roger's head snapped up to fix a gaze on her, but she had taken my arm and was steering me from the room. Alain's head bowed as we walked by him.

Back in my rooms-left only that morning?-Yasmine relented and grew tender as she undressed me. Only when I was swathed in one of the full cotton nightgowns that I had grown to detest for their itchy stiffness did she embrace me.

288

After a while, I pushed her away and untied the ribbons and slid off the hated gown. I climbed into my bed and threw back the covers, holding out my arms to her. "I want to know I'm loved," I said and hoped it would be enough for her.

And later, much later, after we had slept in each other's arms, I woke and remembered Jules and the terror and the dread and the pain, and I felt I might begin to take it all in. But I could not, would never, let him go. I promised myself.

I woke again to find *Monsieur* Roger at the door, watching us. "You have aristocratic tastes for forbidden pleasures, it seems," he said.

Yasmine must have wakened when I did, for now she laughed in his face as though she thought he might be joking. "*Monsieur,* you know better than anyone the pleasure of what is forbidden." He hesitated, staring at us as though he could not make up his mind what to think.

Eventually, the candle he held decided him. When its hot wax dripped and burned his fingers, he dropped it, and it snuffed out.

In the darkness, I heard the rustle of his clothes as he discarded them and felt the weight of his body ease onto my small bed. Thankfully, he crawled into Yasmine's arms, and I had only to turn my back on them.

Celeste, coming in to help me wash and dress in the morning, would not look at them, where they slept next to me. I, too, refused to look at them and said nothing about them, as though they were not there.

After that night, Yasmine moved into *Monsieur* Roger's rooms and devoted herself to his comfort and happiness and the running of his household. Within days, I could see why he had kept her so long and put off marrying a European woman who could have given him legal heirs. Yasmine must have been for *Monsieur* Roger like opium was for me.

She anticipated his every wish. The house was a smooth machine of comfort, elegance and ease. Every night, Yasmine seduced *Monsieur* Roger away from his chessboard and papers and pipe and into his bed, as if the desires that must be satisfied there were her own, not his. His home was a dream away from the real world outside.

Sometimes she left him, when he slept, to return to me. "You know, *chere,* I will leave you two soon, and you must watch me carefully so you can do what I do, when I am gone."

"No, you cannot leave, Yasmine! I am content. *Monsieur* is content. You must stay!"

"I must go or *Monsieur* will send you away before it is your time. You know what I mean. So you must watch carefully and bide your time until *he* has come for you."

"But don't you want to stay, Yasmine?" I demanded peevishly. I waved my hand feebly in the dark. "Don't you want all this back? To be *Monsieur's* mistress, like a wealthy freewoman? Stay, Yasmine. I will go. I don't mind. And when Jules comes, you will help him find me, wherever I have gone."

Yasmine kissed my forehead. "You are such an innocent. Now sleep, so I can go back to the *Monsieur* before he wakes alone and becomes angry with me." I held her close as I drifted to sleep. I could not be close enough to her because, besides loving me-which I needed desperately right now-she also knew and was a constant reminder of my secret knowledge that someday Jules and I would have our chance, while I fended *Monsieur* off, telling him in my mind, *Not yet. You see how I cling to Yasmine. I am not well enough to let her go yet.*

And then came the morning that she left.

I woke when I heard arguing and pleading at the stairway from the *Monsieur*'s rooms. I rushed down the short flight from my rooms to the second-floor landing to intercept Yasmine.

I don't know from where she had materialized the beautiful gowns she'd been wearing, but she had on another exquisite creation in bronze and indigo stripes, belted with satin ribbon at the waist that matched the ties restraining her abundant hair. She was a vision of elegance.

I stopped short of grabbing her arm as she rushed for the stairway. *Monsieur* Roger shouted behind her, "You cannot go until I release you."

When she saw me, Yasmine faltered and then turned back to insist to him, "You do not own me anymore, *Monsieur*. You do not tell me when to come and go, but only if I am welcome in your house."

He caught her arm and turned her to face him. "I still own your husband," he said. "Don't push me."

She freed herself of him only to rush straight into my arms. "Don't go, Yasmine," I begged. "Please. We both need you."

Yasmine's face crumpled. "Aurelie, if I don't go now, I will never go," she said and pushed past me.

I chased after her, calling, "Then never go!"

She turned with tears streaming down her face. "You understand nothing," she said angrily. "You frustrate me. It is impossible to help you, for you will not help yourself. You will be sent away, you fool, and all your silly dreams will be nothing, if I stay."

I murmured urgently, trying to remind her, "No! Jules will find me, wherever I am sold away."

Yasmine groaned and shoved her way to the bottom of the stairs and to the foyer, leaving *Monsieur* to yell from the second-floor landing, behind her, "I have not given you permission to go, Yasmine!"

Alone together in the dark foyer, where only I had followed her, Yasmine turned and held my arms. "Listen to me. Can you bear another abortion? I thought not. Stay and make the *Monsieur* content, as you have seen me do. And if you ever escape with your Jules, I promise you I will return in an instant, to take Roger's mind off you and keep him from pursuing you."

I stared after her until Alain came and asked me, "Shall I call Celeste to attend you?"

I stumbled to the stairway and sank to the top step. So it was now. No more madness.

The day dragged through my mire of revulsion. Everything, every cup of tea or coffee, every bite of bread, every ticking and chiming of a clock, every flicker of anyone's eyelid, announced the oncoming night. I could bear it because it would not last, and my bearing it would blind *Monsieur* Roger. I bore it.

Without madness, without escaping to the memories of the inn, I bore the body that became mine and closer than mine and held him when he told me to, and looked into his eyes and did not show him how I felt.

"You don't love me," *Monsieur* Roger would say, panting, staring, pressing me with his weight and his need.

"No, *Monsieur,*" I answered.

"Damn you. Damn you. Damn you," was his cry of release.

It kept us apart in the throes of a despised intimacy. He did not know how to bring us together. Nor did I.

Monsieur began to take me out upon the town.

It was a little scandal. Frenchmen took enslaved mistresses only certain places. It was understood. But *Monsieur* began to take me places that Frenchwomen of the highest rank yearned to go.

I saw their eyes fix on me, bore into me, glide away, sweeping with them the image of my gowns, my hair, the jewels that pinned the hated turban there, for no matter how the turban was beautiful, I kept dear to my heart the belief that my hair was only covered because it was more thick, more rippled and wild, than the tame tresses of Frenchwomen. As we went out upon the town, the night became my refuge from myself.

I learned to drink. I learned to smoke the fragrant herbs that made men laugh and women sleep in expensive salons where the very walls were draped in carpets *Monsieur* said cost more than a household of Africans.

And I came to love storms.

I leaned from my balcony, rained and thundered upon, grasping the wrought iron, screaming for the lightning to strike me if it dared, for I did not fear it.

I even came to love the memory of my dead baby, reliving its stillbirth nightly, seeing again its kittenish size, its skinned appearance, the bloody phlegm that coated it from spiky head to curling toes.

Monsieur Roger beat a Frenchman in the street who called me a whore one night, coming out of a restaurant, rushing to get into our carriage because he was running up to us.

Monsieur beat him with his cane, and as the man fell in his workman's clothes into the gutter at *Monsieur*'s feet, he continued to raise and whip down the cane upon the man's back and thighs, as he twisted to get away.

Jacques helped me into the carriage and closed the door, standing guard.

The man was going to roll over and beg *Monsieur* Roger's pardon, I could tell. But *Monsieur* Roger could not. Or he did not care. And as the cane drove toward the man's face, I screamed at *Monsieur* Roger to stop. "Please stop, for pity's sake!"

Monsieur raised his head to me. Saw me. Came back to himself, aiming the man a savage kick that might have cracked a rib. I heard the muffled snap of something breaking deep inside the wrapped muscles of his body.

As the carriage jolted away, I said, "Let us not go out upon the town anymore, *Monsieur*. I no longer enjoy it."

Monsieur Roger reached for my hand in the dark, and I was amazed that his hand was warm and dry on mine. Not coated with the blood he had just sprayed across the *banquette*.

"It will not happen again," he said. "I promise you."

"For I will not venture out again," I answered. "Please don't force me, *Monsieur*. Give me this."

He said gently, "I hope to give you more, Aurelie."

I thought, *What more there is, you cannot give me.* But I did not say it.

CHAPTER THIRTEEN
SACRED NIGHT OF MIRACLES

At first, the *Monsieur* seemed pleased that I no longer wished to go about the city with him, neither at night nor to the shops.

But after a while, bringing in his gifts of soaps, perfumes, chocolates, and the heavy, sweet tobacco that made life a dream and dreams real, to draw my interest to the new autumn-colored satins and laces, he grew concerned.

"Is it the man?" Roger asked. "The man who insulted you? I have dealt with him. Word will get around, and others will think twice."

There was another reason, but I could not tell it to *Monsieur* Roger.

After the evening when the man was beaten, when I simply had no taste for going out, Celeste, returning an aired gown to my wardrobe, remarked, "Staying in tonight? Well, I told my Alain that it is just as well if you do. What are we going to do when you and the *Monsieur* run into ... " As her voice trailed away, I knew what she would not tell me.

Jules was back, and everyone else had lived in fear that we might meet while I was out with *Monsieur* Roger.

It was this revelation from Celeste that returned me to the ballroom. Now, there was no more fear of the stillness or the darkness that sucked and pulled from its center or peeked through the repaired window pane. There was only the memory that

296

Jules had come when the sisters and I met our ideal lovers, and though he was hurt and angry, he was there. He could come again.

I was there, in the ballroom, feeling the wisps of Jules's presence drift through my arms, always on his way back to some other world where I could not follow, when the revelers hit the streets for All Hallows' Eve.

Roger collected for me bits of a costume from trunks storing wondrous old clothes. So I wore a mask of gilded lace and pearls, a golden and scarlet satin gown with matching scarlet slippers that teetered on heels under the arch of each foot, and a high tiara of real gold from which my hair kept tumbling, for neither Celeste nor I could control it. And I danced alone in the center of the ballroom floor, for still *Monsieur* Roger would not allow his daughters to come back home and visit me.

Jules was out there, so near. I embraced the emptiness as if it could destroy my longings.

As I turned, I saw from the corner of my eye that *Monsieur* Roger leaned on the doorframe in the entryway. Sticky sweet smoke wound in and out of the locks of his hair. He did not approach.

I began to hum the tune I had learned from the frescoes, when they used to sing for me. Now, faintly, their tentative voices whispered into harmony with mine and filled out the melody.

Monsieur Roger broke the spell. "Where did you learn that tune?" The voices faded and were gone. My dance dragged to a halt.

I dropped my arms and turned to him.

297

I had lit a few wall sconces, circling the room with my candelabrum when I first entered. His face avoided their light. Staring from the center of the room, it seemed almost as if a brighter light shone from behind him, though I could not guess its source.

"The room taught it to me," I said, and even from my distance, I could hear his sigh.

He pushed himself off from the doorframe and came toward me, stepping on his tossed hand-rolled cigarette. "Why do you do that?" he said.

"Do what, *Monsieur*?"

"Say things that cannot possibly be, just when you look so heavenly sweet, so tasty and-I never know what to think."

"Neither do I, *Monsieur*."

'You look beautiful, Aurelie. Do you like your costume?" He smiled at me.

"Yes. Thank you, *Monsieur*."

"Why don't you want to go out with me tonight, *ma chere*?"

"I never want to go out anymore, *Monsieur*."

"I know." He reached me at last and touching me, as if to make sure I would not startle and move away, said, "But this is different."

And though I had many other things in mind to say, now that *Monsieur* Roger's chest came against my cheek and his arms took me into their warmth, I put my head to the intimate thump of his heart and, shuddering, clung to him.

"What is it?" he insisted.

"This is the night I ran away with Jules, and it all began. We ran to the inn. I was so frightened. I didn't know where we were going, and there were dogs eating glass in the street, and beggars and demons and urine in the wine. I wanted to go back home, I truly did, but Jules-"

The story came out. Though he paled and shook his head, saying, "No. I never thought ... " and flushed sometimes, his high cheekbones reddening even as the color drained from his long, grooved cheeks, though we moved from room to room, and he carried me, when he could take no more, to a balcony I didn't know the ballroom had, where we watched costumed devils and priests, wine gods and princesses making love between the bonfires lit in the street below, and even though he swept me up and carried me again, this time to his bedroom, hoping to make love and then turning from me, shaking his head instead, *Monsieur* Roger listened for hours.

"Did you always love him, then?"

"Always, *Monsieur*."

"You are like a loyal dog. I have always thought so."

"You can't insult my love for Jules, *Monsieur*."

"Even if he is your brother?"

"I don't believe it, *Monsieur*."

"Did he believe it?"

"Maybe. Sometimes. But I don't think he cared, *Monsieur*."

"Do you care, Aurelie, if you are Jules's sister?"

"I care only that I am the woman he loves, *Monsieur*."

Monsieur Roger blinked and pulled away, his hand moving from my bared thigh across the satin

299

coverlet of his bed to fold in his own lap with his other hand.

I argued, "I have heard that there are owners who prefer to breed brothers and sisters, to bring out the best traits in a family, *Monsieur*."

"Enough," *Monsieur* Roger said. Then, "Do you think he still loves you?" he whispered.

"Yes, *Monsieur*."

"Why do you think so?"

"The swamp witch said it would be so, *Monsieur*."

"Tell me about her."

"It is too soon, *Monsieur*. I cannot talk about her."

"Tell me something else about the inn, then."

"Only the first night. For this is the anniversary of that night, *Monsieur* Roger."

"Did you make love?"

"Not that night, *Monsieur*."

He sighed, as if relieved, and reached for my thigh again.

When there was nothing more to say about that first night, and gray lightened the dark blue drapes of *Monsieur* Roger's windows, and we had held each other and murmured about unimportant things and still we couldn't sleep, sweating in my costume and his dinner clothes, he undressed us both, and we made love.

I woke screaming in the dawn's soft light, crying out for someone to come and help me.

"What is it?" *Monsieur* Roger demanded. He had twisted to put his arms around me. When that did no good, he shook me until I was fully awake.

But I couldn't tell him that the face that rose this time in my dream from kissing and lapping at the blood at the grandmother's neck was Jules's own.

Not his brother. I was sick with terror and yet with longing, too, to be the body that Jules clutched with such desire and tenderness.

I held onto *Monsieur* Roger and trembled, afraid to sleep again. *Monsieur* held me and kissed my forehead and assured me that no one could hurt me now.

And this was how we lived through that time of memories that seized me because of the chiming of cathedral bells, or the smell of croissant rolls at breakfast, or the graying of the morning that is fall, or the first twinge of cold that says the seasons have changed again, or even the careless laughter of a freewoman passing in the street.

I had never finished reading Jules's poems, and it came to me that I must find the lost volume of his poetry. I must know what he had written to me. Maybe the nightmares would stop, and with them, the yearning. *There is something vital in there. I know it.*

I begged *Monsieur* Roger at dinner one night for the lost poems. "*Monsieur*, ask his parents what became of the book he had bound for me."

"I cannot do that."

"Why not, *Monsieur*? You are a rich and powerful man. What do you care about the law?"

"No one is above the law, Aurelie, particularly not this damnable American law. They throw everyone into jail. They execute everyone else by firing squad. But I do not speak with Jules's parents anymore."

"Do not speak with them, then, *Monsieur*. Ask for me. Say it is mine, and I have a right to it. *Monsieur*"-but I could not say his name aloud to my new owner-"owned me when he gave it to me. Does that mean nothing?"

"Aurelie, leave it alone. I could command you to do as I say, but I'm begging you."

I was stunned but persisted. "And, *Monsieur,* I'm begging you to help me get that volume back, for Christmas. It was given to me for Christmas."

"Why do you need it?"

"*Monsieur,* I don't know anything except that I must have it. There is something in it I must see."

"You are not supposed to be able to read."

"Then you can read it to me, *Monsieur.*"

"I will not!"

"You can read it *for* me, *Monsieur.*" I would find a way to steal it away and read it to myself.

At that, *Monsieur* Roger relented. "I will see what I can do," he said at last and raised a hand to ward off my thanks.

We no longer fought. I no longer screamed from my balcony or welcomed storms to my uncovered breast. I had no rage left, and *Monsieur* Roger seemed satisfied with me, after all.

Except when I needed, at night, to talk about the inn so that I could fall sleep.

"And even when Jules was gone from the inn at night with his friends, you did not think to leave and go home?" *Monsieur* Roger asked me one night, frustrated.

"No. I would not have left him, *Monsieur*." *I did not know the way home.*

"And even once you saw me watching you through the window, and you knew I was concerned, and Arc brought you my messages telling you that you had another friend, you still would not leave him?"

I was more afraid of you than of Jules. "We have not come to those days, yet, in my stories, *Monsieur*. It is not even Yule, yet. First, there were whores. You could see their lovers press their naked backs to the windows of their rooms while they made love, making sure everyone passing the inn knew that these women would do anything, in any way, to please them."

"*Monsieur* Jules made you visit them? Whores? And still you loved him, Aurelie? Why?"

"Because he was who he was, *Monsieur*. Jules was my life and my hope for a better life."

"And so you loved him, no matter what he did to you."

"Yes, *Monsieur*." *I still love him. And I don't love you.*

But he never asked this. And still the tales went on.

In between the words, the pictures that our talks fleshed out, were the sensitive moments of coming together to see who we were to each other, and what we could reclaim of all we'd never really had together. Perhaps *Monsieur* Roger was simply too proud to send again for Yasmine.

I thought often of Yasmine, of her daughters' freedom, and of the swamp witch in her cozy shack

303

filled to overflowing with her gaudy prizes, such as my beautiful Easter dress. How had these women gotten what they most wanted out of life?

For I knew that Yasmine most wanted her children's freedom, as I had wanted mine. And I could guess that the swamp witch wanted her shack, her gewgaws, her power over wealthy men such as Jules's father. And perhaps she also wanted the silent, strong man with the river of black hair who had helped her tend me.

What had she said to me? *Sacrifice,* as I kissed my dead baby.

This is why I wanted to see Yasmine: to ask her what she had sacrificed to get her daughters' freedom, when other adult children freed by their slaveowning fathers were slaughtered by the invading American military. I guessed Yasmine had sacrificed being mistress of *Monsieur* Roger's home and heart.

I would never know what the swamp witch might have sacrificed. But she had made me sacrifice my baby. And what had I asked for in return? I tried to remember. Jules? Or his love, only? What if he loved me from a distance, as I now loved him? Was that all that my suffering and sacrifice could bring us?

And though it made no sense, I began to feel that, since the shadow that had watched and the hand that had paid for our lodgings and sent me food on Arc's tray had been *Monsieur* Roger's, to welcome him into my arms and my heart was to reach out to what I could still touch of my time and my dreams with Jules.

Monsieur Roger, his sweat and mine mingling on our faces, said, "You make love to me as if you've never loved anyone else. I don't think you know what love is. You love me, and you don't know it, Aurelie." Mouths shut on kisses to open again on cries of anguish, the rupture of aloneness, and the kind of pleasure that follows too much pain.

I would give *Monsieur* Roger a Christmas gift that would make him as much Jules as he could be to me. This was our child that I now carried: Jules's because he had my heart, *Monsieur* Roger's because he had my body, Yasmine's because I wanted to be like her, and mine because I was trapped being myself.

On Christmas Eve, *Monsieur* Roger and I sat over goose and plum sauce. I asked through the candles if *Monsieur* Roger knew for certain that Alain had delivered a roast turkey to Else and Arc, the simple satin gowns I had ordered to his daughters, and my own lovely burgundy velvet gown to Yasmine.

"They have been delivered," *Monsieur* Roger said distractedly. "Don't bother me about them, Aurelie."

"Will we share our gifts to each other after dinner?" I asked. "You could light the Yule log tomorrow, if you wish."

"Lighting the Yule log half a day late is for those too poor to find one on Christmas Eve."

We had grown unused to arguing, so "As you like, *Monsieur*," I said gently and reached for his hand.

He stared into my eyes. "Why do you really want the book, Aurelie?" he asked.

No point lying. "How can you ask, *Monsieur*? I have dreams I cannot tell you about, they would shock you so. Do you want to hear again how crazy I feel, *Monsieur*?"

He looked away. "No. No, I don't."

We rose to burn the Yule log and open gifts in the parlor. But there was a knock at the door.

Alain entered as the log flared to say, "*Monsieur* Jules."

And there he was.

It had not been so long-less than a year-and yet I would not have known him upon the street. I suppose I can only say I had forgotten. How I could have forgotten, I don't know. This was certainly not the man I had seen in the ballroom.

He was older, taller, more stooped. Gray had drained his face of hope. Purple rose beneath the pallor, as if in response to the evening's cold and mist. Black rimmed his eyes and curled itself about the line of silver in his hair.

I would never have spoken to him, in passing, nor followed him home. And yet, staring into his eyes, I could see clearly that he was my very own Jules.

His eyes held mine. And was it just a look, left from the past months' suffering? Or were his eyes actually pleading with me?

"*Joyeux Noël,*" Jules said from where he stood in the doorway with a package wrapped in plain paper. "May I come in?"

Monsieur Roger was dumbstruck. So it fell to me to be the sole voice that said, "Please, *Monsieur* Jules."

"*Monsieur* Roger, I believed that *Madame* would want a copy of this little book of poems," Jules said. "I flattered myself that I might be allowed to deliver it in person, as a Christmas gift"- bowing-"as it is not yet available in the bookstore. Excuse me if I am mistaken in inviting myself."

I rushed to assure him, "You are not mistaken, *Maitre* Jules," and wondered immediately why I had used the offensive title of "Master," the crux of our argument so long ago.

At this, Jules straightened and, looking only at *Monsieur* Roger, said, "*Monsieur*, may I present my little book to the mistress?"

Again I said, "Please, *Monsieur* Jules," and held out my hand where I sat.

Jules bowed again, this time toward *Monsieur* Roger, and straightening, came toward me quickly and was gone even more quickly. He backed up to the threshold of the room without bothering to turn away.

When he was out of reach again, the plain package, tied with coarse paper ribbon, lay on my lap, and his words and the breath that had carried them to me still lingered on my ear: "The wrapping paper."

I couldn't lower my eyes from his face to consider the paper and what he meant about it. But *Monsieur* Roger finally spoke. "You *dare*. You damnable upstart, you *dare* come into my home and speak to her!" he roared.

Jules snapped to attention. "I see, *Monsieur*, that I have acted wrongly. Allow me to apologize, and on the occasion of my wedding in the morning, to say only that I wish you both well, with all my heart, and am sorry that my impetuosity so sorely hampered your acquisition of your property, *Monsieur* Roger. My father has explained that you had long expressed an interest in *Madame* Aurelie and even made your down payment, some months before. What I did was steal from you and from my father, *Monsieur*. I recognize now that my behavior was inexcusable."

Monsieur Roger, mollified only a little, raised his head with pride. "Yes, I had made a generous down payment for her, to get your father out of debts he dared not share with his wife." I gasped at *Monsieur* Roger's deliberate rudeness. *Is he trying to provoke Jules to a duel of honor?*

When Jules refused to be baited, *Monsieur* Roger continued. "My intentions toward Aurelie had long been recognized by your father, *Monsieur* Jules."

"And yet," Jules began but did not finish his opposing thought. He snapped, instead, into another bow, and without having glanced at me again, was gone.

I heard the front door close on Alain's hearty Yuletide greeting.

Trembling, the breath knocked out of me, I rose, clutching my gift to the gift I had not announced to *Monsieur* Roger, after all.

"I am unwell, *Monsieur,*" I said to *Monsieur* Roger, who had not asked me how I felt. "I must go to my rooms."

Monsieur Roger still said nothing and did not offer me his arm.

As I passed through the doorway where Jules's faint cologne lingered, *Monsieur* Roger said, "I will come to you, when you've had time to collect yourself."

So used had we grown to treating each other gently that I said, "Of course, *Monsieur,*" without pausing to reflect on Jules's message and its meaning.

I unwrapped the package as I lay on my bed in the cream-colored silk I had worn for Christmas Eve.

Jules had said, "The wrapping paper." So I peeled it cautiously away, checking for a note to fall out of it. There was none. I lifted away the precious booklet and caught my breath at the sight of the familiar binding. This was it, the book Jules gave me just last Christmas, handwritten and bound as a gift for my eyes, before all others.

My hands trembled and my breath came in spasms in my chest. I ran my fingers over the familiar cover, once so hated. Could I possibly bear to look at the words? *No. Not yet.*

It was when I reached for the paper, to wrap up the book again, that I noticed the ink scrawls inside it.

I snatched it up, dropping the book, and read what Jules had written in the wrapping.

Midnight Mass at the Cathedral. Come with Yasmine when she calls for you. Tell Roger you feel the need for prayer. If you cannot go at midnight, I will wait there for you until morning. Search the steps. If Roger insists on coming to Mass with you, it is no matter. We will get away. I will always love you. Jules.

I balled the wrapping in my hand and, leaping from the bed, tucked it into the fire in my room's small neat fireplace just as Celeste let in *Monsieur* Roger.

He searched my face. "Are you all right?"

"How could I be, *Monsieur*?"

He dropped his head.

"*Monsieur* Roger." *I need to be alone. I feel ill. Just go away.* I returned to my bed and stretched out upon it.

"Should I read to you?" *Monsieur* Roger reached for the book of Jules's poems and sat down on a chair beside my bed.

"Please don't, *Monsieur*." I closed my eyes while he read to himself. *I cannot go to Jules, like this. But I cannot stay here, if he wants me.*

Somewhere in the long nights, moist with shared cries and the whispered breath of my stories and his questions, *Monsieur* Roger had become a part of the relationship I'd shared with Jules at the inn. He had stopped the flow of picture memories with questions that almost seemed to have come from my own mind. "Why was Jules angry with you, Aurelie? What had you done that could possibly displease him?" *Monsieur* Roger sided with me and drew too many secrets from me.

There was very little *Monsieur* Roger didn't know, up to the anniversary of each passing day, as well as I could reconstruct that day's events. "Why were you afraid of the sword?"

That was our first night, when shortly before dawn I tearfully confided, "*Monsieur,* Jules had killed his brother, protecting me. No one knows but us, and it haunts him. Please don't tell his parents."

Roger had said only, "I see." But now, I worried, knowing everything, what would *Monsieur* Roger do, how would he react, if I betrayed him and disappeared?

Worse, what would become of me if I went to Jules tonight, and he did not want me?

If Jules tired of me, as Roger had tired of Emilie and Yasmine, before me-but no. Why would I think such a thought? *Because Jules kept me with prostitutes, and Monsieur Roger beat a man bloody for only calling me a whore.*

And Jules said he will be married in the morning.

Everything had shifted and blended. I wanted Jules. But did I want to leave the safety of my new truce with *Monsieur* Roger, who could send gendarmes after us? What had he reminded Jules tonight? *Stolen property.* He could tell Jules's parents and the authorities that Jules had killed his brother. *And drunk his blood.*

No. Even in the throes of my night terrors, I had not told *Monsieur* Roger about that.

But the child? *He doesn't know about that, either. Unless Yasmine has told him. Surely, that's what she meant when she left.*

But it was one thing to tell myself-and someday, perhaps, *Monsieur* Roger-that this was the child of the four of us, his and mine, his lover's and my lover's. But how to tell Jules that I now carried *Monsieur* Roger's child, when his own lay rotting to bones in a swamp?

Jules will want to kill Roger's child, as Roger was the reason Jules's parents had our child killed. Or maybe he will sell Roger's child, to humiliate him. To bring him down to the level of an American, with his flesh and blood sold into slavery, for money.

It occurred to me that, just as I would never have recognized this new, mature and bitter Jules on the street, I also did not know his mind. *Can I bear to lose another child?*

I turned my back to Roger and buried my face in the bedclothes. Reality and hope had met and gone their separate ways. And here was I, left behind.

Monsieur Roger put his hand on my back. "Yasmine has come to wish you a joyous Noel. I should have told you sooner, but you seemed so agitated. Should I send her away?"

I sat up. "Please send her up here, and let us visit alone, *Monsieur*. I don't want you to see me like this."

"She doesn't have time for a long visit. She said she is on her way to Midnight Mass."

I stood, swaying, and reached for my silk shawl of that long-ago shopping spree with *Monsieur* Roger's daughters. "I will hurry down to her, then, *Monsieur*."

Roger followed me.

I thought as we descended, my hand on the rail, his eyes boring into my back so that I shivered with anxiety and rebellion, *Maybe Jules will want me, with Roger's child. Roger saw me at the inn and wanted me, with Jules's child.*

But was it in fact *Monsieur* Roger who had my baby taken from me? Or was it Jules's father and mother?

If only I could think clearly. I could perhaps figure this out.

But *Monsieur* Roger and I had not come to that part of my story yet, in our nightly talks about the inn, and the clarity I got with telling Roger, despite his displeasure and my torment in the telling, had not come yet to the loss of the baby.

Yasmine, elegant and poised in a brocade chair, rose so that I might admire the velvet gown I had sent her. She happened to have a silk cloth of a remarkably similar shade to wind as a turban, and we exclaimed together over the perfection of the accidental match, for I had forgotten to include a scarf or name of the dressmaker where I'd ordered the dress, along with the gown. This was sometimes an unforgivable oversight among freewomen.

"All one needs is to be frantic to wear a new gown on Christmas Eve, and yet unable, for lack of a match. Of course, some freewomen keep a length of black or white lace, just in case," Yasmine had explained to me when I sent gifts to her daughters. Not being free, myself, I would have been excused by most women for not knowing, Yasmine explained. But it was best to know these unspoken rules of polite behavior.

Now she amazed me by chattering about how, "Gown-giving is so rare and generous, these days, what with the Americans taxing everyone into poverty. Except of course among near-relations, as we are to each other. You have even given gowns to my daughters, as well! In satin! Your generosity shall be legendary, in the city. And the colors?"

I described the dresses.

"You remembered each daughter's preferred colors? So thoughtful! And speaking of thoughtfulness, *Monsieur* Roger's allowances to you will soon be the envy of all the city, the talk of both freewomen and French, for you must not forget that he is considered quite a catch among his countrywomen, though now that he has paraded you among them, I fear they have quite despaired. Perhaps the *Monsieur* is a rogue and will never marry," Yasmine said to me with a husky loud whisper and a wicked wink.

Monsieur Roger relaxed and opened the volume of poetry again. His face had begun to darken and cloud by the time the cathedral chimes called the faithful to Midnight Mass.

"Midnight Mass!" Yasmine said. "I must go, *Madame* Aurelie. I hope my daughters will meet me there. Oh, I hate to walk alone, even on such a holy night. One never knows." She rose and wrapped her dark shawl about her shoulders.

There was no time to think. Not since Jules had arrived and placed the book in my hand.

I said, "Oh, *ma chere amie,* let me go with you! It will be so good to get fresh air. *Monsieur* Roger, may we walk together? Please do not call the carriage."

But I had said too much. For not only did *Monsieur* Roger allow my outing. With that much enthusiasm, he said he could not resist inviting himself along.

As he swept my cloak about me, confusion fell among us. "That is not my cloak," I said, pulling it off and studying it thoughtfully. It was black satin, lined with burgundy wool inside. But it looked familiar. I extended it toward Yasmine. "Perhaps it is yours?" I suggested.

Yasmine tilted her head in sympathy. "*Pauvre chere,*" she said. "No, it is not mine."

Roger said, "It is yours, Aurelie," and the confusion faded in blinding, humiliating clarity. I had been thinking of the cloak at the inn, chocolate-colored, Jules's gift. Of course, this was newer, and it was certainly mine.

I pulled it back on.

We walked quickly through the streets as Yasmine assured us there was no time to ready the carriage. The mist that had purpled Jules's sallow skin had thickened into icy drizzle. We were soon bitterly cold. "Not a good night to choose to walk," *Monsieur* Roger commented to Yasmine, no doubt hoping she would relent and turn back. But she had her head bent and swept onward.

All the while we walked, she looked furtively from side to side, quickly up each cross street that we passed, sometimes behind us. "You are unused

315

to being free, Yasmine," Roger called to her. "You have become a nervous person."

And this time Yasmine panted, "Perhaps, *Monsieur*," hurrying on so that I skipped steps now to catch her.

So caught up was I in her headlong race that I did not see him until I raised my head as we ascended the cathedral steps, and for a split second, there he was, watching me.

He seemed about to extend to me his hand, come toward me to escort me inside-a dream was coming true! Had I not dreamed of entering a cathedral with Jules?-when he turned from us and was suddenly gone.

I looked over at *Monsieur* Roger, who was just now looking up. He studied the steps, squinting against the fattening slivers of rain, and then turned his head to gaze at me.

I followed Yasmine through the doorway into the vestibule and dipped my right hand into the fount, touching the holy water to my forehead, my heart, my left shoulder, my right. My lips.

As I kissed the blessing, my eyes shifted to a shadow and caught a glimpse of Jules, waiting. He blew me a kiss, and, startled, I dropped my fingers slightly so that my blessing flew to him. *Oh, sacred night of miracles, so like that night of resurrected souls!*

"Up this way," Yasmine said and tugged me toward the steep stairs that wound to the gallery.

Already the shadow whose face was Jules had disappeared again. *Monsieur* Roger came to the bottom of the steps and, biting his lip, seized my free wrist. "You don't have to go up there, Aurelie," he said. "Keep your face cloaked, and no one will dare say a word to me, if you follow me into the church to sit with the French and Americans."

"I will keep an eye on her, *Monsieur*," Yasmine hissed down to him. "You don't want someone ushering her outside while you go up to receive the sacrament. Remember that gentleman a few years ago, when you kept me downstairs, *Monsieur* Roger?"

"I will abstain from taking the sacrament."

"On Christmas Eve, *Monsieur*? Is that wise, for the year ahead?"

And in the instant that he was silenced, *Monsieur* Roger let my wrist slip, and we wound our way up to the gallery without him.

At the top of the stairway, Yasmine stopped so abruptly that I ran into her. "Wait and watch, Aurelie," she whispered. "He will come looking for you as the Mass progresses." And she went forward to watch the priest, arms raised, lead his segregated flock.

No need to ask for whom I must watch. For, too soon, the beloved and feared face appeared below me, at the turn of the stairs. "Aurelie," Jules whispered, and my breath caught, stuttered, started again. That voice. That dear, lost, sacred voice.

"He is here," I whispered to Yasmine's back, and mothers turned, assuming I meant another child, I suppose. It was the night for unexpected children.

"I don't see *Monsieur* Roger," she whispered back. "Go on down, Aurelie. But perhaps *Monsieur*

Roger is seated in a back pew. Look for him before you leave the vestibule."

I slid down the stairway, watching Jules's pinched and anxious face draw nearer, my heart and mind filled with terror and ecstasy, all over again.

I was in his arms too short a time. As Jules pushed me from him and leaned forward to peer past the fount into the darkness of the church, I thought, *I must tell him.*

But then Jules's grip, the slender long fingers strong and tightening on mine, pulled me from the church and down the steps. *I must say something!*

Rain stung my face, and I pulled my cloak lower. Only as Jules tugged me into the tight alley that ran alongside the church did I pull back. "Wait. Jules, my only love, you must listen." Jules drew up short and turned back to me. I stared up into his anxious face, searching for comfort.

"Aurelie," Jules said miserably. "Don't you want to come away with me?"

"Oh, yes, Jules. With all my heart, I want nothing else."

"Then, come." Tugging. He whipped his head, slick with rain and shining with tips of ice, to look up the alley to the darkness ahead. "There will be a carriage for us."

"Jules, please listen."

He whipped his head back to look at me, the eyes lined and puffed but smoother than my vision in the ballroom, the pupils clearly ringed by white, the eyes of a normal man, not a shadow or a spirit or a memory, tinged with horror.

"Jules, there is a child," I said. I did not say, *Will you still have me?*

His face went slack. Tightened. Frowned. Tilted back to catch the sleet and moonlight, faint through thickening clouds. "Yasmine will know how to find the swamp witch."

"Not that!"

Jules snatched my hand back into his own. I had not known I'd pulled it away. "I see," he said. "You can go to the swamp witch to have *my* child killed, but not *his*. Do you want this child?" Jules demanded, teeth chattering with cold. "I thought you would have waited for me."

"I had no choice, Jules! I did not want to lose *our* child. And I did not want *this* one. I am *owned*, Jules. I am not free to choose."

"Do you want to come away with me? This you can choose."

Sacrifice. "I do!"

He gave my arm a yank. "Then *repudiate* that man and your life with him, and come on!"

"Come where?"

The question was mine, but the voice that asked it was neither mine nor Jules's.

It was *Monsieur* Roger's. He shouted and came on through the rain, waving his vicious cane. "Come where, you rogue?" he insisted again.

"Only to *Monsieur* Jules's house, *Monsieur* Roger, to make my peace with his parents and tell them the truth of some things they do not understand," I lied quickly, hating the creeping knowledge that it was already over. Our escape was finished, done and gone.

Now to avoid a duel that Jules could not win.

Monsieur Roger reached me. "What need have you to make peace with *them*, Aurelie?" he said and snatched my arm from Jules. "Unhand her before I knock you to the ground, you *thief*. You *liar*. You *sneak*! You *coward*!"

Jules stood under the barrage of insults and peacefully let my arm go.

When he saw that Jules would not be provoked, *Monsieur* Roger began to drag me away.

Jules said, "I see I have misjudged my place again, *Monsieur*. I should have listened to my parents, in such matters and concerning such persons. They told me such wenches are like dogs in their loyalty toward whoever next feeds them."

Jules cannot be saying that! I whipped around to face him, retreating from us. "I?" I screamed and thumped my chest with the pointing finger of my free hand. "I do not know loyalty?" I tore back the hood of my cloak, began to rip at the strings that tied it shut across my throat, yelling, "*Look* at me, *Maitre* Jules, when you tell me what I am and am not! I have borne *everything*!"

Monsieur Roger rounded the corner away from the cathedral, and Jules was a line of shadow that faded from view and lingered only barely in the darkness. At the top of the cathedral steps, Yasmine clutched at her shawl and stared down at us.

"Don't come near her, ever again, Yasmine! Your husband will hear of this treachery," *Monsieur* Roger bellowed up to her, and she turned and hurried toward the alleyway, her velvet soaking up rain at the hem.

320

EPILOGUE: PERHAPS

This run through the darkness of the sacred night held neither the uncertainties nor the wild dreams of that first escape, long ago. We came into the warmth and grandeur of *Monsieur* Roger's house, and I pushed away from him to run up to my rooms. I had the doors locked against him, and I was alone again, before I thought of what I was doing and what had happened.

I yanked open the windows to the balcony before I asked myself why. The cold gripped me, and I embraced it, stripped off my cloak, my turban, my slippers, my gown, and finally my chemise.

I went forward into the driving sleet and the gaining wind, shivering, and spread my arms wide. Below, the city sprawled, pelted and terrified, trying to close itself around thousands of tiny fireplaces, enclosing itself in comfort and hope. But I knew better. There was no such thing as hope.

I pulled shut the glass doors behind me, as well as I could, and heard the latch click when I rattled them. Now I could not return.

I thought to leap from the balcony. But that would be killing my child. Or perhaps it was not such a high jump, after all.

I worked my way up, digging my feet into toeholds in the brick wall, to the roof.

I was frantic to throw myself down from this height. But when I leaned out, I grew dizzy and heartsick. Perhaps I would jump and smash my child. It would be murder, and I could not bear to kill another one.

So I sat huddled on the roof, clinging with my toes to the tiles where I squatted, huddling in upon myself against the sleet.

The biting wind did not howl or rage but whispered softly around me, as though welcoming me for coming to meet it. *You think that you have suffered? You know nothing about suffering. Feel it.*

I spread my hair about my back and shoulders, a curtain against the cold. This was not what I had meant to do. Through the haze sparkled the passing face of the moon, the bulge to the left. Again.

I laughed despite my misery. Of course. The moon was on the wane. *Offering the end of my story its left hand.*

Our love had met its death under that moon, so long ago. Since it was already dead, now something else must be sacrificed.

My life. Why not? It was a burden to me. I didn't know what to do with it. Everyone told me so.

Perhaps there was no baby, and no sin in dying. Or perhaps I would not die.

The cold stung and burned and turned my limbs and face numb. The stars swung overhead as the night moved. The patter of incessant ice and rain made a drumming lullaby.

Drowsy, I grew oddly warm and thought to rise and stretch.

But pain raced up my cramped legs as they stretched. "Ah!" I squatted again, sliding a little down the roof.

I huddled and decided to stay still, not look at the steep slide to the harsh ground below, but wait out the storm.

I began to think of other days, people I had loved, dear faces passing through my dreams. This was the way to pass the nightmare night. Soon I would waken, rise, and crawl into bed. I could already feel the slide of smooth sheets and the warming weight of the coverlets. I would be soothed to sleep even if I slept alone, not knowing what would become of my love for Jules.

But the night lingered and would not pass. I could not be troubled to open my eyes and see. I pictured stars beyond the closed lids. A night with a clear sky and stars.

I came from a long way to hear urgent voices, men's voices, and the grasp on my limbs with rough, scratching hands that would surely break my bones. "I've got her, *Capitaine!*"

"Easy now. We've got you, man."

"How the hell did she get up there?"

"That's it, boys. Now just ease her over to me. Watch your step."

They were moving me too quickly. Unable to unbend, I came stiff like a chiseled statue through the air and banged like marble against the balcony railing.

I could feel *Monsieur* Roger near. I barely saw him as if through the skin of my closed eyelids, face as pensive and still as his hushed voice saying, "Oh, my God."

Something harsh enveloped me. I had sunk onto the mattress of my bed and was being wrapped in bedclothes that stung like summer ants.

"We only need a story for the authorities, *Monsieur*. We apologize. But perhaps she had a cat?"

"A cat? No."

"And tried to bring it in from the roof? Perhaps she was undressing for bed, and heard a neighbor's cat or pet bird, trapped in the storm?"

"Perhaps, *Monsieur*, she walked in her sleep? They can go dangerous places, sleepwalkers."

"No, no. You see, we quarreled."

"No, no, *Monsieur*. This is no answer for the authorities. You recall that other incident, the woman who had her servant beaten and driven into the storm. We need to help the people see that you did not cause this unfortunate ... yes, you see, *Monsieur*."

Monsieur Roger coughed. Or was he sobbing?

I wished I could open my eyes. I should explain. For, even now, he was lying. "We quarreled. I told her terrible things. Get out of my life, I think I said. If you're unhappy, end it all." He choked on the lie and went on. "I did not mean to hurt her. I did not know she was out in the storm. I was playing chess. Chess! A fool! How did she get out there, with the door closed?" he asked desperately.

"Well, these details, *Monsieur*, are better left unmentioned. What was the nature of the quarrel?"

"*Monsieur*, you know these *mulattas*. Discontented with their lot. Always wanting more. The people will understand. Your generosity is famous."

324

"Oh, God, no. It was all my doing. I challenged her. I drove her. She wanted nothing but love. Say what you will, but not a suicide. Let her rest in peace in hallowed burial ground." *Monsieur* Roger was leaving the room, his voice muffled, perhaps because his face was in his hands.

I thought that now would be the time to speak, to explain that he feared the pagan pit for me, but I was not afraid. Not for myself. Only, our baby deserved better. *Sacrifice.*

Celeste was crying.

I should rouse. Waken. Speak. *I went out upon the roof because I wanted to jump, but I changed my mind and was not able to climb back down.*

I must say it. I would speak and set all their minds at ease.

After I had slept. For I needed so badly to rest.

THE END